Alex Kava is the *New York Times* bestselling author of the critically acclaimed series featuring former Marine Ryder Creed and his K9 dogs, and the international bestselling Maggie O'Dell series. Her novel *Stranded* was awarded both a Florida Book Award and the Nebraska Book Award. Her standalone novel *One False Move* was chosen for the 2006 One Book One Nebraska and in 2007 she received the Mari Sandoz Award. Her political thriller *Whitewash* was also named one of *January Magazine*'s best thrillers of the year.

Published in thirty-two countries with over six million copies sold, Kava's novels have made the bestseller lists in the UK, Australia, Germany, Japan, Italy and Poland. She is a member of the Nebraska Writers Guild and International Thriller Writers. Kava and her pack of Westies divide their time between Omaha, Nebraska and Pensacola, Florida.

Alex KAVA
Before Evil

sphere

SPHERE

First published in Great Britain in 2017 by Sphere
This paperback edition published in 2018 by Sphere

1 3 5 7 9 10 8 6 4 2

Copyright © S.M. Kava 2017

The moral right of the author has been asserted.

A CIP catalogue record for this book
is available from the British Library.

ISBN 978-0-7515-5385-7

Typeset in Sabon by M Rules
Printed and bound in Great Britain by
Clays Ltd, St Ives, plc

Papers used by Sphere are from well-managed forests
and other responsible sources.

MIX
Paper from
responsible sources
FSC
www.fsc.org
FSC® C104740

Sphere
An imprint of
Little, Brown Book Group
Carmelite House
50 Victoria Embankment
London EC4Y 0DZ

An Hachette UK Company
www.hachette.co.uk

www.littlebrown.co.uk

In memory of
Patti El-Kachouti
(Dec 28, 1954–Nov 13, 2016)
Your kindness and bravery will forever inspire.

1

He pushed himself to go faster. Sweat dripped from his brow. He was in good shape, just out of practice. The excitement and adrenaline made his pulse race. It had been some time since he had hunted in this forest though he knew the deep and hidden paths by heart.

Down close to the water there were huge oaks. But up here, the pine trees grew so close that he had to sidestep through them. The crossbow felt heavier. It slowed him down despite looping the strap over his head and onto his left shoulder so he could let the weapon ride across his back. Still, it kept getting snagged on low branches, jerking him backwards. He reminded himself that he'd done this dozens of times. He was just a bit rusty. And it was a new crossbow, better than his old one. Faster. Laser beam fast.

The sporting goods clerk assured him that 75 to 125 pounds of draw weight would be more than adequate to drop a white-tail deer at moderate ranges.

'How fast?' he'd asked the man.

'Fast enough.'

But the man had only glanced at him as if he were some ordinary guy and not an experienced hunter.

'I need enough weight for an initial velocity of at least 300 feet per second. That'll give my arrow enough kinetic energy to reduce the arrow's trajectory, increase accuracy and cleanly take down my prey.'

That's when the man stared at him. A smile slowly crept across his face.

'The state of Virginia doesn't have any regulatory minimums or maximums for draw weight,' the man told him.

'Bigger is faster.'

'Yes, sir.'

'Let's go to 200.'

The man simply smiled again and nodded, now recognizing that he was dealing with no ordinary hunter.

Ordinary men were often underestimated. Most of time he considered it a gift to be seen as ordinary. He liked that he fit in, that he looked like he belonged. Others tried too hard to be noticed. He strived, instead, to blend in with the crowd – or in this case, the landscape.

A fog had started to move in like wisps of clouds sinking from the sky. Now on level ground he shuffled his feet making the pine needles sound more like squirrels playing rather than a predator's stalking footsteps. From this viewpoint up above he already had the advantage, but being an expert hunter meant knowing your prey. Predicting every move. He'd been watching and observing for days. This stop along the creek was a safe haven. The water ran crystal clear over the rocks. It was the perfect place to quench a thirst.

He scouted out the area the day before and got to work. He created a rock-solid rest to balance the crossbow. The scope sight was at the perfect level when he kneeled down. He had cocked the weapon before his hike, confident that the three built-in mechanisms would prevent it from dry firing. All that was left was to slide a bolt on the shelf, slip off the safety and aim.

And wait.

It didn't take long. Through the fog he saw movement down below and he smiled to himself. Just three days and even out here in the middle of the woods, routines were formed and followed. Routines provided comfort. They could ward off fear. But they made you predictable.

His pulse began to race again. The hairs along the back of his neck stood up. Every nerve ending seemed to come alive, as he stayed hunched in position. This is what he had been missing for too long. This glorious swell of excitement that ignited all his senses.

He kept his fingers in place, ready and waiting as he watched through the scope.

Seconds turned into minutes.

Patience, he told himself and tried to ignore the sweat sliding down his back. He didn't move a muscle. He didn't blink. He watched as his target eased slowly into the crosshairs of the scope. The fog had grown thicker, making it difficult to see, but he concentrated on the one flash of color he recognized, he depended on.

Holding his breath, he took aim. He knew he'd only have one chance.

Laser beam fast.

He watched the arrow hit. A clean shot straight through the leg.

He smiled again.

Three days ago when this game began, he'd told the woman that she'd probably regret buying those fluorescent orange running shoes.

TWO WEEKS LATER

TWO WEEKS LATER

2

Special Agent Maggie O'Dell escaped into her cramped office and closed the door. The mailing envelope she had tucked under her arm was bulging and much thicker than she expected. The slight surge in adrenaline irritated her. At least she recognized that, yes, it was strange – and some would say morbid – for her to be excited about the package's contents.

For several years now law enforcement officers from across the country had been sending her information on cases they couldn't solve. Usually they sent very little – scraps of evidence, blurry Polaroids and rudimentary copies of coroner reports – all in the hopes that Maggie could take those bits and pieces and put them together like a jigsaw puzzle.

More times than not, she'd been successful producing comprehensive profiles. And she did it without ever stepping foot onto an actual crime scene. From her small office in the depths of the Behavioral Science Unit, she had managed to develop criminal profiles that helped lead to the apprehension and arrest of eight – possibly nine – murderers in the last twenty-six months. She'd built up quite a reputation, but with that success came an insurmountable amount of requests.

Lately she carried around a file or two with her. Over lunch, in between meetings, or curled up on her sofa at home, she found herself sifting, reviewing, searching for pieces she may have missed. The cases filled almost every waking hour. Her husband, Greg accused her of being obsessed, and in the last couple of months she began to worry that he might be right. Even today she'd skipped lunch, anxious to see the details of this new case.

The fact was she had stopped killers from adding victims to their lists. With each apprehension came a sense of power. But with that power came an overwhelming obligation and responsibility. So much so, that she hated turning down a single request, hated having to be so selective, picking and choosing. Unfortunately – or perhaps for the sake of her mental and physical health she should consider it fortunate – her boss, Assistant Director Cunningham, restricted her caseload.

'You need to take a break every once in while, Agent O'Dell,' he had told her when she first started. 'I can't have you burning out before you reach thirty.'

Now alone in her office, Maggie opened the envelope carefully and slid the contents onto her desk. Immediately her eyes caught a glimpse of the photos. These weren't blurry Polaroids. A close-up of the victim's neck showed what could be rope burns. Another captured bite-marks, red gashes in the soft flesh of the inner arm.

She stopped herself from picking up any of these for a closer look. Instead she left everything where it landed when it slid out of the envelope. She stood back, restraining her hands, keeping them on her hips as she cocked her head to take in an overview of the contents.

She focused in on the medical examiner's report without swooping. Instead, she scanned it all the way to the middle of the first page before she found what she was looking for. This victim's name was David Robards. Twenty-one. Five feet, nine inches tall. A hundred and fifty pounds.

The autopsy listed the manner of death as 'undetermined,' but Maggie already knew that early police reports indicated that Robards' death 'appeared to be alcohol-related drowning.' Those were the few things Maggie had allowed Detective Michael Hogan to tell her. He seemed stunned when she stopped him from providing more details.

'I need to see the photos first,' she had explained. 'The next time we talk I'll ask you to take me through the crime scene as if I'm walking right beside you.'

Hogan accepted this without argument. They all did. Sometimes it surprised her how few of them questioned any part of her process, almost as if she were clairvoyant and they dared not disrupt the magic they didn't understand but respected.

She was impressed and maybe a bit too excited to see that Hogan had provided a good deal of documents, photos and even several plastic bags of trace evidence. This was more than she usually received.

Again, before digging in, Maggie went over the details she had committed to memory. David Robards was one of three victims in nine months. All of them were young, white males. College students but not from the same universities. Each had been drinking with friends before they disappeared, only to be found in a river days – sometimes weeks – later.

Maggie glanced at the array of photos. 'Alcohol related' didn't exactly explain the rope burns left on Robards' neck or what appeared to be a bite-mark left on the inside of his upper arm.

A knock on her door startled her.

'Come in,' she said when she really wanted to say, go away.

Preston Turner eased the door open just enough to tuck his huge head and right shoulder in between. The agent reminded her of an ex-linebacker, and she was sure he could crush his way through the door if he chose.

'O'Dell, boy, am I glad you're here.' He grinned at her. 'Delaney has a family thing. Wanna go with me to an autopsy?'

She hesitated, not because of the interruption but because of the unexpected invitation. None of the guys ever invited her to come along.

'Sure,' she said, trying to sound casual. Trying to sound like one of the guys – that's how she needed to react. With all that in mind she decided to add, 'Can we stop on the way and pick up lunch?'

She carefully slid all of Hogan's case back into its package, so her back was to Turner when he said, 'Very funny, O'Dell. So Delaney already tipped you off.'

'Tipped me off?'

'About how much I hate autopsies.'

She turned to look at him and now saw his clenched jaw and his right hand fisted over the door handle. Agents Turner and Delaney had been treating her like their little sister ever since she helped them break open a three-year old serial arson case. Last week they waved her over to join them and three other male agents at the coveted 'guys' table' in the cafeteria for lunch. Delaney had even stopped by a couple of times to see what she was working on.

She didn't mind. Both were well-respected and in this male-dominated department it was a relief to have some of her male counterparts more interested in her profiling skills rather than how she filled out her navy blue suit. However, she never would have guessed that the tough but charming Preston Turner had a queasy stomach when it came to autopsies.

'Delaney never told me.'

'He didn't? Huh.' Turner pretended it wasn't a big deal, now glancing at his watch as if suddenly the time was more important.

'I skipped lunch,' she explained.

'Then by all means, we'll drive through and get you some lunch.' He held the door open for her. 'Actually, I wouldn't mind if we were a little late getting there.'

3

WARREN COUNTY, VIRGINIA

He took a different exit off the interstate. It was never good to get too comfortable and follow the same route. Although it meant depending on his mobile GPS more than he liked. Life was about taking risks, seeing opportunities where others simply drove by. Being unpredictable had always served him well.

Until now.

He hadn't been on the two-lane blacktop for ten minutes when he saw the cruiser in his rearview mirror. His eyes automatically glanced at his speedometer. Two miles per hour over the limit, if that. And yet when he looked up again, the cruiser's flashing lights filled his rearview mirror, rushing up behind him.

This was ridiculous. He hadn't done anything to warrant notice. And it was much too early for the car to have been reported as stolen. He slowed down and pulled carefully to the edge of the highway, allowing only one set of tires to drop off the blacktop and onto the muddy side.

He listened, holding his breath as he sat perfectly still. He didn't fumble for his driver's license. Nor did he reach to check the glove compartment where he could only hope the car's owner kept the registration papers. Instead he sat quietly, listening for anything unusual while he watched the side mirror. He could see the asshole taking his time. Was he running the license plate number? Finally the officer climbed out of his cruiser and strutted toward him.

He recognized that strut. Uniform tight across the chest and arms to emphasis the muscles he worked so hard to develop. Hat brim low so there was no space between it and the frame of his sunglasses. He held back a smirk when he noticed the man's sunglasses had mirrored lenses. Of course they did. It was all part of the training package – asserting authority 101.

He waited until the asshole was one step away from his car door before he hit the button to bring down the window.

'Good afternoon, officer.'

That took the guy a bit off guard. Most people wanted to know immediately what they had done wrong. But to find the driver friendly, and not confrontational or defensive? That was unpredictable.

'License and registration.'

Direct, demanding to the point of being rude. The asshole thought he was – again, asserting his authority – but what he had just revealed was that his confidence level wasn't high enough to exchange a friendly greeting without losing that precious piece of authority.

'Yes, sir.'

He slowly pulled his wallet from his jacket pocket. All careful, deliberate movements. He didn't need this guy suddenly feeling threatened by what he might misinterpret as a jerk or a grab. He slid the driver's license out and handed it up. The license was a fake but he knew it was professional enough to fool even a digital scanner. The identity was one of his many and it matched his current physical appearance – a harmless, ordinary middle-aged guy.

Fact was, he hadn't used his real name in years. Only a handful of people still knew him as Albert Stucky, but even they would never recognize him because he changed with each new name and identity. He was like a chameleon, shredding his skin and pulling on a whole new persona. Three weeks ago he was a blind veteran with a pronounced limp.

However, the vehicle registration might be trickier.

'Is it okay if I get the registration from the glove compartment?' he asked before he reached for it.

'Go ahead.'

'This is my friend's car,' he explained as he popped the compartment open. He was only informing the good officer. No hint of excuse or reason to be defensive. 'She hates leaving it at the airport, so I usually drive her.'

Under the pack of tissues and three tubes of lipstick, he found the paper he recognized as the registration. As he grabbed it he glanced over the type, committing the address and full name to memory: Susan R. Fuller. He left the compartment open to show he had nothing to hide then sat back and held the paper up through the open window.

The officer didn't take his glasses off as he examined the driver's license and looked over the registration.

'Where'd she go?'

'Excuse me?'

'Your friend.'

It wasn't at all the question he had expected.

'Florida. Fort Lauderdale.'

'Vacation?'

He had to think quickly. This guy was good. If he was her friend why wouldn't he have joined her on vacation?

'No, unfortunately, business.'

The hat bobbed but he couldn't tell behind the mirrored sunglasses if the officer was still reading the license and registration or if he was looking for some tell. A tell was a clue, an indicator that signaled someone was lying.

'What kind of business?'

'Excuse me?'

'What kind of business is she in?'

'Susie owns a little boutique in Gainesville. Costume jewelry, bright colored scarves, that sort of thing. You know where the Red Lobster is?'

Actually she worked at a pastry shop next to the boutique, but the trick was to take the asshole off guard a bit. Turn it around. Ask him a question that seemed totally unrelated. If nothing else, the guy would be thinking about where the Red Lobster was. But he didn't wait for the man to respond.

'It's in that upscale shopping center off the interstate. You've probably driven by it.' But in saying that he was hoping the officer would probably never notice a women's boutique nor would he have any reason to in an upscale neighborhood that rarely had any police incidents.

To his surprise the officer handed the registration back to him but kept his driver's license. He waved a hand at the back of the vehicle.

'One of your taillights is out. I'm gonna have to give you a ticket.'

He stopped himself from saying, 'But it's not even my car.' Instead he watched the man march back to his cruiser and now every nerve in his body came alert.

He knew the asshole wanted to run the license plate and worse, he wanted to run the driver's license. Whether he believed the story or any portion of it, didn't matter. The guy was still going to bust his chops, make him sweat, push a little harder just to see if he could get him to crack.

Son of a bitch.

The driver's license was solid. He needed to relax. He always made sure he had a credit card in the same name. Those were easy to come by. For this identity he'd even gotten a library card. Other times he'd added a membership card to Costco or Sam's Club. He tried to change it up a bit. Never wanted to get too comfortable, take anything for granted. Part of that being unpredictable creed.

The guy was finished and on his way back.

He cocked his head and listened hard. *Nothing.* But he wasn't sure how much longer this would take. Those damned sunglasses wouldn't allow a hint of what came next. *Just be patient*, he told himself. *And prepared*. The heel of his right foot tapped the hunting knife he kept under the driver's seat. Its presence calmed him by the time the officer arrived back at the car door.

Then without a word the asshole handed him his driver's license . . . along with a ticket.

Even as Stucky took the two items the man's attention was drawn away. His head tilted and his body turned to look back toward his cruiser. Stucky took the opportunity to glance at the officer's nametag then he held back a smile.

Mr Tough Guy living up to his name.

He shifted to look in the rearview mirror, now anxious to see the new focus of this asshole. A vehicle was approaching. The first one he'd seen since leaving the interstate.

The guy was obviously done with him but he stood in place, making no move to leave. And now there was a hint of emotion. Stucky saw it in the way the guy's jaw clenched as if he were grinding his teeth. He glanced in the rearview mirror. It was a black pickup but it didn't seem to be speeding. And yet it held the officer's attention almost as if the guy was expecting it.

The pickup slowed a little, not much, weaving into the other lane to give the officer on the side of the road plenty of room. Stucky watched the asshole's face. With his head turned Stucky could see the guy's eyes behind the sunglasses, and he was intrigued to witness a slip of anger. Stucky was so focused on the asshole that he barely saw more than a glimpse of long blond hair in the passenger window as the vehicle drove by.

It took a second or two before the officer realized he still had a car pulled over. Suddenly the guy tapped the car door with his knuckles, signaling he was finished and dismissing him.

'Move along,' he said, his emotions back in check or so he pretended.

As Stucky shifted into gear he saw the officer glancing over his shoulder, still watching the taillights of the pickup blink then disappear around a curve. He pulled out before the officer got back into his cruiser. He accelerated quickly to the speed limit, wanting to gain some distance. When he rounded the curve he looked up and couldn't see the cruiser. He almost missed an old pasture road on the other side of a line of trees.

He skidded to halt. Glanced in the rearview mirror. He backed into the two-track road, spitting up dirt into the tire wells until he knew his car was hidden from the road by the pine trees.

Then he waited.

He wanted to see what the hell had gotten this guy all bent out of shape. Something told him there was more to this asshole under that carefully crafted surface. Not to mention the fact that he had almost caught Stucky. That pissed him off. But with his relief came a swell of power. A feeling of being invincible.

He wanted to tell the asshole, 'You didn't discover my secret, but maybe I can find out yours.'

He had several hours before he needed to worry. It wasn't like he was in a hurry. Still, he cocked his head and listened as he watched the road, expecting the cruiser any minute now. Susan R. Fuller wasn't going anywhere. The injection worked like it always did. Except she must have kicked out the taillight.

4

'Whoa! She is seriously messed up.'

This was the first thing out of Turner's mouth when they arrived. No 'hello.' No apology for their delay. With only a glance at the corpse, Maggie realized that was an understatement even before the M.E. scowled at them over his half glasses. They were twenty minutes late though it took only five to go through the fast food drive-thru.

'I'm sure you won't mind that I started without you, Agent Turner.'

Stan Wenhoff was clearly not happy. But it was hard to tell. Head down, shoulders hunched, his eyes didn't leave his fingers. He had already sliced the body open and started to examine the internal injuries. Maggie had worked with the medical examiner about a dozen times. His facial expression rarely changed as if it were stamped on with an eternal look of disapproval. She knew lack of emotion could be an advantage in his line of work.

Wenhoff finally glanced up. To Maggie he nodded and said, 'Agent O'Dell, good to see you again.' Back to Turner. 'Gowns, masks, shoe covers—' He pointed with his scalpel to a metal rack against the far wall behind them.

'This is not the missing councilwoman from Boston,' Wenhoff told them, getting down to business.

The story had made the national news, a constant loop with photos and interviews of panicked family members. The woman had gone missing several days ago, her car found in the parking lot of a restaurant she frequented.

Now that Maggie stood over the corpse she wondered how Wenhoff could be so certain. The tangled hair, the bruises and gashes on her swollen face made her unrecognizable.

As if reading Maggie's mind, Wenhoff said, 'This woman's been gone more than a few days. I'd say a week, maybe even two.'

'She doesn't look like she's been dead for that long,' Turner said, towering over Maggie's right shoulder.

She noticed Turner hanging back behind her instead of alongside her, his facemask clasped firmly in place. She left hers dangling at her neck. Autopsies didn't bother her. She'd considered pre-med in college until she realized a medical doctor might require social skills she didn't have. Fact was, she felt more comfortable with dead people, and yes, she had a minor in psychology so she also knew that preference wasn't quite normal.

'I'm guessing she was dead for only a few days before her body was discovered.'

'Where was she found?' Maggie asked and watched Wenhoff nod his head toward Turner for him to answer.

'Shenandoah County.'

'That's northern Virginia,' Maggie tried to picture the area. But she also knew there were four district offices in Virginia's medical examiner system. Wenhoff was the forensic patholo-gist for the Central District. Shenandoah County wasn't his jurisdiction.

'Filmer's on vacation,' Wenhoff told her. 'I'm covering for him. Lucky me.' He pointed to the counter. 'Forest worker noticed a flash of color in the woods.'

On a separate tray sat one lone running shoe. Despite the mud, Maggie could see the shoe was a fluorescent orange.

'Any chance she got lost while out for a run?'

'From what I understand there's only one service road that winds into the forest,' Turner said. 'That forest isn't open to the public. Almost 600 acres. No trails. No hunting. No fishing. No access.'

'So she could have gotten lost.'

'And wandered around for two weeks?' Wenhoff shook his head. 'I know that area. She would have needed to drive there. It's an old watershed at the base of the mountain. The land was donated to the state and about all they could do with it was make it into a wildlife sanctuary. It's called Devil's Backbone. Not exactly someplace you go to jog.

'Who knows how she ended up out there,' he continued. 'But she definitely was left stranded to fend for herself. She's dehydrated. Undernourished. Welts from insect bites. Scratches and cuts on her legs and arms.'

The medical examiner put down his scalpel and reached around to grab a basin. Maggie and Turner both leaned forward to see inside. When Wenhoff announced that it was the women's stomach contents, Maggie heard Turner suck in air. She avoided looking back at him. Wenhoff either didn't notice Turner's discomfort or he didn't care, because he poked around the goop, eager to show off what he had discovered.

'Tiny little berries. Maybe crabapples. I'm not sure. And this,' he stabbed at a more solid piece. 'I think it's some kind of raw fish.'

'Not sushi?' Turner asked, almost hopeful.

Wenhoff shook his head. 'No, the scales are still attached.'

A moan from Turner and she heard him take a step back.

'You're saying she may have had to eat raw fish that she caught? So she could have gotten lost in the woods,' Maggie persisted.

'I said stranded, not lost.'

'What's the difference?' Turner asked.

'Lost suggests she did this to herself. Stranded implies someone left her in the middle of nowhere.' Wenhoff placed the basin back on the counter and returned his attention to the corpse. 'She didn't do this to herself.'

He reached and pulled down the cloth he had draped over the woman's lower body. Immediately Maggie could see what the medical examiner meant. The woman's left calf had been pierced with an arrow and part of it was still intact.

Turner let out a low whistle. 'I knew I should have read the entire sheriff's report.'

'Someone shot her with a bow and arrow?' Maggie leaned in for a closer look.

'A crossbow,' Wenhoff corrected her. 'I'm speculating about that, but I do believe much more velocity would be needed. Lots of crossbow hunters in these parts. But these carbon arrows? There're difficult to break. Can splinter and cut your hands.'

Wenhoff pointed at her hands. The palms were covered in small cuts.

'At least she knew not to pull it out,' Turner noted.

'Looks like the wound started to heal around the arrow,' Maggie said, examining both sides. 'That's why you think she was stranded in the forest for several days.'

'Correct.'

'If a lot of hunters use crossbows these days, you sure this wasn't an accident?' Turner pointed out.

Wenhoff shook his head, and he looked a bit frustrated with Maggie and Turner. 'Still doesn't explain this.'

Now the medical examiner grabbed the cloth where it had bunched up at the victim's feet and pulled it completely off.

The woman's big toe on her left foot was missing. It had been cut off.

5

From his perch on the pasture road Stucky had watched the black pickup turn into a long winding driveway just on the other side of the curve. The officer obviously knew where the pickup was headed because he moved at a leisurely pace. In fact, Stucky had parked his car and waited for a good ten minutes before the cruiser came by then parked at the end of that driveway.

Through the trees Stucky could see a double-wide trailer and a couple of other outbuildings. He pushed aside the small cooler and grabbed his duffle bag from the floor on the passenger side. Without dipping his eyes from the cruiser or the double-wide, he let his hand dig deep until he felt the binoculars. The pickup was parked alongside a dirty tan SUV in the front yard. Sheets whipped on a clothesline like bright sails in the breeze. He couldn't see beyond the trailer's curtained windows.

The asshole stayed parked on the side of the blacktop about twenty feet from the driveway's entrance. Stucky wondered what the occupants of that black pickup had done to warrant such attention. And rile such emotion.

He checked his watch. Susan R. Fuller wasn't going anywhere even if she woke up. He started the car and slowly backed farther uphill on the pasture road, careful to keep to the tires to the worn tracks. He didn't need to get stuck in the mud out here in the middle of nowhere. There was a line of trees on one side of the path and on the other were thick woods that would hide him and the vehicle from view.

He cranked the steering wheel and the front tires to the right then shoved the parking brake into place so the car wouldn't roll back down the hill. He wanted to get a better look from up here. Just as he grabbed his binoculars and climbed out, he saw the cruiser making its way over the winding driveway.

What the hell are you up to?

He hurried into the thick growth of trees now scrambling for a better view of the front yard and the double-wide. He saw movement and shoved at the branches in front of him. The officer was out of his vehicle, walking to the front door of the trailer.

Damn it!

Stucky couldn't see the front door. There were too many trees and they stretched all the way down to the property. He could only see slivers – bits and pieces.

Maybe if he climbed a bit higher.

He rushed now, anxious and breathing hard. Branches slapped in his face. Vines snagged his pant-legs. Pine needles crunched underfoot. He needed to see what this asshole was up to.

What made you so angry?

It was a long way to go just to give somebody a ticket.

Finally Stucky found an opening and swung the binoculars to his eyes. He pinched and turned the focus knob, frustrated that it was taking too long. The magnified blur was making him dizzy and he leaned against a tree trunk. The trailer became crystal clear. But he still couldn't see through the curtains. Once he thought he saw a shadow move but that was all. He was too far away to see or hear anything.

Stucky checked his watch. Fifteen minutes passed but no one came out the front door. Back behind the trailer he saw motion. Maybe it was only the laundry whipping around on the clothesline. The binoculars gave him tunnel vision, only showing him magnified pieces. When he pulled them away from his eyes he was certain something or someone was back behind the trailer.

Damn it!

He was missing whatever was happening.

His eyes searched the forest. Farther downhill he noticed another pasture road. This one was closer to the property. There'd be enough trees to hide his vehicle. He needed to see what this asshole was up to.

He jogged now, watching his feet as he weaved through the trees and jumped over fallen branches. By the time he got back to his vehicle his heart was thumping, his pulse raced. He climbed in and immediately heard a tapping sound coming from the trunk.

'Go ahead and kick out the other taillight, Susan,' he yelled over his shoulder. 'No one can hear you.'

When the engine started, the tapping stopped. He thought about a second injection. Glanced at the duffle bag on the floor. Checked his watch. No time if he wanted to see what was going on over at that double-wide.

His excitement rammed the accelerator. The mud sucked at the tires and sent the car swerving.

Slow down, he told himself while he lifted his foot off the pedal and kept it from slamming on the brakes. He hadn't realized how steep the incline was when he had backed up the hill. Coming down was starting to feel like a mudslide. He jerked the gearshift into neutral. The tires continued to slide but the momentum slowed the car until finally it skidded to a stop. And that's when he heard a banging coming from the trunk.

He shoved the gearshift into park. Slammed down the parking brake and shut off the engine. With teeth clenched he grabbed the duffle bag, digging into the side pocket where he kept an extra loaded syringe. Then he swiped his hand under the driver's seat and picked up the hunting knife. Before he opened the car door he noticed movement out of the corner of his eyes. Down below on the main road. It was the police cruiser.

Son of a bitch.

Stucky slouched down in the seat until he could barely see over the steering wheel. His vehicle was only about a hundred feet from the main road. Would the trees be enough to hide him? Because the bastard was headed back this way.

The banging grew louder.

He swore he could feel the entire car rock with each thud. And yet he caught himself holding his breath as if that would make a difference as he watched the cruiser getting closer and closer. He sat perfectly still, clutching the syringe in one hand and the hunting knife in the other, prepared to use both.

Sweat slid down his back. His jaw was clenched so tight it began to ache. And now the thump of his heartbeat joined the tempo coming from the rear of the car. Then suddenly he saw the cruiser speed up. In seconds it flashed by the entrance to the pasture road. Stucky could see the silhouette behind the wheel, the officer's hat still in place, low over his brow.

The sunglasses facing straight ahead. He didn't even glance Stucky's way.

He watched the taillights blink only for a second before they disappeared around the curve. Then he was gone.

Stucky stayed put, waiting, almost expecting the asshole to backtrack. He checked his watch and endured another five minutes. He was used to waiting and watching. Used to blending in and becoming invisible. Although Susan R. Fuller was unraveling his last bit of patience.

Another five minutes passed and the cruiser never returned.

Stucky tossed the syringe back into the duffle bag. He slid the hunting knife into his jacket pocket. Then he shifted into gear.

'Okay, let's see what the hell you did.'

6

The rain had started with a light drizzle and by the time they arrived at Ollie's Bar and Grill Maggie regretted not bringing along her FBI windbreaker. Who knew it could be this chilly in the middle of summer?

Turner had talked her into having drinks with him and Delaney. He insisted she needed to help him go over the autopsy details.

'I'll never do it justice,' he told her.

Having drinks with Turner and Delaney after work was beyond inviting her to the cool guys table in the cafeteria. It wasn't like she had never had drinks with her co-workers after hours, but it was usually a whole group, meeting for some celebration like a birthday. This was different. This was talking about a case, after hours, like colleagues.

She left a voice message for Greg, though it hardly mattered. Ever since he made partner at his law firm he'd been working long hours and most weekends. She couldn't remember the last time they sat down to dinner with each other. They were like roommates, crossing paths and leaving messages for each other. Maggie usually found herself eating takeout food at the kitchen counter. She actually didn't mind all the alone time.

Who was she fooling? She *preferred* the alone time. It beat listening to Greg berate and lecture her about her job.

Recently he decided he didn't like his wife being an FBI agent, and he no longer bothered to keep that opinion to himself.

Delaney looked exhausted, his short hair tousled and damp from the rain. But he smiled and waved them over to the coveted corner booth he'd managed to snag. Coveted for sure. The place was packed.

'Everything good?' Turner asked him.

Only then did Maggie remember that Turner had said Delaney had a family emergency. No, not an emergency. A family 'thing.' On closer inspection she noticed his eyes were bloodshot. He rubbed at his jaw, a full palm over and across. So when he answered Turner with, 'Yeah, everything's good,' Maggie knew it wasn't.

She scooted into the booth across from Delaney. Turner slid in next to her, and he was already searching for a waitress. Maggie continued to study Delaney while pretending to be interested in Ollie's single sheet menu.

'You can't go wrong with a burger,' Delaney told her.

'Is that what you're having?'

'Just beer for me. I'm meeting Karen later.'

Karen was his wife. And now Maggie wondered if perhaps the 'family thing' wasn't quite finished. That Delaney had simply interrupted whatever was going on just to meet about the autopsy.

Stop it, she silently admonished herself.

Lately she did this with everything and everyone. She examined and analyzed as if her mind couldn't shut down. As if every piece of information about anyone became a means for profiling. A test exercise. Yesterday she caught herself coming up with an entire profile for the grocery store clerk. In her own defense, the line of customers was long and the clerk exceedingly slow. The poorly concealed bruise above the woman's left eye didn't help matters.

Turner managed to snag a waitress.

'Sweetheart, you are a lifesaver!'

He rewarded the young woman with a wide smile. Maggie had seen him do this before. He might look like a badass linebacker but the man knew how to be charming. And now he extended that charm to Maggie when he told the waitress, 'I think we're looking at some dinner. Whadya say, Maggie?'

He was allowing her the courtesy of ordering first. Ordinarily she bristled at male agents being polite with her, but she squelched the impulse. The fact that she was here with Turner was because he respected her expertise.

She remembered that all she had eaten for lunch was the greasy French fries and a Diet Pepsi on the drive to the autopsy. So she ordered a burger and side salad. Added a bottle of Sam Adams. By the time the food arrived Maggie had to pace herself. She wanted to scarf it down. Instead, she took small bites in between describing the murder victim's wounds and ignoring Turner's groans.

'It was pretty gross, man,' Turner told Delaney. 'What kind of madman shoots an arrow into a woman's leg then takes a toe as a trophy?'

'Is the toe a trophy?' Delaney asked.

When Maggie glanced up from her salad she realized he was asking her.

'From the looks of it, the toe was obviously taken post mortem,' she said, as if that answered his question. Both men continued to stare at her, waiting, and she realized it obvious only to her. 'Yes, I think he took it as a trophy.'

'Twisted bastard,' Delaney said.

Turner shook his head and pushed his plate away even as Maggie took another bite of her hamburger.

'That's a bit over the top, right?' Turner's eyes were on Maggie. 'I mean, we know it's not random. And we can pretty much toss out some revengeful boyfriend or pissed off husband, right?' He took a sip of his beer, still looking to Maggie, waiting.

'Killers have taken all sorts of odd things as trophies: underwear, teeth, drivers' licenses. Jeffrey Dahmer kept a collection of penises in his refrigerator.'

Turner winced and Delaney smiled at his reaction.

Maggie continued, 'Jerry Brudos stored the sliced-off foot of one of his female victims in the freezer. He liked to pull it out and try on his collection of stolen high heels.'

'A toe doesn't sound so weird after all,' Delaney said. 'But you're talking about serial killers. You think this guy's killed before?'

Maggie stopped with her forkful of salad in midair. Again, both men stared at her, waiting for a response that she thought was obvious. Maybe the only thing obvious was that she spent way too much time researching and studying serial killers.

'I have no way of knowing whether or not he's killed before,' she told them. 'But I can tell you this, one-time killers rarely take a trophy.'

7

Miserable rain!

If only he hadn't taken a detour and spent his afternoon off spying on that stupid bastard. He could have missed the downpours that now made this forest road a muddy obstacle course. Stucky's reward, however, had almost been worth his botched plans. What he found at that double-wide trailer surprised and impressed him. He couldn't wait to return. Already he was anxious to watch and see the reactions of the first responders.

His next shift didn't start until tomorrow evening. In the morning he planned to call the county sheriff's department. He knew exactly which pay phone he'd use – a busy gas station off of the interstate. The next exit after the one he'd barely left when Officer Tough Guy stopped him. His mind played over and over what he'd say, 'Can someone please check. I think something awful has happened.'

Then he'd give them the address of the double-wide.

He knew the sheriff's dispatcher would want to know who he was and his relationship to the occupants. But he prepared himself for that, as well. Being an expert at impersonation wasn't just about physically changing hair or eye color, gaining or losing weight or developing a limp. He knew how to play each role and he was certain he could do whispered hysteria.

'No, I can't leave my name. He might come after me, too.'

'Who do you think will come after you, sir?'

'I'm just a concerned citizen. I can't say anything more.'

He'd give the address again and hang up. Simple as that. And then he'd tuck his vehicle into those trees – closer this time – and he'd hike to a place where he could wait and watch.

But first he needed to introduce poor, restless Susan R. Fuller to her new home.

8

'Agent O'Dell. Come in.'

Assistant Director Cunningham waved for Maggie to come into his office even though he remained behind his desk and after only a glance in her direction. His head remained down, eyes focused on the yellow notepad that he continued to scribble on.

Maggie had never been summoned to her boss's office. Nicknamed 'the Hawk,' Cunningham rarely missed a detail. He also didn't smile. Now that she thought about it, she had never heard him raise his voice either. He didn't need to. His agents knew when they disappointed him. And none of them wanted to do that. Maggie imagined disappointing Cunningham would be similar to losing your father's trust. Once lost, an uphill battle to win it back.

'Agent O'Dell.' He looked up this time.

Only then did she realize she hadn't come into the room yet. Instead she hovered close to the door as if she wanted to keep open the option of escape. In her mind she tried to go over what she might have done wrong to deserve this summons. Usually Cunningham left her alone in her cramped window-less office. He stopped by to toss files on her overloaded desk on a regular basis. Otherwise there was a conference room meeting once a week. But if he wanted to reprimand her he'd do it in private . . . in his office.

'You can sit,' he told her.

She shook off her reluctance and took the lone chair that he pointed to in front of his desk.

'I'll be just a minute.' And his head went back down.

She crossed her legs. Uncrossed them. Gathered her hands in her lap and intertwined her fingers. The chair was wooden. Hard back. Hard seat. Cunningham didn't want his guests to be too comfortable or want them to stay long.

This close, she caught a glimpse at the open file folder on the corner of the desk's pristine mahogany surface. Her name was up at the top. Her file.

This couldn't be good.

He was scribbling again on the notepad. Blue ink, not black. Notes filled the margins. Block printing used for emphasis. Crazy the things she noticed. She wanted to shake her head. And once again she reminded herself that not everything needed to be analyzed. Maybe Greg was right. Her professional life was starting to consume not just her private life, but perhaps her total consciousness. Even the simplest, day-to-day tasks spurred her mind into analytical mode.

This morning she'd gotten to work early and decided to have breakfast in the cafeteria. She wanted to get a head start on Detective Hogan's package. She hadn't gotten back to it since Turner pulled her away for the autopsy. But at breakfast she realized she couldn't order eggs without wondering if there was a correlation to the personality type of people and the way they liked their eggs prepared. Were hardboiled people more disciplined, for instance? It took fifteen to twenty minutes, after all, to boil an egg. Did the preference for sunny-side up suggest a more flexible personality? What about scrambled?

'Agent O'Dell?'

'Yes, sir.'

She sat up straight. Stopped short of flinching and giving away the fact that her mind had wandered. But Cunningham still caught it. She could see it in his eyes as he studied her, now giving her his full attention.

'I don't think I ever asked you where you're from.'

'From?'

'Where did you grow up?'

It wasn't at all the question she expected and she waited a beat too long as if waiting for the real question.

'I was born in Green Bay, Wisconsin.' That detail would be in her file, and she stopped her eyes from darting to the corner of his desk. She didn't add the fact that she'd only lived there until she was twelve. That was the year her world fell apart. Her mother moved them to Richmond, Virginia, leaving behind all their friends, neighbors and family along with Maggie's childhood.

'Your father's deceased.'

Another unexpected question – not really a question but he was waiting for an answer. She wasn't sure where he was going. Why all of a sudden ask about her childhood ... and her father?

'That's correct.'

This wasn't a subject she wanted to discuss.

'How did he die?'

Definitely not a subject she wanted to discuss.

'He was a firefighter. He died in the line of duty when I was twelve.'

Maggie held his eyes as if daring him to ask more. She loved her father. No, she adored him. She hadn't stopped wearing the medallion he had given her. Even now she could feel the chain around her neck, tucked inside her blouse, the small medal pressed against her skin.

Over fifteen years had gone by and she missed her father terribly. She caught herself wondering if he'd be proud of her. She still watched the Green Bay Packers games every chance she got, usually wearing his oversized jersey. She'd never forget the morning she found that shirt in the dirty laundry basket – almost a week after his death.

She'd grabbed it, rolled it up and hid it in various secret places where she knew her mother would never look. Then she'd take it out just to smell his scent. Some nights she wrapped herself in the shirt. It helped her sleep. But one morning she made the mistake of leaving it in her unmade bed when she went off to school. She panicked as soon as she realized her mother would find it. That afternoon she raced home relieved to see the jersey still on her bed. But then her heart sank. It was neatly folded, and freshly laundered.

Thankfully, Cunningham's eyes and attention were back on the contents of the file folder. He picked up the top sheet, giving it only a glance.

'Pre-med, masters in behavioral psychology, forensic fellowship here at Quantico, now special agent. All very impressive. And you've built quite the reputation using the skills you've acquired.'

He was referring to the long-distance cases she had helped solve. Was that what this was all about? Had she been spending too much time on those? Was he going to shut her down?

No, it couldn't be. He had added to her pile. There had

been several times he brought her a new case and told her, 'Tell me what you see. Tell me who did this.'

Cunningham actually seemed proud of her when she'd been able to supply investigators with specific details about the killer. What type of job he had, the model of car he drove, whether he lived close to the crime scene, or how old he might be. She'd like to believe her success was due to statistics and logic, but some of it was dumb luck. It certainly wasn't magic, but Maggie knew that's what a few of her colleagues said behind her back. Better that they called it magic rather than voodoo. Whatever 'it' was, she had garnered a reputation.

Now as she sat across the desk from him she realized maybe she wasn't here to be reprimanded. Perhaps he was getting ready to present her with another test.

'It's not just about skills,' he told her. 'You have something special, Agent O'Dell. Something beyond your educational background. It has nothing to do with your childhood or the fact that you lost your heroic father.'

He waved his hand over the file folder like it didn't matter. Then he leaned forward, elbows rested on the desktop, fingertips together creating a steeple. He held her eyes again.

'You have a talent for seeing what others miss. Details that appear insignificant to the rest of us. You have instincts about people ... about killers. While all that is, indeed, a skill, a talent – whatever you want to call it – while it all seems like a good thing, I want you to be aware that oftentimes there's a price to pay for climbing inside the mind of the evil.'

She stayed quiet, not breaking eye contact, trying to take in his message. Still the good student wanting to learn. She'd heard Cunningham call murderers evil before. The first time, she had to admit that she was surprised. None of her psychology classes or other studies of criminal behavior used the term 'evil' as an explanation. It seemed like something relegated to her childhood catechism lessons.

When her father gave her the medallion he told her it would 'help protect her from evil.' She could hear her twelve-year-old voice whispering in the back of her mind, 'But it didn't protect you, Daddy.'

Evil. For Maggie it belonged only in the mythical realms of religion, like heaven and hell. Maybe that was the catch. In order to believe in evil, you had to believe in hell. And you needed to believe in heaven.

All these years she wore the medallion not because she thought it might protect her. She wore it simply because it was a precious gift from her father.

So she was always surprised to hear Cunningham use the word 'evil' as if it were a term from one of the textbooks he'd co-written on criminal behavior. But before she had time to respond, he announced the reason she was here—why she had been summoned in the first place.

'I think you're ready for a real crime scene.'

9

'I've never seen so much blood,' Sheriff Geller warned them. 'It's like a slaughterhouse in there.'

Maggie knew he was referring to the double-wide trailer that sat in the middle of the acreage.

'Smells like one, too,' he added.

Hard to believe. From outside Maggie thought the property looked like picturesque rural Virginia. A forest lined one side of the long driveway. Tall pine trees grew and climbed up the hill, standing so close together it was impossible to see between them. Less than a hundred feet away she could see a riverbank and the shimmer of rolling water.

Quiet and tranquil – the type of place people go to escape.

'Your deputies didn't touch anything?' Cunningham asked.

Geller shook his head. 'We didn't go in. Saw enough from the doorway.'

From the look on the sheriff's face he wouldn't be joining them.

Maggie tried to take in everything. She made mental notes. The yard had two well-maintained berms with flowers in bloom and several ceramic gnomes. A cobbled-stone path led to the front door. In the back she caught a glimpse of bed sheets hung from a clothesline, flapping in the breeze. From somewhere she could hear the soft delicate tinkle of a wind chime. Someone had made this place a home. And now it was a crime scene with yellow tape stretched from tree to tree all the way to the poles of the clothesline.

The sheriff and his deputy – introduced only as Deputy Steele – had parked a safe distance away as they waited for A.D. Cunningham and his three agents. Turner and Delaney were veterans. They didn't flinch at Geller's warning. They'd probably seen worse. Maggie had seen dozens of bloody crime scenes as well. But she'd viewed them secondhand from photographs or – if she was lucky – videotape. Autopsies didn't count. So this crime scene would be her first real one.

Of course, it didn't take long for her to understand there were benefits to seeing crime scenes secondhand.

The first thing she noticed was the smell. Then the heat.

Agent Delaney opened the trailer's door and the wave of hot foul air hit them all. No amount of training could have prepared Maggie for this. She fought her gag reflex. She didn't want the men to notice. Didn't want to remind them this was her first scene.

'Whoa!' It was Delaney who complained.

He pulled the door shut and took a step backward, delaying their entrance. Maggie tried to refocus, grateful for his hesitation and the opportunity to suck in a few more breaths of fresh air.

She could do this. She had to be able to do this.

She felt Cunningham tap her on the shoulder. Immediately she thought he was prodding her forward, ready to observe her initial response. But when she glanced back, his hand stayed outstretched. It took her a few seconds to realize he was handing her shoe covers, latex gloves and a small jar of Vicks VapoRub.

She took the covers and gloves but started to wave off the Vicks. The last thing she wanted was special treatment, but then she got a whiff and saw the greasy ointment smeared on his upper lip. Turner already had some, too, and out of the corner of her eye Maggie could see Delaney waiting for his turn. She swabbed on a layer and passed it on.

When Delaney opened the front door to the trailer a second time, the dab of menthol under her nose made no difference.

10

At first glance, Maggie thought it looked as though every surface had been splattered with blood. The walls were a Jackson Pollock masterpiece of horror, spaghetti streaks that crisscrossed in layers. One of the victims hung from the ceiling. Electrical cord tied his feet and hands.

Although the man's body was now bloated Maggie knew it was his blood on the walls. It didn't take a blood spatter expert to speculate that his throat had been slashed *after* he had been hung upside down.

'Looks like he fought for a while.' Turner said what the rest of them were thinking.

She had to look away, and that's when she noticed the bloody prints on the carpet.

'Someone was barefooted.'

All of them looked up at the man's feet, corded together at the ceiling and still laced up in tennis shoes. Turner took off down the narrow hallway to the back of the trailer, careful where he stepped. Maggie could hear him opening doors.

She tried to concentrate. She needed to look at this no differently than she would look at the photos she received of other crime scenes.

Focus, she told herself.

But the smell was overwhelming. Like suffocating inside a dumpster filled with rotting meat. Sweat slid down her back. Strands of hair stuck to her damp forehead and she swiped it with the back of her arm. It didn't help matters that she couldn't shake an annoying buzz from inside her head. And the heat – she was burning up.

'Feels like he cranked up the furnace,' Cunningham said.

So it wasn't just her. Little relief came with that revelation.

'Heat accelerates decomp,' Maggie told them, all the while fighting the acid backing up from her stomach.

'And speeds up the work of our little friends.' Delaney pointed at the mass of black, a stain on the victim's T-shirt.

She thought it was dried blood, a possible stab wound to the abdomen. But now she saw movement.

Maggots! Oh God, she hated maggots.

She swallowed bile. Tried to breathe.

Stupid gag reflex.

Yes, there were many advantages to observing a crime scene from photographs and video.

Concentrate. Focus.

Then she realized the buzzing wasn't in her head.

Flies. There had to be hundreds although she couldn't see them. The others had finished here and were working in the next room. Carefully watching her steps, she followed the sound. A mass of flies swarmed what looked like dinner left on the kitchen table. An open takeout container was black with flies. As were the melted puddles surrounding it.

'Victim number two is in the bedroom,' Turner announced from down the hall. 'Female.'

Cunningham shot a glance at Maggie. If he was worried about protecting her sensibilities it was a little late.

'Throat's slashed. Clothes haven't been pulled down or off. Her hands are tied in front. And she still has her shoes on. No bare feet.'

'Electrical cord?' Maggie asked.

Turner looked back into the bedroom then said, 'Yah, looks like it. What are you thinking?'

Maggie pointed to a capsized lamp. Its cord had been cut. 'He didn't bring rope or ties. He used what was already here.'

Turner nodded.

'The killer wasn't organized. He didn't come prepared,' she said.

'Or is he cocky enough that he knows he could kill them without much preparation?' Cunningham asked.

'No forced entry,' Delaney said as he examined the doorjamb.

'I didn't see any broken windows,' Turner added. 'Back door's not kicked in.'

'So chances are they let him in,' Delaney said. 'Someone they knew?'

'Any signs of drugs?' Cunningham's eyes darted around.

Turner shook his head. 'Not out in the open like a drug deal gone bad.'

'So are the bloody footprints his?' Cunningham asked. 'Could we be that lucky?'

'If they are, he's a small guy,' Delaney said.

'Charlie Manson's only five foot two,' she told them as her eyes tried to follow the smeared bloody steps.

'Come on now,' Turner said, sliding his words into a jive on purpose. 'Don't it freak you guys out that she can come up with crap like that so casually?'

Maggie smiled. The other two men ignored the comment. She walked back into the living room, following the bloody steps. They seemed to start at the upside down body. They backed up then they turned around in small smeared circles and headed in the other direction.

'If he didn't bring restraints maybe he didn't bring a weapon either.' Maggie headed back to the kitchen.

What were the chances he used a knife from the victims' own utility drawer? It certainly wouldn't be the first time. A wood block with knives sat on the counter by the sink. Several were missing from their slots.

It was difficult to concentrate with the buzz of flies. Despite putting distance between herself and the hanging victim, the smell was strong in the kitchen, too. But it was different. Less metallic. More like rotting fruit.

Cunningham was already at the table when Maggie turned to take a closer look at what held the flies' interest.

'Did he interrupt lunch or dinner?' Cunningham asked.

There was a takeout container and two small plates with forks. Each plate had crumbs and the gooey remains of what Maggie guessed may have been cream or ice cream.

'Maybe dessert,' Maggie said, pointing to the bakery box on the counter.

Cunningham glanced behind him. 'Looks like pie. So what's in the takeout container?'

That's where the flies were piling together, bypassing the plates.

Cunningham pushed his eyeglasses up and bent over the container. He took one of the forks in his gloved hand and used it to flop open the lid.

Maggie joined him despite the increasing smell he had just released. She was nauseated again. It didn't help matters that the buzzing was even louder now.

'Melted ice cream?' Cunningham asked, waving off a couple of flies not pleased with his presence.

'Pie à la mode,' she said, just as she realized there was

something added on top, something that definitely didn't belong.

This time there was no pushing back the bile. She covered her mouth with her hand and raced out the door, barely getting down the steps. The retching seemed to last forever until there was nothing left in her stomach. She felt a hand on the back of her neck, the soft swipe to remove a strand of hair from her cheek and then she saw Cunningham's polished shoes peeking out from the protective covers. As much as her stomach hurt, the embarrassment hurt more.

All of that was short-lived. Still on her knees, she had a perfect view of the storm cellar about fifty feet away. At this angle she could see the heavy wood door was tilted. It was opened several inches.

Just enough for someone inside to be watching them.

11

Maggie eased herself up, grateful that Cunningham didn't offer to help. He was pretending this was no big deal, and yet she could see concern in his furrowed brow.

She waited until her back was turned to the storm cellar. Waited for Cunningham's eyes to meet hers. Then she said as quietly and slowly as she could, 'We're being watched.'

He didn't flinch. Kept his eyes on hers. Slowly he shifted his weight, spreading his feet a little farther apart. All of this done casually as though they were simply chatting. He crossed his arms and she saw his fingers tuck in close to his shoulder holster.

Maggie's mind was racing, trying to remember if she had noticed another door to the trailer. There had to be one. The clothesline was in the backyard. She remembered a small utility room – sink, washer and dryer. No windows. Dark. She pictured Turner coming out announcing that the back door hadn't been kicked in.

'Ready to go back inside?' Cunningham asked.

His eyes darted around but his head stayed tilted as if he were listening intently to her.

She nodded.

His arms stayed crossed. To anyone watching, it was a casual, almost bored stance unless you noticed his right hand tucked and grasping his weapon. He gestured for her to go first, but he wasn't just being polite. He was covering her, following behind, keeping his body between her and the front yard. Even as she stepped up into the trailer she noticed that he was moving sideways, arms still crossed, hand still gripped and ready to draw. He never turned his back until the very last step inside.

'Where?' he asked as soon as the door was closed.

'The storm cellar.'

Maggie was already walking past Turner and Delaney to where she remembered the utility room.

'What's going on?' Turner asked.

'Agent O'Dell thinks we might have company in the cellar.'

'Crap!'

'Wouldn't be the first time a killer came back to watch,' Cunningham said. 'But would he choose a place where he could get trapped?'

Maggie's pulse was racing. With her stomach empty the smell didn't affect her as much. The buzzing flies still set her on edge. It took a second to realize Cunningham was asking her and waiting for a response.

'Except they never believe they'll get caught,' she said. 'Edmund Kemper met with his psychiatrist while he had a body in the trunk of his car. Berkowitz started fires then stood and watched with other bystanders.'

Her husband Greg hated that she could conjure up this kind of trivia with little effort. But here and now, it could justify their next move.

'Then we proceed like it's him,' Cunningham told them.

'If we can approach from the backyard he won't be able to see us.' Maggie headed for the utility room and the others followed.

'He'll hear us,' Delaney said.

'Not if it's only one of us. And not if there's a distraction in the front yard,' she said. Glancing into the room she saw a plain wood-paneled door to the outside.

'Agent O'Dell.' Cunningham's voice stopped her. 'This is your first time in the field – sorry, but you're not going to be the one opening that storm cellar.'

He didn't wait for an argument. To Turner he said, 'Give us a little time. I'll send Sheriff Geller and Deputy Steele away. Make it look like we're all getting ready to leave.' Then he waved for Turner to move around Maggie to get to the back door.

'The clothesline is between here and the cellar,' she told Turner.

He stared at her, waiting for an explanation.

'Bed sheets,' she said, as though that should be enough. When she saw that he still didn't understand, she added, 'They were whipping around in the breeze. Should provide some cover.'

Turner nodded.

'The bedroom at the end looks out that direction,' Cunningham told Delaney.

'Good idea.' And Delaney started down the hall to take up his post.

'Give us a chance to get in position,' Cunningham reminded them.

12

Kyle Cunningham had started to regret bringing O'Dell as soon as he smelled the insides of that trailer. He didn't blame an agent for giving in to a weak stomach, especially in a case like this. Besides, O'Dell had great instincts, a special talent in itself. He liked that she bounced right back. Maybe bounced back a bit too cocky, but he could control that. What he regretted more than anything else was that he had brought her to a crime scene that had now become an active threat.

Turner and Delaney were pros. Sheriff Geller and his deputy? Cunningham suspected, not so much. No way would he risk his agents' lives by giving Geller and his deputy the benefit of the doubt.

Truth was, he didn't trust the sheriff. There was something the man wasn't sharing. Cunningham wasn't sure what it was, but in a situation like this, he didn't appreciate the locals holding back information. Knowing whether these murders might be a drug bust gone bad or a family feud or even a vengeful lover – that information could be paramount, especially now when Cunningham had to guess what threat lurked down in that storm cellar.

Because he didn't trust the man, he simply wanted him gone.

Sheriff Geller's cruiser was parked alongside Cunningham's SUV, about a hundred feet from the front door of the double-wide. Cunningham walked out casually to the men, his back to the storm cellar the entire time, leaving O'Dell to cover him. He wasn't worried. He'd seen her at the firing range. If a weapon poked up out of that storm door he knew O'Dell would fill the planked wood with lead in a matter of seconds.

'It's a mess, huh?' Geller asked, shaking his head before Cunningham had a chance to say anything.

'I have a CSU team on their way,' Cunningham said. 'I'm hoping you and your deputy could meet them back at the interstate exit. Make sure they find this place.'

'Oh sure, we can do that.'

The man couldn't hide his relief. But Cunningham noticed the deputy almost looked disappointed, like he expected more information.

He watched them leave and stopped himself from glancing over his shoulder. Earlier, he'd noticed that there were spaces between the wood planks that made up the storm cellar door. Impossible for them to see down into the dark, but someone on the steps looking out into the light would be able to see slivers of what was going on out here. At least that's what he hoped. He wanted that someone to think they were all leaving.

Cunningham continued to their black SUV. He opened the passenger door and waved to O'Dell. Then he went around the back of the vehicle and opened the driver's door. It would be a distraction, but at the same time, he wanted to put some metal between them and that cellar door just in case the killer was armed with more than a kitchen knife.

By the time O'Dell reached the SUV, Turner had made his way across the backyard. The storm cellar looked like a mound of dirt. The wooden door was on this side of the mound. Although someone might be able to see through the thin slants, he wouldn't be able to see Turner sneaking around the back. Once he was able to position himself above the door, the intruder still wouldn't be able to see him. Opening the door would be heavy and awkward from that angle, but Turner was probably strong enough to rip the door off its hinges, let alone open it.

Now in position, Turner stood silently in place waiting for Cunningham's signal. Cunningham took off his jacket, allowing easier access to his weapon. He tossed the jacket into the SUV. That was the signal.

Turner grabbed the edge of the wood door and heaved it open. Even from where Cunningham stood he could see was a flash of movement.

'FBI,' Turner yelled.

Too quick. Someone retreated down the hole.

Cunningham raced toward the cellar's entrance, his weapon gripped firmly in both hands. O'Dell followed, matching his movements. They joined Delaney who rushed out of the trailer. Cunningham was close enough now that he could see the concrete steps that disappeared into darkness.

'FBI. We've got you surrounded,' he yelled. 'You may as well come out. Or we'll start throwing down tear gas.'

They waited.

He didn't dare look away. Not even for a second. Underneath his button-down, his T-shirt stuck to his back like a second skin. He resisted the urge to wipe at the perspiration on his forehead.

Suddenly there was more movement.

He felt his agents tense beside him, all weapons in position.

Then slowly emerging out of the darkness, a young girl peered up at them through a tangled mop of hair.

'Please don't shoot me.'

13

Stucky watched from his hiding place. He'd found a new one. This one closer. With the aid of binoculars he could see the surprise in the investigators' gestures. And he had to admit, he was as surprised to the see the girl as they were.

He pressed the binoculars against his eyes, squinted and adjusted the focus.

Stupid trees were blocking the view.

He repositioned himself. A branch poked into the small of his back and his boots sunk into the mud. He wanted to see the woman's face and her reaction. He hadn't been able to take his eyes off of her ever since she arrived. It thrilled him the whole time she had been inside the trailer, knowing that she was about to discover his contribution. And when she raced out the front door, it thrilled Stucky even more. He smiled as he watched her vomit, down on her hands and knees.

There was no bigger compliment.

Her windbreaker matched her male counterparts – navy blue with white FBI letters on the back. Hers was slightly too large. So were her trousers.

My dear, are you trying to hide a lovely figure underneath that uniform?

That thought alone was enough to captivate him. He couldn't look away. Immediately, he became obsessed with her every movement even as she swiped the damp hair off her forehead. Just a few minutes ago, right before they flung open the cellar door, he noticed as she tucked her hand into the front of her jacket. Her legs spread further apart as she took up a shooter's stance, and Stucky felt a tingle throughout his body.

What would it be like to hunt this woman?

The need, the urgency distracted him when he should be focused on the pale little girl who had immerged like a ghost from a dark grave.

How the hell had he had missed her?

Stucky had meant to go in and out lickety-split. He simply wanted to see what the asshole had done. But what he found stunned him, which wasn't an easy feat. Mr Officer of the Law had managed to do much more than Stucky had ever imagined. And yet, he really shouldn't have been surprised.

Stucky had seen the flash of anger in the guy's eyes as the pickup passed them on the road. Maybe he even recognized it. Anger like that could boil over if not tended to. And then it explodes. The insides of that trailer certainly looked like an explosion had gone off. Stucky used to feel those kinds of rages. But that was before he learned how to control them.

So the guy had killer instincts. Stucky should have felt a sense of camaraderie, but in fact, the asshole disgusted him. He was an amateur. He allowed his rage to overpower him. The result was a slaughterhouse. Still, it seemed the perfect place for Stucky to leave his package – his contribution. A gift for the investigators to appreciate.

He had gone back to the car, back to get the takeout container from the small ice chest he kept with him for opportunities just like the one inside the double-wide trailer. But even doing all that, he'd spent less than ten minutes.

No, it may have been fifteen minutes, because he ended up having a slice of that apple pie. No sense in wasting all of it.

Still, he'd been careful. He was always careful. He would have sensed if someone was watching him. So how the hell did he miss seeing this girl?

Had she been inside the trailer? Was that possible? Could she have seen what happened? Watched it from some hiding place? Or had she already been down in the cellar?

Thinking about the container made him regret that he couldn't see the investigators opening it. Those damned curtains. Now he realized he could have pushed them open when he was inside. He needed to perfect the placement of his containers, so he could watch the initial reactions. Each time he learned something.

Humans were curious by nature. An abandoned container, a paper bag left where it didn't belong – it was so interesting to see who would stop first and look inside. There would be a casual glance usually followed by a double take, like they couldn't believe their eyes. Then the sheer horror came across their faces.

Priceless.

The discovery made it a shared experience. What artist didn't enjoy sharing his masterpieces? And now he had that in common with this lovely, shapely investigator – yes, he was sure the body beneath those baggy clothes was shapely. Strong, independent – he loved them that way. They had so much fight in them. They were a worthy prey. And this one – who just wanted to be one of the boys – what a challenge she would be.

But the little girl ... What to do about her?

It bothered him that he missed seeing her. What was more interesting was that the asshole had missed her, too.

Stucky checked his watch and groaned. He wanted to stay and watch, but he needed to get back. He had the evening shift. Actually he didn't need the money, but jobs were great alibis and often presented remarkable opportunities. The discipline provided yet another level to his games. He'd shed one identity and crawl into another. He'd gotten quite good at it.

And besides, it would be easy to keep track of what was going on here. He'd even be able to track where the girl was. All he had to do was make another anonymous phone call, this time to someone in the media.

Stucky shook his head at the irony of it all. He'd taken a detour from his plans just for a little fun and in the hopes of tripping up this bastard. But as it turned out, this ghost of a girl might trip up both of them.

14

Maggie shivered even as sweat slid down her back. The weather had been erratic these last few weeks. Now the sky had turned to gray with heavy rain clouds rolling in and threatening to burst. With them came a damp and cool breeze.

Delaney took off his jacket and attempted to wrap it around the girl's bare shoulders. She flinched and he stopped short. The girl kept blinking and wiping at her eyes as if the gray sky seemed too bright. Delaney continued talking to her, gentle and slow and without taking another step. Instead he explained to her who they were, that they were there to help.

'No one will hurt you. I promise.'

Maggie watched, mesmerized by him, lulled by the tone of his voice, and she could see the girl was, too. Delaney specialized in hostage negotiations. He knew how to convince criminals that he was on their side, that he was willing to listen and help, but Maggie realized this wasn't just the hostage negotiator talking. This was a father talking to a child. A cold, hungry and scared child who was also in shock from what she had seen.

Obviously the girl hadn't witnessed the murders or she wouldn't be alive. But there was no doubt in Maggie's mind that she had seen the dead bodies. One look at the girl's bloody bare feet and she knew the footprints on the carpet were not the killer's.

'My name's Richard,' Delaney was telling the girl. 'What should I call you?'

The girl batted at her hair but didn't answer. She wore a T-shirt and cropped jeans. Maggie remembered that the weather had been warmer the day before.

She was guessing the murders had taken place twenty-four to thirty-six hours ago from the condition of the bodies and from the presence of maggots. A housefly maggot usually took fourteen to thirty-six hours to pass through all the larvae stages, but environmental conditions could change that. Turning up the heat in the trailer would definitely speed up the process.

Even so, it meant this girl may have been hiding in the dark, damp cellar for more than a day.

'My name is Katie,' the girl finally said, so quietly her words were almost lost in the breeze and the whip-snap of the bed sheets on the clothesline.

'How old are you, Katie?'

But now she just stared off into the distance like she didn't hear Delaney. Every few minutes she glanced over her shoulder as if she might be expecting someone to come up from behind. Was she worried the killer was still here?

Maggie guessed the girl was eleven or twelve. Unfortunately, she understood all too well what it meant to be twelve, to be scared and to be alone. Maggie didn't believe the killer had seen the girl. If he had, he wouldn't have left her alive. But had Katie seen him?

'Your parents,' Delaney started to say and Maggie could see him struggling with the next question. 'Are they the people in the trailer?'

Cunningham and Turner had backed off. They'd left Delaney and Maggie, giving the girl space. Now Maggie could see Cunningham on his cell phone. But Katie wasn't interested in the law enforcement men. She was glancing back in the other direction. Back toward the river. She wasn't listening to Delaney anymore either.

'My daddy,' she whispered, and then she pointed. 'He fell in the river.'

'Your dad?' Delaney shot a look at Maggie. 'He's not in the trailer?'

She shook her head, a quick back and forth like she was shaking the image out of her mind. 'Uncle Lou and Aunt Beth.'

Maggie started walking toward the riverbank. Delaney stayed with the girl. She felt Cunningham rush up beside her just as her fingers gripped her Smith & Wesson once again.

'Stay calm,' he told her when he noticed her hand inside her jacket. 'We're simply taking a walk to look around.'

But Maggie felt her adrenaline kicking in. Earlier she felt like they were still being watched even after Katie had come out of the cellar.

'What are you thinking?' she asked. 'Did Katie's father fall into the water or—'

'Or did he jump in,' Cunningham finished her sentence. 'After he killed Uncle Lou and Aunt Beth?'

15

Dense fog had settled in like smoke hovering above the surface of the water. Maggie guessed they had two hours at the most before they lost daylight. Thankfully it wasn't raining yet, but the breeze had turned brisk, especially here on the river's bank. She wished she had more than the thin windbreaker. Everywhere on her body that had moments ago been hot and sweaty was now cold and damp.

She thought the rowboat looked new. So did the fishing gear inside. It was tied to a post, gently rocking with the river's current.

'That's a beauty,' Cunningham said, coming up behind her. 'It's a kit boat. Red and white cedar. Still freshly polished. Probably just put it in the water.'

'Kit boat?'

'Build it yourself. You order it. Comes in pieces.'

Maggie was more interested in the surface of the water. With the fog it was difficult to see more than ten feet. If Katie's father was out here, his body might be miles downstream.

'CSU team and the medical examiner are on their way,' he said.

Then Cunningham stepped up beside her on the riverbank. In silence they studied the area, looking and listening. Both stood motionless. The slush-slap of water against the boat was the only sound. Twice Maggie saw something riding the current. Once it was a branch. The second time was debris.

'What are you thinking, Agent O'Dell?' Cunningham finally asked, and she wondered if he was asking as a mentor testing his student or simply as her boss looking for an answer.

'I don't think Katie's father is the killer.'

'Why not?'

'A father wouldn't want his daughter to witness a mess like that. Even if she just saw the aftermath. But if he didn't mind letting her see him murder two people then he might not have a problem killing her, too.'

'So that means if she's still alive . . .'

'Her father is most likely dead.'

She felt his eyes on her now. Without looking she could see him push up the bridge of his eyeglasses and cross his arms. A gesture she was used to seeing.

'I think you're right.' And he stared back out at the river.

They stood side by side, again, in silence. Several minutes passed and suddenly Cunningham's arm shot out.

'There. On the other side of the river.' He was pointing to his right, head tilted, body bent at the waist, trying to get a better view.

Maggie saw it now, too. Something bobbing in the water. Something large but not moving with the current. Obviously tethered down.

'Let's check it out.' Cunningham started to untie the boat.

He caught her off guard. Was that the way they did things in the field? Weren't the CSU techs supposed to recover the bodies? What about evidence? And she found herself digging in her pockets for another pair of latex gloves.

Cunningham glanced up and saw her hesitancy.

'We're just going to take a look.'

'But the boat –'

'If it's been used we're adding only our prints – easy enough to discount.'

She wasn't so sure about that, but how could she argue with her boss who was already climbing down into the boat?

She looked over her shoulder. No one else had followed. From this angle the double-wide seemed far away and insignificant. All she could see of it was its roofline. The bed sheets continued to flap on the clothesline, blocking her view of Delaney and the girl. A good thing. The girl was dehydrated and in shock. The last thing she needed was to watch them fish the bloated body of her father out of the river.

Cunningham rowed. It was obvious he'd done this before. He knew how to maneuver the oars to keep the small boat going in the right direction despite the current. Surprisingly it wasn't any easier to see once they were in the water. What had looked to be a large mass suddenly disappeared as the fog moved in thick layers. Twice Cunningham stopped rowing and waited until one of them could spot the object again.

'There.' Maggie pointed at what looked like a pile of debris bobbing and bumping against the opposite bank of the river.

Three feet away she could see the arms tangled in the branches. As Cunningham brought the rowboat parallel to the rubble Maggie saw the bloated face of a man before his head dipped under the surface again. The constant wash of water was probably the only thing that discouraged the insects.

'I don't think his throat was slashed like the others,' she told Cunningham who was working to keep the boat beside the debris while she got a better look.

Frustrated, she grabbed at the prickly vines and branches that made it impossible to see. The water was cold but the biggest tangle was just beneath the surface. Cunningham didn't stop her. Instead he worked the oars, encouraging her to tell him what else she could see.

'Do you think he drowned?' he asked.

'I have no idea.'

Maggie pulled and tugged at the tangled mess as sharp sticks poked at her. The water was murky. She couldn't see what was anchoring the body down. His arms were twisted inside the debris. At times his face bobbed up, eyes wide open almost as if staring at her, imploring her to help. She tried to focus instead on the snarled mess that kept him submerged, working her fingers until her hands were numb from the cold water.

'Is it possible he was hiding out here?' Cunningham asked. 'Why not hide in the cellar with his daughter?'

'Maybe he was trying to lead the killer away from her so that she could hide.'

'She said he fell in the water,' Maggie said, sitting back now to rest. 'But she didn't say anything about the killer. Do you think she saw him?'

Cunningham shrugged. 'Might not make a difference. You know how reliable witnesses are. Compound that with the shock and her being just a little girl. But I know someone who can help her remember.'

Maggie turned back to the debris.

'Agent O'Dell, stop,' he told her this time. Then pointed. 'Your hands – they're bleeding.'

She hadn't even noticed.

'There isn't anything more we can do. We'll let the CSU techs bring him in.'

He focused on turning the boat around against the current.

Maggie rubbed her hands, trying to warm them and wiping the blood on her jeans. She'd pricked several fingers and scraped the back of one hand. It looked worse than it was. Not that big of a deal.

But something didn't feel quite right. That's when she realized that something was missing. Somewhere in the murky water she had lost her wedding ring.

16

DEVIL'S BACKBONE STATE FOREST

Susan Fuller woke with a tremendous pounding in her head. Her mouth and throat were cotton dry, her eyes bleary. She tried to move but her head threatened to explode. It had been a long time since she'd had a hangover like this. What was worse, she had no idea where she was.

Somewhere close by, birds were singing. A soft wet breeze caressed her face. The scent of cedar and fresh rain soothed her aching head. But there was also a faint smell like overripe fruit.

She waited for her eyes to adjust to the dim light while her fingers investigated. A thin mattress and scratchy blanket separated her from the floor. She was on her back, and as she attempted to roll over, pain shot out and stopped her.

It came to her in short clips of memory. In a panic, she grabbed at her wrists to find they were no longer bound together, but she could feel the cuts that the flex-ties had left. A slight kick and she realized her feet were now free as well. But the movement also revealed the pain in her right knee.

She pushed herself to sit up and rubbed at her eyes. The room started to come into focus – wooden rafters and wood paneled walls. She guessed they were made of cedar, the scent strong and damp. Two windows were boarded up from the outside though the glass in neither had been broken or cracked.

What was this place? And how the hell did she get here?

A quick glance down and she could see her blue jeans and leather slip-ons, no socks. Her thin knit sweater had ripped at the hem. The front of it was sticky and filthy. Then suddenly the smell of eggs and raspberries made her remember.

She had been going to work early for weeks, ever since she landed the new job, but getting up in the wee hours of the morning was still a challenge. She loved her job as a pastry chef. It was a dream come true, so she dismissed how much she hated going to work when it was still dark out.

Her apartment complex was huge, three buildings in a community-like setting. No early risers at this time of morning. She'd barely gotten inside her car when she noticed the older man struggling with two large paper sacks. She recognized the logos stamped on the sides of the bags. There was a twenty-four hour grocery store three blocks away. She remembered smiling because she thought she was the only one who shopped there at the oddest hours of the day.

The guy had looked familiar. Probably lived in one of the buildings. He walked slowly with a slight limb and hunched shoulders. He wore thick-framed glasses and a windbreaker that had a logo on the back for some veteran's association. Even before she saw him trip and spill one of the bags she knew she was going to stop and help him.

She pulled up beside the curb and opened her window.

'Need some help?'

He looked startled as he stared up at her. He was already on his knees while he attempted to gather the apples that rolled over the sidewalk. She could see the glass in his frames was so thick it magnified his eyes two sizes larger. He looked a little pathetic and totally harmless.

Yes, she remembered thinking that he looked harmless.

Now Susan pulled up the sleeve of her sweater to see the needle marks, as if needing to validate that she hadn't been dreaming.

The man had caught her completely off guard.

He told her he lived in the building around the corner and at the far end of the complex's huge parking lot. Susan was already picking up the bruised apples for him when she offered to drive him to his building. The engine was still running when she popped the trunk. She took one of his grocery bags and started to put it inside.

He was incredibly strong. She remembered being surprised by his strength, and now she could see the evidence in the black and blue marks where he'd grabbed her.

It happened so fast.

One second she was bending down to put the grocery bags inside the trunk and the next second she felt the stab of the needle in her arm. He shoved her off balance, pushing her face first inside the bed of the trunk.

Whatever he shot into her system left her paralyzed almost immediately. She couldn't move her arms or legs even as she knew he was quickly binding her wrists and then her ankles. She couldn't seem to move her lips even to scream, but he still slapped a piece of duct tape across her mouth. Then he slammed the trunk shut, leaving her bound, paralyzed and in complete darkness.

All of it had taken only seconds.

She examined her arms. There had been other injections. She counted three puncture marks. Perhaps that explained why she couldn't remember anything after the attack. Or how she had gotten here?

A sick feeling swept over her. What else didn't she remember?

Reluctantly, she forced her hand down the front of her pants. Would she know if he had violated her while her body was paralyzed and her mind had shut down? No soreness, no bruising. Nothing sticky left. As repulsed as she was by the thought, she wanted to cry from relief. But just because he hadn't done anything didn't mean that he wasn't going to when he came back.

Susan looked around the room again. Only one door. Perhaps a one-room cabin or shed. She held her breath and listened. All she could hear were the birds and a soft tap-tap of a gentle rain. The breeze she felt earlier came from an air vent in the roof.

Her body ached. She attempted to stand, but pain stopped her again. Her right knee was on fire. Through her jeans she could tell it was swollen. She managed to get to her feet, keeping pressure off the knee. He had taken off her restraints. Maybe she could find something inside the cabin to break the door or its lock. But as she started to search she noticed the door didn't have any kind of lock.

Had he barricaded or padlocked it from outside?

Susan stopped and listened again, ignoring her aches and pain and her labored breaths. Then she grabbed the door handle and without much effort, pushed the door wide open.

17

Maggie tucked her hands under her arms. Suddenly the damp chill felt like it had seeped bone deep. For some reason she felt a sense of defeat because she hadn't been able to untangle Katie's dad from the debris. She hated leaving him out there in the murky water.

She wasn't sure where these feelings were coming from. Bringing his body back to the girl wasn't going to bring him back to life. It'd been over fifteen years since she'd lost her own father and yet she remembered all too well how raw that loss could feel for a twelve-year-old girl.

Cunningham had insisted that Delaney crawl into the ambulance when Katie had refused to get in. Not just refused but started screaming, arms flailing, bare feet ready to kick if anyone dared to grab her.

'I can't leave without my daddy.'

Maggie wasn't sure what Delaney told her, but somehow he had convinced her. The role he had taken on – negotiator, friend, and surrogate father – was now the only bond the girl had. The ambulance had just left, and a few minutes later the sheriff's cruiser, followed by the CSU mobile crime lab, pulled in.

Now Cunningham took Sheriff Geller and Deputy Steele aside to update them. The CSU team unpacked equipment onto the front lawn. One of the men started setting up floodlights. Someone mentioned that the medical examiner was only a few minutes away.

Maggie stood quietly, watching it all. Her job was done here. There was nothing more she could do. She'd have to wait for the evidence to be collected and the autopsies to be processed. Her first crime scene and she found herself feeling completely and totally powerless.

'You think that girl saw something?'

Maggie startled at the sound of Deputy Steele. She hadn't heard him come up beside her.

Without taking her eyes off the CSU techs, she shrugged and said, 'It's hard to say.'

'Your boss said she was in the cellar. I'd think it was hard to see anything from that angle.'

Maggie glanced at him. He was staring over at the cellar as if trying to calculate the distance.

She guessed the deputy was around her age, late twenties or early thirties, but something about him seemed younger. Too much swagger. Maybe a bit too cocky. He was as tall as Turner but smaller built, narrower in the shoulders and waist, still lean and muscular. His brown uniform shirt fit tight across his chest. His shirtsleeves bulged at the biceps, almost as though he wore a size smaller to emphasize his physique.

He wore no jacket and didn't seem affected by the damp weather. He kept the brim of his hat low over his eyes and stood with legs spread apart and his thumbs looped on his utility belt. He reminded Maggie of a gunslinger in a classic Western.

'Pretty gruesome inside, huh?'

She certainly didn't want to talk about what she had seen. Deputy Steele, however, did want to talk.

'Sheriff didn't want us contaminating the scene, but I got a pretty good look.'

'I've seen worse,' Turner answered from behind them. He took a place on the other side of Maggie. 'That piece of pie though – that was the craziest freakin' thing I've seen in a long time.'

'What are you talking about?' Steele wanted to know.

Immediately Maggie glanced up at Turner, looking to see if he meant to let that piece of information slip out. There were details of a crime that you held close. Certain things that only a handful of investigators and the killer knew about. Technically the deputy was part of the investigation, but Maggie wondered if maybe this particular deputy didn't need to know. Obviously he had *not* gotten a 'pretty good look,' despite his bragging claim.

'Son of a bitch left something in a takeout container,' Turner said, then shot a quick glance at Maggie, as if checking to make sure it didn't still make her nauseated. She wanted to remind him that she had done just fine at the autopsy yesterday when he was groaning. Then he continued, 'Looked like pie à la mode with something added.'

'Wait. What d'you mean, something added?'

Turner looked at the deputy, and he raised an eyebrow waiting for the man to figure it out. But Maggie could see Steele still mulling it around like it didn't make sense.

'That doesn't sound right.'

'Tell me about it,' Turner said. 'Ruined one of my favorite desserts.'

'Sheriff is convinced we got a serial killer on our hands,' Steele told them. 'You think that might be the case?'

This time Turner didn't blink. Maggie was too chilled to have this conversation. She glanced over her shoulder and was grateful to see Cunningham and the sheriff on their way back.

Steele noticed, too, and his entire demeanor changed like he'd flipped a switch.

'Nothing more for us to do here,' Sheriff Geller said, tucking in his shirt as if to emphasize that they were finished. 'How 'bout I buy all of you a drink before you head back home?'

'Thanks, Sheriff. Unfortunately we'll have to take a rain check,' Cunningham told him. 'My team might be finished out here but we still have some work to do.'

On that same note, Maggie asked the sheriff, 'Did you know them?'

He stared at her like perhaps he didn't understand her question.

'The victims,' she explained. 'Katie said they were her Uncle Lou and Aunt Beth. Did you know them?'

'We might all live out in the sticks, Agent, but no, we don't all know each other.'

'I don't believe Agent O'Dell meant any disrespect, Sheriff Geller,' Cunningham said. 'It's our job to gather as much information as we can. We have the girl and her safety to think about.'

'Sure, sure, I understand.' He tilted his hat back but he kept his eyes on Maggie. 'I can certainly offer some assistance there if you're worried about her.' Now he looked over at Cunningham. 'Let me know which hospital you have her at and I can have a deputy outside her room.'

'That would be helpful,' Cunningham said, then he turned and headed for their SUV.

Maggie could feel the tension between the two men. Neither Cunningham nor Sheriff Geller offered to shake the other's hand. Nor did they promise to keep each other posted.

She glanced at Turner to see if he noticed. He was climbing into the backseat, leaving her to ride shotgun alongside Cunningham. He winked at her and shot her a grin like he was doing her a favor.

They drove down the long driveway in silence, but as soon as they turned onto the main road, Cunningham said, 'No information gets shared with Geller. If he calls, direct him to me. Understood?'

His tone was matter-of-fact. No anger. No frustration.

'Yes, of course,' Maggie said in unison with Turner's, 'Okay, sure.'

Maggie waited for more explanation. There was none.

18

WASHINGTON, DC

Dr Gwen Patterson's heels clicked all the way down the tiled floor of the hospital hallway. She had been heading out to the Kennedy Center when Kyle Cunningham called her. Her date was with a professor at John Hopkins – tall, dark and handsome with an M.D. *and* a Ph.D. behind his name. He had invited her to see the Washington National Opera's performance of *Carmen* followed by drinks at the Columbia Room. She hadn't had a swanky night out like this since ... forever. And yet, the second she heard Kyle Cunningham's voice, she felt that damned flutter in her stomach. Her palms were sweaty and by the end of the conversation she had made a promise to him that completely derailed her entire evening.

Damn it!

She hated that he had that effect on her. He was a married man – off limits. But the chemistry between them was so tangible Gwen swore others had noticed, no matter how careful she had been.

They had worked together only a few times – three to be exact. Gwen was a psychiatrist and had her own successful practice in the District. Her clients – she referred to them as clients, rarely patients unless they required hospitalization – included senators and congressmen, even a five-star general, but she specialized in criminal behavior. Sometimes she wondered what the hell she was thinking, but the subject fascinated her.

She'd written a book, published dozens of articles and suddenly became the go-to-expert that the media loved to call on. A year ago her guest appearance on a national talk show had attracted the attention of the Assistant Director of the Behavioral Science Unit at Quantico. He wanted to hire her as a consultant on a murder case. Then came another case and another. It didn't take long and Gwen was wishing Kyle Cunningham would think of her without there being a dead body involved.

She thought this might be the time when she answered her phone and he said, 'Gwen, I need you.'

Yes, those very words and the tension in his voice had made her knees go weak, although she tried to blame the cracked sidewalk and three-inch heels. He'd literally caught her on the street before she climbed into the waiting town car.

Even when he asked his favor and it was all about business, she didn't once consider saying, 'no.'

What in the world was wrong with her?

Why hadn't she told him that she had a hot date and tickets to the opera? That she was wearing a little black dress with a slit up her thigh – totally inappropriate attire for a hospital visit. Not to mention that the three-inch heels were already killing her feet.

He asked his favor and before she knew it she heard herself instructing him which hospital to use and telling him, 'I'll be there as soon as I can.'

Then she got in the town car, redirected the driver and made the phone call to cancel her swanky night out. That's just what friends did for each other, she told herself, knowing full well she and Cunningham were not really friends. But that was how she explained it to Professor Hottie.

Now she stopped at the nurse's station. The unit secretary looked up at her and Gwen didn't flinch as the woman's eyes traveled down, checking out Gwen's dress but without a flash of judgment. She had probably seen stranger things in the last several hours. She thought the woman looked familiar but didn't take anything for granted and introduced herself.

'I'm Dr Gwen Patterson. I'm meeting a young girl the FBI's bringing in.'

'Already here.' She pointed down the hall. 'They have her in room 333. Finally got her sedated.'

'I was hoping they'd wait for me to talk to her before they did that.'

'If they'd waited you would have needed a helmet.'

'That bad?'

'Mostly scared. They said her daddy was one of the victims.' The secretary got up from behind the counter and grabbed something from a drawer. She handed it to Gwen and said, 'No sense in ruining a perfectly awesome dress.'

Gwen unfolded the garment. The white lab coat would be too large but she smiled and said, 'Thanks.' She slipped it on and started rolling up the too-long sleeves as she made her way to room 333.

Before she got to the door, a man came out of the room. His hair was tousled, his tie loosened and his suit wrinkled. He looked exhausted. She barely recognized him.

'Agent Delaney,' she called out to him.

Relief crossed his face. He wiped his left palm over his jaw as he offered her his right.

'Thanks for coming Dr Patterson.' Then he noticed her dress and heels. 'Looks like we interrupted your evening.'

She shrugged like it didn't matter and told him, 'I've seen

Carmen several times. I already know how it ends.' It wasn't Delaney's fault, after all. She could have said, 'no.'

He nodded and smiled then led her farther down the hallway so the girl couldn't hear them talking outside her door.

'Her name's Katie. They had to sedate her, so I'm not sure you'll get anything more out of her. A.D. Cunningham was hoping she might tell you a last name or what other family she has. If what she's told us is true, she lost an aunt, an uncle and her father.'

'Did she see what happened?'

'We're not sure. General consensus is that if she had, she wouldn't still be alive. But there were footprints on the carpet, and she was barefoot when we found her with bloody soles. Not from cuts on her feet. So she might have wandered in and saw the aftermath.'

'How bad was it?'

'Bad.' Delaney's eyes darted back up the hallway, making sure no one was in earshot. 'Uncle Lou was hanging upside down from the ceiling when his throat was cut.'

Gwen closed her eyes. Shook her head. No little girl should ever have to see such a thing.

'It's possible she spent a whole night in that storm cellar. Maybe longer. Attending doctor says she's dehydrated. Still in shock.'

'And her father?'

'She said he fell in the river. They were still retrieving his body when we left the scene.'

'Does she know he's dead?'

Delaney swiped his hand over his jaw. 'She asked me about him in the ambulance. Wanted to know if they were taking him to the same hospital.' He met Gwen's eyes and she could see the pained look when he added, 'I didn't know what to tell her.'

'You did fine, Agent Delaney. She was lucky to have you there with her. How old is she?'

'Maybe eleven or twelve. I'm guessing she's about the same age as my oldest daughter.'

That explained why this was extra hard for him. Gwen knew he wasn't just comparing the two girls' ages.

'I'll talk to her. Go on home, Agent Delaney.'

'You sure you don't want me to stick around?'

'I promise I'll be gentle with her. It's actually better if she only has me to lean on. If you're there she'll look to you as a mediator. Go home and hug your daughters.'

She watched him leave, then Gwen found the girl's room. The sedatives had kicked in. Katie was asleep. She looked tiny and fragile in the hospital bed with IV-lines going into her thin arms.

Gwen glanced at her watch as she sat in the chair next to the bed. She had cancelled her entire evening to sit and wait. It wasn't the first time she'd done this with a client and it most likely wouldn't be the last.

She slipped the heels off and stretched her legs out in front of her, crossing them at the ankles. She studied the girl's face. It was calm except for a slight pouting of her lips. Every once in a while her eyelids twitched.

There would be nightmares and possibly a fear of the dark. Maybe even claustrophobia. She would grieve for her aunt and uncle. She would cry for her father. There was nothing Gwen could do to make any of that hurt go away.

But maybe, if they were lucky, the girl would lead them to the killer. And hopefully she could do so before he realized he had left a witness behind.

19

QUANTICO

Maggie had been at her desk computer for almost an hour when Turner tapped on her office door even though it was open.

'Don't you have a husband expecting you at home?'

'You didn't ask me that last night when you kept me out late.'

She wasn't sure if black men blushed but from the shake of his head, she knew she'd zinged him. Isn't that what colleagues did to each other? He and Delaney did it all the time.

'Whadya know. O'Dell has a sense of humor,' he said as he leaned against the doorjamb. 'Don't worry. I won't tell anyone.'

She smiled at that.

'But seriously, O'Dell, you're starting to make the rest of us look bad.'

'I've been searching ViCAP.' The Violent Criminal Apprehension Program was essentially a database that recorded and analyzed violent crimes, allowing investigators access to track killers with similar M.O.s. 'Two victims with missing body parts within days of each other and within – what would you say – a hundred miles of each other?'

'You're thinking of the woman hiker missing her toe?' Turner finally seemed interested.

'Yes.'

'But that thing in the trailer,' he grimaced. 'We don't even know what all that mess is yet.'

'I had one of the crime scene techs email a photo. I'm pretty sure it's a spleen. Maybe a liver.'

'Do you know for sure that's even human? Calves' livers are pretty disgusting. Probably more so after being in a heated trailer for over twenty-four hours.'

'I'm pretty sure it's human.'

'So where did it come from? That dude hanging from the ceiling looked stabbed. I don't think he was sliced open.'

'How could you tell with all the maggots?'

He shrugged. 'True. Guess Wenhoff will let us know. Did you get any hits at ViCAP?'

'Not in Virginia. But there was something interesting in Massachusetts. The Boston area. About three months ago. A truck stop off Interstate 95. Someone found what they believe was a lung. It was left in a brown paper bag outside the restroom.'

'Holy crap! How come we never heard about that?'

'They've never found a body. ViCAP notes that it could have come from an organ donor facility. Warns that it could have been a prank.'

'That's some frickin' prank.'

'Isn't that missing councilwoman from the Boston area?'

'Could be. I don't remember.' He pushed himself off the doorjamb. 'Seriously, O'Dell, it's been a long day. You need to go home. Get some rest.'

She promised him she would. But as soon as he left Maggie started another search. Property taxes would tell her the last name of Uncle Lou and Aunt Beth. Finding out more about them could help lead them to their killer. This wasn't like the other cases she had worked on. The long distance ones. She wasn't obsessed with figuring out the puzzle and solving the mystery. This was different. There was an urgency. She could feel time slipping away, causing her pulse to race and her brain to throb. She felt a sense of obligation to the little girl named Katie. She knew what it was like to lose a father. Not just lose him, but tragically.

That wasn't all. O'Dell had tracked enough killers to know that as soon as this one discovered he'd left behind a witness, he would be back.

20

Cunningham had gotten an update from Agent Delaney, so he knew that Dr Patterson had arrived hours ago. He was pleasantly surprised, however, to see one of Geller's deputies already stationed outside Katie's room. He flashed his ID at the man and they exchanged only a nod.

He tapped on the door and eased it open slowly, coming in quietly. Gwen glanced up at him from a chair beside the bed. The girl was asleep.

'Sorry it took me so long to get here,' he said as he ran his fingers through his damp hair. He'd gone back to Quantico to take a shower and change clothes. He needed to get the smell of that trailer off of his body.

'Has she said anything?' he asked.

'She hasn't woken up. They had to sedate her before I arrived.'

He came all the way into the room before he noticed Gwen's dress. Actually it was her bare feet that his eyes caught sight of first. She had one foot tucked under her, pulling up her skirt and revealing enough of her thigh to be distracting.

'I pulled you away from a special evening.'

She looked surprised that he would even notice. There was very little he didn't notice about Gwen Patterson.

She shrugged like it wasn't a big deal. Which made Cunningham think it was, in fact, a big deal.

'I owe you one,' he told her and caught her eyes to make sure she knew he was sincere.

There was a groan and movement from the bed. The girl's eyes started to flutter open.

Cunningham looked to Gwen and she put a finger up to stop him where he stood. Then she sat up and leaned in. She touched the girl's hand and waited a second.

'Hi, Katie.'

The girl's eyes darted around the room. She noticed the IV, saw the needle in the back of her hand. Panic sat her up and Gwen came out of the chair, calming her with gentle but firm hands on her shoulders.

'It's okay. You're safe. You're in the hospital but you're okay.'

The girl's head swiveled, taking in the surroundings. She saw Cunningham and her eyes stayed on him. She recognized him.

'My daddy ... he fell in the river. You went to look for him.'

Cunningham looked to Gwen for instruction. She nodded her head, indicating it was okay for him to tell the girl. He wished they had had a chance to discuss this. He didn't know how to say it, but he wouldn't lie.

'We found your dad in the river, Katie.'

The girl sat completely up. Gwen rubbed her shoulder and back. Cunningham realized she was keeping her hands close in case she needed to hold the girl down. They didn't want Katie to jump out of the bed and rip the needle out of her hand. But the girl seemed to be taking it well.

But then she asked, 'Is he here at this hospital?'

And Cunningham felt his stomach nosedive.

She was looking at him with all the innocence and hope of a child. Why hadn't he expected a child's response? But Gwen saved him.

'Katie, your daddy didn't make it.'

She was still staring at Cunningham as if she hadn't heard Gwen. Or maybe she needed to hear it from him. He was the last one to see her father. In her mind, he was the one who had gone to pull him from the river.

This was exactly why he had called Gwen to be here. To rescue him from saying the wrong thing. She was the expert. She was supposed to know what words to use. How to say them. What to say. It had been a long time since he had a conversation with a child. But one thing he remembered – kids didn't like it when adults lied to them.

'I'm sorry, Katie. He was already dead when I found him in the river.'

Silent tears slid down her face. The sedative was probably still in her system. She didn't thrash around. She didn't move. In her eyes he could see a sad, quiet acceptance.

'Did you pull him out of the water?' she wanted to know.

'Yes, we did.'

'That water's still really cold even though it's summer.' She said this like she was repeating what someone must have told her.

'Katie,' Gwen said, waiting for the girl to finally look at her. 'I'm Dr Patterson. I'm here to help make sure that you're going to be okay. And this is Mr Cunningham. You already know that he's a law officer.'

'FBI,' Katie said, nodding and watching Cunningham.

'That's right. You remembered.' Cunningham allowed a smile though he was thinking, of course she remembered.

They had yelled it down the storm cellar how many times before they realized there was no threat?

'He's going to find out what happened to your daddy,' Gwen told her. 'We're both going to make sure nothing bad happens to you. Okay?'

Gwen sat on the bed now and put her hand over Katie's. She gestured for Cunningham to take the chair that was now right behind her. He understood immediately. She didn't want them towering over the girl. They needed to be on her level, less threatening and more trusting. He sat at the edge of the seat, the space that Gwen had just vacated. It was warm and smelled like her. The high heels she had slipped off were at his feet.

'Are you hungry?' Gwen asked.

One of the IV lines was probably providing nutrients but sometimes food was one of the best ways to gain a child's attention and trust. Cunningham knew it always worked with his boys. Still worked, even now that both of them were in college. If he needed to talk to them, getting a bite to eat added a layer of comfort.

'How about we order you some soup? Do you like grilled cheese?'

The girl nodded. Gwen glanced at Cunningham. Without a word he scooted the chair backward so he could reach the phone. There was a menu card on the stand with instructions. Gwen talked to the girl in a low soothing voice while he placed the order. As soon as he finished, Gwen scooted even closer to Katie. She was holding her small hand between both of hers, and he could see Gwen's thumb rubbing the girl's palm, a tactile method to calm and relax her.

'Katie,' Gwen said and paused while she waited for the girl

to look at her, again. 'Did you see what happened to your daddy?'

She stared at Gwen then her eyes drifted over Gwen's shoulder to Cunningham. No, he realized, she wasn't looking at him. She was staring past him, too.

'He told me to hide,' she said in a small, quiet voice. 'Something was wrong.' Then in a whisper, she added, 'Something bad.'

Gwen waited. Neither she nor Cunningham moved. Katie's eyes continued to stare just over their heads. He wanted to turn and see what held her attention, but realized it didn't really matter. Her mind was back at her aunt and uncle's.

Gwen decided to gently prod her. 'He told you to hide.' Her voice was soft and warm as though she were reading a bedtime story. 'So that's when you went down into the cellar?'

She nodded but her eyes still didn't return to Gwen's.

'And you closed the door to the cellar?'

Another nod.

This time Gwen let the silence fill almost a full minute before she said, 'Katie.'

A few more seconds slid by, and she called the girl's name again, waiting until Katie's eyes made their way back to Gwen.

And then Gwen asked the million-dollar question. 'If you were in the cellar how do you know your daddy fell in the river?'

21

Stucky's shift didn't end until midnight. His mind had been distracted the entire evening. He'd made a couple of mistakes. Nothing drastic. No one seemed to care and if they did, they never mentioned it to him. According to the owner, he was a 'diligent worker.' Besides, he'd already established himself as a quiet loner in order to avoid chatty conversations with co-workers or even the owner.

As soon as he left work he headed for a payphone he remembered seeing earlier in the week. It was getting more and more difficult to find the contraptions. Whenever he did see one he jotted down the location in a little notebook. This payphone was attached to the dark corner of a dilapidated gas station, which made it even more valuable. Rundown businesses didn't spend money on parking lot cameras. The station was closed. There was no one else around.

He dialed the number of a local TV news station. Not the information line. At this hour, he knew that would only be a recording telling him when to call back. No, he dialed the actual news desk. From past experience, he knew the staff would always pick up. As soon as someone answered, Stucky took on a slightly hysterical tone.

'My neighbors. I think someone killed them. I saw cops, FBI agents, an ambulance—'

'Sir, slow down,' the woman interrupted. 'Where exactly is this?'

He gave her the name of the main road and the interstate exit number, estimating how many miles to the double-wide's driveway. Somewhere in the middle of his description he heard a click and slight buzz. Someone else had picked up on the connection or she had put him on speakerphone.

'There's a little girl. The lone survivor. My wife's real close to the family. We just need to know if she's okay. That sheriff won't tell us.'

'We don't have any information—'

He heard a man's voice somewhere close by. Then Stucky heard tapping. She was checking on a computer.

'Look, I got to go, I just thought—'

'No, please stay with me for a minute.'

Stucky stifled a smile. Even though she couldn't see him he didn't want it seeping into his tone. He knew if he sounded reluctant she'd want to harvest whatever information he had.

'Can you just stay with me for a minute?' she asked, but the man's voice was right beside her now and distracting her.

Stucky heard him well enough to know he was telling her about an ambulance call in that area. She must have put him on speaker, so her colleague could listen in, but they forgot that Stucky could also hear them.

'Looks like they took a patient to Sacred Heart in DC.'

'Not the local hospital?'

He hung up the phone. He had what he needed. As he climbed back into his car he heard the payphone start to ring.

Wasn't that sweet? She was calling him back.

He had a small studio apartment close to work, but long ago he'd gotten into the habit of renting a motel room when he needed to change his identity. He usually chose one off the interstate. Tonight's desk clerk barely looked up at him as he handed over the room key in exchange for the night's payment in cash.

Stucky's traveling cooler and the oversized duffle bag always stayed in the trunk of his car. Along with his crossbow encased in a waterproof, zippered bag that the sales guy had upsold him.

Preparation was an art. There were other risks that made the game worth playing. But the basics? No need to trip over the basics. That's what separated him from the amateurs like the raging asshole. What a mess he had left in that trailer.

And then of course, there was the girl.

Inside the cramped motel room, Stucky peeled off his work clothes like a chameleon shedding his skin. He popped out the contact lenses that made his brown eyes blue. He added some gray to his temples, and although he hated hair gel, he put in a generous amount. Then he slicked his bangs back.

From the duffle bag he pulled out and unfolded the specially padded T-shirt. It added a layer of fat around his middle. When he put his shirt on over it, the buttons looked ready to pop. He carried a pair of baggy jeans that accommodated the new waistline. In a couple of minutes he had added about ten years to his age and what looked like ten pounds to his body.

Stucky was curious why they'd taken the girl to a hospital in DC. From his viewpoint she hadn't looked injured. It seemed overly cautious, but it also told him that the FBI was definitely in charge. Not a bad thing. It would make it more difficult for Officer Asshole. And maybe it would give Stucky an opportunity to see that pretty FBI agent again. He so liked the impression he'd already made on her. Given the chance to see more of his work, he knew he could win her respect. He welcomed that challenge.

He left the vehicle in the far corner of the hospital's parking lot. Then he went through the front doors, walking into the place like he had been there many times. He crossed the lobby with confident strides and passed the reception desk without a glance at the woman behind it. He wanted it to look like he didn't need any directions or instructions. He wanted it to look like he belonged here. So he kept walking. It wasn't until he stood in front of the elevators that he allowed himself a glimpse at the directory.

When he saw that no one was looking, he left the elevators and continued down another hallway. He found a door marked EMPLOYEES ONLY. He tried the door handle. Not locked. He pulled it open and walked inside the small supply room. By the time he exited, he was wearing a janitorial uniform and pushing a rolling bucket and mop.

He took the elevator to the first floor of patient rooms. The rollers on the bucket were tricky. Splashing water would draw attention. At the same time he couldn't afford to look tentative. He stopped at the nursing station and waited for the woman behind the counter to notice him. The longer it took the more pleased he became. Already he had managed to blend in. Still, being polite and patient were not traits that came easily for him.

When she looked up, he simply said, 'They sent me to clean up some little girl's vomit. Said the ambulance brought her in last night. Didn't give me no room number or anything.'

She pulled out a chart and started flipping pages. She didn't even question his lack of information.

'Only child we admitted by ambulance last night is up on the third floor. Room 333.' Then she shook her head and looked back up at him. 'Poor thing. Hopefully she won't be sick all night long.'

'You and me both,' he told her and she smiled at him before turning back to her work.

He headed back for the elevators, a kick of adrenaline making it difficult to keep his pace slow and the bucket from sloshing over its rim.

This was almost too easy.

22

WASHINGTON, DC

Katie had no answers for them. Instead, she shut down.

Cunningham could see that Gwen had expected it. But of course, she had needed to ask the question. She understood the urgency. She had told him once during another investigation that in medicine, they called it 'the critical hour.' Those first forty-eight hours were crucial as to whether a patient moved toward recovery or slipped away.

So Gwen understood that the same concept applied in criminal investigations. If there was no lead, a suspect or an arrest within forty-eight hours, the chances of solving the case were cut in half. With eyewitnesses it was even more important to capture their accounts while it was fresh and not manipulated by hearsay, the media or second-guesses. But when that eyewitness was tragically affected, let alone a child ... well, Cunningham had no idea if Katie would be able to help them.

They agreed to let the girl rest. No more questions. At least for now.

When her tray arrived, Katie slurped spoonfuls of the chicken noodle soup and took several bites of her grilled cheese sandwich. Her eyes brightened when she saw the treat Cunningham had ordered for her – a bowl of ice cream with chocolate syrup.

It wasn't until a nurse came in to do her routine check that

Cunningham realized it was long past midnight. The nurse seemed surprised to find Gwen still here. She mentioned the cafeteria then offered to sit with the girl, promising she wouldn't leave until they returned.

Cunningham stopped short when he recognized the uniformed deputy stationed outside the door.

'Deputy Steele. You must be pulling a double shift?'

The man shrugged and said, 'Feel bad for the girl. What she must've seen. No kid needs to see that. Hopefully she got a good look at the guy.'

Cunningham almost said that they might never know, but he stopped himself. Instead he asked the deputy if he could get him anything from the cafeteria.

'I'd kill for a cup of coffee,' he said, rubbing his eyes and totally unaware of his poor choice of words.

'Cream or sugar?'

'Black.'

As they got on the elevator Cunningham explained to Gwen that the Warren County sheriff had volunteered his deputies to watch over the girl.

'That's a generous offer,' Gwen said. 'Considering it's about an hour's drive into the District.'

Cunningham shrugged and kept it to himself that maybe it was Sheriff Geller's way to make up for whatever information he was holding back from them.

The cafeteria was almost empty except for two doctors at a table close to the door. It was too early for breakfast, but Cunningham managed to convince the grill cook to scramble some eggs and throw on some bacon. The man even added some wheat toast, buttering it and warming it on his grill.

While he waited, Cunningham watched Gwen select a table

in the huge dining room clear on the opposite side of where the doctors were. She had gotten their coffees. He noticed that she stopped at the counter to add cream and sugar to his. He pushed up his glasses and rubbed at his eyes, stifling a smile. They'd only worked together a handful of times and she remembered how he took his coffee.

He paid for their trays then stopped at the same condiment counter. He absentmindedly grabbed napkins, salt and a half dozen tiny grape jelly containers, bypassing the strawberry and pushing aside the marmalade and cherry. The last time they had had breakfast together was at Quantico's cafeteria. He teased her about slathering so much grape jelly on her toast.

Silly of him to be thinking about that. Odd that they both remembered such stuff.

'You must be exhausted,' he told her when he placed the tray in the middle of their table.

As if only now willing to admit it, she ran her fingers through her hair. 'Food will help.'

'Do you think she saw something?' Cunningham asked as he sipped his coffee. He already believed that the girl had, but he still wanted to hear what Gwen thought.

'How else would she know he fell in the river?'

Gwen picked up two of the jelly containers and began squeezing generous portions on her toast. Her fingernails were manicured and freshly polished, reminding him that he had pulled her away from an obviously planned evening. Gwen noticed him watching and caught his eyes. They stared at each other a beat too long. He looked away, took another sip of coffee. Pretended he was interested in the two doctors now leaving the cafeteria.

'The door to the storm cellar is made up of wooden planks,' he told her, 'with spaces in between. She was watching us by lifting the door just a fraction.'

'So she could have watched what happened to her father from the cellar?'

He shook his head. 'The door faces the driveway and the front yard. No way she could see the river unless she was standing outside the cellar.'

He glanced back for her reaction. She was digging into her eggs and he appreciated this about the woman – she was a professional. She set aside her exhaustion and the emotion of the morning and she continued to work the puzzle.

'Delaney said that she might have spent the entire night in the storm cellar.'

He nodded.

'The mental shock, the physical toll on her body could affect what she thinks she saw. Her father told her to hide. He may have said that he was going to take the boat and get help. Maybe when he didn't come back, she worried that he fell in the water.'

'Is that you believe happened?'

Without hesitation she said, 'No. I think she actually saw him fall in the water. Do you know how he ended up in the river?'

'He was shot in the back. Probably at the river's edge.'

She sat up straight, and when she rubbed at her eyes he could see the exhaustion.

'Agent O'Dell and I found him tangled in some debris. CSU techs recovered his body. They're still out there processing the trailer.'

'Tell me what you believe happened.'

'I think Katie and her father may have been out in a rowboat when the killer arrived,' Cunningham said. 'The river's about two hundred feet from the back of the house. The killer wouldn't have needed to go around back. There's an incline. Lots of trees. It's not easy to see the front of property or the trailer from the river.'

'So could Katie have even seen—?'

'Looking down at the river from the backyard, yes, she could have seen her father fall in. But not from inside the cellar.'

'So they came back after their boat ride. Katie said something was wrong. Something bad.'

'Her father might have sensed something was wrong. Maybe he saw a vehicle parked in front. Whatever he did see, it concerned him enough to send Katie down the cellar while he checked it out.'

'You think he interrupted the killer?'

'Or the killer saw him when he was finished and on his way out of the trailer. Her father made a run for the river.'

'And he shot him before he got to his boat.'

Cunningham nodded.

'Here's the odd part.' He pushed his plate to the side then leaned his elbows on the table. 'Neither of the victims in the trailer was shot. They were both stabbed. It looked and smelled like a slaughterhouse in there because the killer turned the heat up full blast. It looks disorganized, like he didn't bring anything with him. We think he may have used a kitchen knife. He even used electrical cord to tie them up, so he didn't think to bring rope or flex-ties. And yet, he was carrying a gun.'

'Inside the trailer was personal,' she said. 'Outside he was just taking care of business.'

'I suppose you're right.'

'So where was Katie if she wasn't in the cellar?' Gwen asked.

'She had to be in the backyard. Maybe behind the trees.'

'Do you think she saw the killer?'

He pushed up his glasses, sat back and crossed his arms over his chest.

'I think it's possible,' he said.

'But he didn't see her.'

'No. She wouldn't be alive if he had seen her.'

'If he didn't see Katie then he has no reason to believe she exists. So why have the deputies outside her room?' she asked.

'Because there's no way I'll be able to keep it a secret for very long that she does exist.'

23

Maggie could smell ashes, something burning. No, the fire was already out. It wasn't smoke she smelled but singed hair and burnt flesh. She searched but couldn't see through the fog. Where was the smell coming from?

Then she saw it.

Another boat was floating on the river. She kept her eyes fixed on the boat while she pointed at it.

'Row up a little closer,' she told Cunningham without looking back at him.

He didn't say a word, but obeyed.

Closer. Just a little bit closer.

The fog grew thick. Now she wasn't sure if it was fog. Or was the air filled with ashes?

Suddenly the boat appeared right in front of them. Too late to stop. Their rowboat crashed into it. Only it wasn't another boat.

It was a casket.

Smooth, dark wood, polished with brass rails and soft, tufted fabric peeking over the edges. The lid was gone but Maggie hesitated to look inside. Her stomach felt sick again. She was shivering from the cold, damp air. She could hardly breathe without sucking in the thick ashes.

She didn't want to look. She felt like she was twelve years old again. She already knew what she would find inside. It was the same every time, and she didn't want to see her father lying there in a crisply pressed brown suit that she'd never seen him wear before.

She couldn't bear to see the side of his face where the mortician had painted over his burned flesh in an attempt to salvage what skin remained. She remembered the crinkle of plastic under his sleeve when she touched him. She remembered how his hair was combed all wrong. She had reached up to brush it off his forehead and snapped her hand back when she saw the blisters and the Frankenstein scar that the flap of hair had been hiding.

'I told you not to touch him,' her mother scolded her.

But how could she not touch her father?

And now this casket was floating here in the river. It couldn't be her father's. That was ridiculous.

Maggie stood up in the rowboat. She braced herself and leaned over the edge of the casket to see inside.

Empty.

'It's empty,' she told Cunningham, relieved and able to breathe again.

Then she turned to look at him. But Cunningham was gone. Her father sat in his place. He smiled at her, dressed in the brown suit with his plastic-wrapped hands gripping the oars.

Maggie jolted back so suddenly that her feet slipped. She fell backwards over the side of the boat.

Falling with arms flailing. Nothing to grab onto.

Falling and falling.

Where was the water?

She jerked awake. Sat up and searched the dark surroundings. Her heart pounded in her ears. Her breathing came in gasps. Sweat drenched her body. In the shadows she searched for the boat, searched for her father.

Then finally she recognized her own small living room. She heard the familiar hum of the refrigerator behind her. Smelled the air freshener Greg insisted they use. She eased herself back down on their worn, but comfortable, sofa. The afghan she had covered herself with was in a tangled ball at her feet, and she pulled it up now that she was shivering.

Her pulse still raced as she tried to calm her breathing, as she tried to remember.

She had gotten home late last night. All she had wanted to do was wash the smell of that trailer full of death off her body. She wanted the water and the steam to return some warmth deep inside her. She wanted the smell gone. After a hot shower she snuggled down on the sofa under the afghan, not wanting to wake Greg.

Truth was, she didn't want to talk to him about any of it last night. She was too exhausted. And he'd have questions, which he'd be sure to follow up with a lecture. She already knew he wouldn't be happy that Cunningham had taken her to such a bloodbath for her first real crime scene.

She was so tired and wanted to give in to the exhaustion. Closed her eyes. Tried to think about something other than the crime scene or the body hanging from the ceiling, or Katie's father bobbing just under the surface. But her dream hadn't included any of those images. Instead it had been her father, his casket. Her father replaced Cunningham in the boat.

She needed to just shut off her mind. She could do that. She used to dream about her father inside his casket.

Used to. It had been a while.

Had Cunningham's questions about him prompted the nightmare's return?

Or was it Katie?

Maggie could relate to the girl's loss. Earlier that feeling of vulnerability, of fear – all of it had been palpable.

She kept her eyes closed. Concentrated on her breathing. If she tried hard enough she could conjure up images of good times with her father. Saturday afternoons watching college football. Or Sundays if there was a Packers game on.

Her mother didn't have the patience to learn the rules. She'd go shopping and leave the two of them in front of the TV. They'd have popcorn. Sometimes they'd order a pizza. If Maggie thought about it hard enough she could even smell the Italian sausage and Romano cheese. Her dad's favorites became her favorites.

She used to wear his old Packers jersey as a sleep shirt until Greg complained. She needed to find it. She no longer cared what Greg thought or said.

That decision made, she started to fall asleep as she tried to remember where she might have packed it away. Like counting sheep, Maggie opened and closed drawers in her mind. She unfolded and folded, looking for the jersey. She knew it was here. Maybe at the back of the closet. There was no sense of panic. Instead it became a quiet and lulling search. Comforted by its softness and the memory, even if it no longer smelled like her father.

She drifted off into a deep sleep until the banging of pots and pans woke her up. Behind the sofa in the kitchen she could hear a skillet being pulled from the hanging rack. The refrigerator door opened and closed. A metal whisk click-clacked against a glass bowl. Fresh brewed coffee filled the air.

Greg never made breakfast. He even picked up coffee on his way to work. But of course, he would make breakfast this morning. And she realized she hadn't avoided anything despite going to great lengths to not wake him last night.

Instead, she had only made things worse. He was upset. She hadn't avoided his lecture. She'd only just delayed it.

24

Stucky heard the whispers in the hospital hallways. He had gotten close enough to hear pieces of the conversations. No one seemed to notice a middle-aged, slightly overweight janitor with a mop. He was practically invisible. He'd even been inside the little girl's room to empty the trashcans.

In and out, just like that. No questions. Hardly a nod from her captor outside the door.

From what Stucky had learned, the man in the river was the little girl's father. Apparently he had tried to run away and Mr Law Officer shot him in the back.

Brilliant sense of justice.

Interesting how this asshole had convincingly funneled his rage into his authoritarian job and no one had noticed. Or perhaps they noticed and didn't care. The bully had found a safe haven.

But this – this was another major screw up. Another amateur mistake.

There were all kinds of ballistic tests they could do on that bullet once they pulled it out. The poor bastard couldn't just throw away the gun. How would he explain to his superiors that he'd lost his service revolver?

Or was that exactly what he had done? Perhaps he had another gun no one knew about. How easy would it be to borrow one from evidence? Or never report it when he made an arrest? If a police officer took an unregistered gun during a traffic stop would anyone complain?

Whatever the explanation, he didn't seem too alarmed. He certainly didn't look frantic.

Stucky heard the elevator doors then the click-clack of high heels and a soft tap of flat-soled shoes behind him. Without looking he simply moved his bucket out of the way and off to the side.

'Thank you,' he heard the woman say.

He nodded and kept his head down so that she'd think he was being humble and polite when he was actually admiring her legs. The pretty redhead returned — actually strawberry blond and that was a better description because it sounded as yummy she looked in that short black dress. She was with the FBI guy from the trailer, the oldest of the three FBI men. Lucky bastard and he hardly noticed the way she looked at him.

That's when Stucky realized he had forgotten all about Susan Fuller.

25

DEVIL'S BACKBONE STATE FOREST

It had rained off and on since Susan left the shed. Three times she had followed overgrown paths, battling the branches and shrubs that poked and grabbed at her. And three times those overgrown paths led right back to the shed.

Without the sun, she had no idea what direction she was going. The pine trees rose high above and were clustered so closely together she could barely see the sky – or rather the clouds. The pain in her knee was overwhelming. Even the sturdy branch she found to use as a makeshift crutch didn't alleviate the pain. She had bitten her lower lip until it bled. Her arms and face were scratched from twigs. She'd given up swatting at the mosquitoes. Her shoes were mud-caked and heavy. Her clothes, soaking wet, stuck to her skin. At times she heard her teeth chattering from the chill that had settled deep inside her.

When darkness started taking over the woods Susan planted herself close to the shed. She discovered she was afraid to leave the familiarity of this area. And the longer she remained exposed to the rain and the chill and the bugs, the more that she wanted to return to the shed. Still, she hid up in the trees where she could see the front door, the only door. He hadn't come back. In her circular journey she hadn't seen anything that looked like a road. If he did come back, Susan was certain of one thing. He'd have to return on foot.

Sometime during the night – numb from being wet and cold and now hungry – Susan had sneaked back down to the shed. The soiled mattress and the scratchy blanket would feel luxurious. She left the door open at first, comforted by the flickering of lightning. If he did come back she wanted to see him in the doorframe before he could see her in the dark corners. She even moved the mattress to the other side of the room where it would be in shadows.

By accident she discovered one of the grocery bags in the corner of the shed. Whether he left it by accident or on purpose, it didn't matter. She scavenged through it like a wild animal, sucking down a bottle of water and gobbling one of the bruised apples all the way to the core. Inside the bag – now torn from her overenthusiasm – was a smorgasbord of damaged fruit and packages flattened from her body being thrown on top of them. She ripped open a box of smashed crackers and began shoveling the crumbs into her mouth.

Thunder rumbled closer, so close she could feel the vibration. The rain was coming down hard. From the vent in the roof she could feel the mist.

Surely, he wouldn't come back in weather like this.

She tried to convince herself as she curled up on the mattress and pulled the scratchy blanket up over her aching, wet body. She didn't mind that it smelled of body odor. Someone else's body odor. How many others had he brought here?

Stop it! Don't think about it.

She needed to rest. She needed to warm her body and heal the aches and pains.

Just for a few hours.

That's all she wanted. She'd stay here through the storm, until the rain stopped. Maybe until it started to get light.

Then she'd be strong enough to head back out. She'd find a road. Find someone. Yes, she'd be stronger after a rest. After some more food. And a little more water.

But right now, she needed to rest. She was exhausted and her head felt too heavy to move from the mattress. She started thinking about the little pastry shop where she worked. In her mind she mixed flour and powdered sugar, eggs and milk. She rolled out dough and pressed out pieces until she could almost smell the scent of freshly baked cookies and scones and turnovers.

And somehow Susan Fuller managed to lull herself to sleep.

26

QUANTICO

When Maggie arrived at the forensic lab she realized she shouldn't be so relieved to be at work instead of at home. But she felt like she had dodged a bullet this morning. She had made it through breakfast and managed to switch the conversation quickly from her first real crime scene to Greg's upcoming trial. His law firm was taking on a mega lawsuit and Greg would be the lead attorney.

When they'd met in college he couldn't wait to get into a courtroom. They used to laugh about how Maggie would hunt down the criminals and Greg would put them behind bars. Somewhere along the way he decided to take on the bad guys in corporations instead of killers and rapists.

Actually she was glad he enjoyed what he was doing. She only wished he felt the same way about what she was doing. These days, too many of their conversations turned into yelling matches. If he wasn't lecturing her, he was trying to convince her to come work for his law firm as an investigator.

'Seriously, Maggie, wouldn't you rather be digging through computer files than dumpster-diving for body parts?'

Maybe something was wrong with her, but the thought of spending hours going over cell phone records and credit card statements, hunting for indiscretions of a scandalous nature seemed mind numbing to her. And yes, as crazy as it sounded and as nauseated as she felt back at that double-wide trailer, she would *not* trade places.

Thankfully this morning Greg was more anxious to share his good news than he was about sharing hers. And she almost got out the door when she saw him notice her hands. She had treated the cuts and scratches but she knew they still looked a bit raw.

'What happened to your wedding ring?'

Of course, that's what he would notice. Not that her hands looked like she had fought off a rabid raccoon, but that one finger was missing a ring. She knew he would be angry. Maybe less so, if the reason was something he already expected.

'You know, you were right. I should have been more careful.'

'Oh Maggie, for God's sake! I told you a dozen times.'

'I know. At least a dozen.'

'What am I always telling you? Take it off when you're washing dishes or you'll lose it down the sink.'

'I'm sorry I wasn't more careful.'

On the drive to Quantico she wondered why she wasn't more upset about losing the ring. Yes, she was sorry she hadn't been more careful. But why wasn't she upset? In some ways she wondered if losing the ring was just one more piece of their relationship that had slipped away.

She walked into the lab and saw that Keith Ganza had already started without her. Pieces of evidence were lined up on the counter – at least those that didn't require refrigeration.

He nodded at her as she gloved up. Yesterday had been her first visit to a real crime scene but she had been working together with Ganza on evidence and trace for several years.

The law enforcement departments that sent in crime scene photographs for her to analyze also included bags of evidence. The two of them would work the puzzle pieces.

She valued his expertise even if he looked more like an aging drummer for a rock band than a forensic scientist. Tall and lanky, he slouched a bit and appeared out of sorts in the long white – more gray than white – lab coat. Underneath, he had on jeans and a black T-shirt emblazed with a white skull and crossbones graphic. He kept his stringy hair tied in a ponytail. Sometimes he wore a just soul patch. Lately he extended that to a full goatee.

'Heard you won a trip to your very first rodeo yesterday.'

Immediately she felt the heat flush her face, but Ganza remained bent over a slide he was preparing. She shouldn't have been surprised that the news would already be making the rounds.

'So you heard about me flipping my cookies.'

Now he looked up, wire-rimmed eyeglasses almost at the tip of his nose.

'No, I didn't hear about that.'

'Seriously?'

'Turner just said what I just said – that you won a trip to your very first rodeo.'

She could see he was telling the truth. She was surprised but pleased.

'Sorry about the cookies,' he said, and went back to his slide. 'Was it the pie?'

'More or less the combination of pie and flies and whatever he left on top.'

'It's a spleen.'

She had guessed right.

He pointed to a photograph on his left. It was a duplicate of the one she received from the CSU techs last night. Without the smell, the gooey concoction didn't look worthy of her vomitfest.

'Dutch apple pie and French vanilla ice cream,' Ganza told her.

'You can actually tell it's French vanilla?'

He shrugged and said, 'CSU tech found the container in the freezer. Brought it in for us to test.'

'How can you be sure it's a spleen?' she asked, even though she was sure.

'I have the takeout container zipped up in the fridge if you want to take a look. Wenhoff's doing the autopsies later today. He'll make the final determination, but I'm pretty sure it's a spleen.'

'It doesn't make sense.'

'You mean mixing Dutch and French?'

She rolled her eyes at him. He grinned, pleased with himself.

'Killers have done stranger things,' he told her.

'The scene was chaotic. He improvised. Used electrical cords from a couple of lamps at the scene to tie their hands and feet. I'm guessing he took a knife from the kitchen to slit their throats. Doesn't seem like the type of guy who'd know where the spleen was, let alone expertly extract it.'

'Expertly?'

'I saw the two bodies. Other than slitting their throats he didn't carve them up. There were maggots already in what looked like stab wounds. I guess it's possible that there's an incision. But a spleen isn't something you slice open a body and accidentally pull out. It sits under your ribcage tucked in at the upper left part of the abdomen. And it's actually toward the back.'

Ganza was staring at her and bobbing his head. 'Interesting,' he said.

From the look on his face, Maggie was grateful he didn't follow it up with, 'How the hell do you know all that?' But he had worked with her long enough to know there was nothing boastful in her regurgitation of information. This was just how her mind worked.

Instead, he pulled off his latex gloves and washed his hands, drying them as he headed for the refrigerator in the corner. For a second she thought he was going to pull out the bagged takeout container, but thankfully he grabbed a couple cans of Diet Pepsi instead.

He handed one to Maggie and popped the tab of his, guzzling it. It used to freak her out that he kept his lunch and his stash of Diet Pepsis in the same refrigerator that housed the specimens from crime scenes. When he wasn't looking she wiped down the top of the can. Maybe it still freaked her out a bit.

'Okay, so we don't know if the spleen belongs to either of these two victims,' Ganza said. 'We'll have to wait for Wenhoff's autopsy results.'

'I'll be surprised if it did come from one them. This killer just seems too disorganized. He didn't bring any rope to tie them up. He used a knife he found in their kitchen. But I have to admit, if it didn't come from the residents of the trailer, where else did he get it? And why would he just happen to bring along a spleen he cut out of someone else?'

Ganza's ponytail bobbed with another shrug. 'Again, I remind you, we have seen stranger things.'

27

'Property taxes list Louis and Elizabeth Tanner as the owners,' Maggie told Ganza.

He was studying a piece of carpeting the CSU techs had cut out from the trailer's living room floor.

'Not the girl's parents?' he asked without looking up.

'Katie called them Uncle Lou and Aunt Beth. We found her father in the river.'

'No ID in his pockets?'

'Could be at the bottom of the river.' In her mind she added, *along with my wedding ring.*

She took a break to stretch and ventured over to Ganza's side of the counter.

'Did the techs recover any shoe prints?' Maggie asked.

'They said this was one of the best ones. I have three others.'

'Actual shoe prints?'

He gestured for her to take a look at the piece of carpet. He was right. The heel was from a shoe.

'I'm guessing all the bare foot prints have been ruled out?' He laid out those photos on the counter like cards from a deck.

'The girl had blood on the soles of her feet. She must have gone inside at some point.'

Maggie took another stack of photos Ganza had and started working her way through them, using his same method. One by one she fanned them out on the counter above the other set with the footprints. There were various shots of the blood-splattered walls along with several close-ups of the wounds filled with maggots. She was relieved that Cunningham hadn't asked her to attend the autopsies. She hated maggots.

Something bothered her about the photos.

'There was a lot of blood,' she said, talking it out with Ganza as was their usual routine. 'He had to be close enough to slit Mr Tanner's throat. It splattered all over the walls. It would have sprayed him, too. Why are there none of his footprints?'

'Maybe he had his shoes off, too. Some of the footprints are smeared so badly we probably won't be able to determine size. Sure the girl might have gone in with bare feet, but maybe he did, too.'

'Or he put on shoe covers,' she said absently.

She came across the photos of the ceiling.

'He had to tie up Mr Tanner and suspend him from the ceiling before he cut his throat,' she told Ganza. 'How difficult would that be?'

'Not as difficult as it seems.' He reached over and pointed at a close-up photo of the hook in the ceiling. 'Hard part was probably subduing the victims first. He had to tie their hands and feet. Then once he looped the extension cord around this hook, all he had to do was pull down on it. It'd work like a pulley, yanking the body up.'

'Wouldn't it have been easier to kill him first?'

'Maybe that wasn't a part of his plan.'

'You think he wanted him to suffer?' Maggie asked.

'Hey, I analyze the evidence. You psychoanalyze the killers.'

'There was no forced entry. So they may have known him well enough to let him in. But he didn't know about Katie and her father.'

'Sometimes in the rural areas people don't lock their doors,' Ganza said.

She came to the photographs of the pie. 'It's not unusual for killers to take trophies from their victims. If this spleen isn't from one of the Tanners that would mean the he brought it with him to the scene.'

'Does the spleen signify something in particular?'

Maggie shrugged. 'I have no idea.'

'Was the girl's father cut? Maybe it's his spleen,' Ganza suggested.

'CSU techs didn't mention it. And that's another mystery. He uses a knife to kill both victims inside the trailer, but when he needs to stop Katie's father he shoots him in the back. So he had gun. Why not just shoot all three of them?'

'Bullets can be traced back to a gun.'

'Could just throw it in the river.'

'Maybe he didn't want to get rid of his gun.'

Maggie thought about that. 'Very few serial killers have used guns. Not personal enough.'

'And this was personal.'

'Personal enough that he wanted Mr Tanner to feel fear. Why else string him up and hang him from the ceiling?'

'But the female victim wasn't strung up,' Ganza reminded her.

'No. And we don't think she was sexually assaulted. Of course, we won't know for sure until Wenhoff's autopsy.'

The wall phone started ringing, and Ganza grabbed it on the third ring.

'This is Ganza.' He listened and his eyes darted up to Maggie. 'Yep, she's here. You wanna talk to her?' Ganza listened again, nodding, still watching Maggie. 'I can do that.'

He hung up. Stripped off his gloves and put on a new set. 'Cunningham's still at the hospital with the girl. He asked for you to come over. Room 333.'

'Does he need me to bring anything?'

'I think he just wants an update and doesn't want to do it over the phone.'

'You said he's still at the hospital? He went there last night.'

He shrugged like he couldn't be bothered by Cunningham's schedule.

'Before you leave, there's something else I thought was very strange,' Ganza said, and he headed for the refrigerator again.

This time he did pull out the takeout container with the pie. He opened the plastic evidence bag and slid the gooey mess out onto the counter. Maggie was relieved to find that without the flies and with a reduced smell it no longer turned her stomach.

'Is there any way to figure out where the takeout container came from?'

'I'm guessing they're generic. I'll check. Might be a lot number or something like that.' With the tip of his gloved finger, he lifted a corner of the piecrust to show her. 'There's something underneath.'

It looked like a slip of paper.

'Is it a note?' she asked.

'I saw it earlier, but I didn't want to take it apart until you were here.'

Now he grabbed a butter knife and some forceps. He gently lifted the crust with the knife and tugged the object out. Ganza held it up with the forceps, gripping it carefully by the corner. It looked like a soggy receipt, only it was a bit thicker than paper. The print was smeared. Piecrust stuck to the bottom portion.

'Can you retrieve any of that?'

'You know me. I do love a challenge.'

28

Stucky knew there wasn't much time left. He'd need to take care of this. Before the asshole made yet another mess. And he needed to do it soon.

This entire detour had become a distraction. He didn't want to play this guy's game anymore. It was boring. There wasn't much challenge. He had prey waiting to be hunted. And Stucky certainly wouldn't allow himself to get caught up in this amateur's collateral damage. Because without Stucky's help, he was sure the asshole would only makes matters worse.

His janitorial status provided him access to a wide variety of places within the hospital. On his nightly rounds he had acquired quite a treasure trove of surgical instruments. It was always good to restock his supply, but most of these he'd need to use now.

From just one glance, Stucky saw the man's bloodshot eyes. His fingernails were chewed down to the quick. His foot tapped out his nervous energy. He looked anxious. Too anxious, though he hid it whenever anyone else was close-by. It looked like he had changed clothes before he'd arrived, but these were already wrinkled from hours of sitting.

He was so obsessed watching the girl's room that he didn't pay attention to the janitor mopping the hallway floor right in front of him. He barely even looked at Stucky when Stucky handed him the folded piece of paper, mumbling that the unit secretary had asked him to pass the note to him. The asshole accepted the lame explanation, glancing at Stucky's mop and bucket longer than he looked at Stucky. By the time he did look up, Stucky was mopping his way down the hall with his back to the guy. It didn't matter. He never would have recognized Stucky anyway.

Before he headed toward the elevators Stucky looked over his shoulder. The asshole didn't know what to do. The poor bastard truly looked torn. Because just at that moment, the FBI man and his lovely companion were getting ready to leave the room again. The nurse passed Stucky in the hallway. She'd sit with the girl like she did the last time they left. But nurses had emergencies. They could get called away. And in a matters of minutes – seconds, really – anything could happen.

Stucky got in the elevator as he fingered the syringe he had in his pocket. He caressed his thumb over the cap to make sure it was still snapped in place.

He found his clothes where he'd left them in the supply room. He put on scrubs then rolled his shirt and jeans – along with his newly acquired surgical supplies – all neatly into a towel, which he tucked under his arm. He still had time to throw them inside his vehicle and get what he needed from his trunk.

Then he walked out of the supply room, confidently down the hallways, passing the reception desk, through the lobby and right out the front door.

29

More clouds. More rain. It slowed down traffic but Maggie was almost to the District when she got a call from Ganza.

'It's a speeding ticket,' he said without a greeting.

'Excuse me?'

'The piece of paper under the piecrust. I was able to perform some magic and resurrect the print. Looks like Louis Tanner got the ticket last week.'

'He must have had it someplace in the kitchen. Maybe on the refrigerator? People do that sort of thing, right?'

'I suppose so, but why would it be something the killer thought should go into the pie?' Ganza asked.

Maggie knew it might not mean anything except for a madman having fun, another sick piece to a puzzle. He could have found Louis' speeding ticket on the refrigerator or taken it from the counter.

Rather than discount it, she asked, 'Is there anything different about it? Maybe he's pointing out something on the ticket. Perhaps the date it was issued?'

'There is one thing I thought was a bit odd. The officer took the time to write ARGUMENTATIVE in the comments. All caps. That's a long word to take time for.'

'Is it that unusual? I would imagine quite a few people are argumentative when they get a speeding ticket.'

'Yes, but Deputy Steele thought it was important,' Ganza said.

'Wait a minute. Did you say Steele?'

'Can't make out the first name, but yes, Steele – S-T-E-E-L-E. Does that mean something to you? Warren County Deputy.'

'There was a Deputy Steele at the crime scene with Sheriff Geller. The sheriff claimed they didn't know the Tanners, but to be fair, at that time none of us knew the names of the residents. Steele could have given Louis Tanner a speeding ticket and not known where he lived.'

'Just a coincidence then,' Ganza said.

Except neither of them believed in coincidences.

Twenty minutes later Maggie pulled into the hospital's parking lot, found the first slot and called Cunningham.

'Agent O'Dell, you probably just missed us. I'm headed to the cafeteria.'

'I'm still in the parking lot, but I wanted to run something by you right away. Ganza found a piece of paper inserted under the piecrust.'

She explained it to Cunningham while she watched the few hospital employees leave and arrive. She realized she was in the wrong lot. This was for employees, not guests. In her rearview mirror she saw a woman in a white lab coat getting into her vehicle. A man in blue scrubs walked through the lane in front of Maggie's car. He was carrying a small red cooler – probably his lunch. It looked like there was a bloodstain on his tunic.

Surgery, the ER, she reminded herself as she continued to tell Cunningham, 'It may be a coincidence but—'

'Steele is posted outside of Katie's door right now,' Cunningham interrupted.

He sounded more alarmed than Maggie expected. She could hear him tell someone that he needed to leave.

'Deputies write dozens of tickets,' she said. 'He might not even know that the man he wrote a speeding ticket for last week was the victim in the trailer.'

'We left him up there with her. Probably fifteen, maybe twenty minutes ago.'

His voice broke in and out.

'I'm on my way back to the room.'

Maggie was climbing out of her vehicle when she saw a police cruiser two lanes from where she was parked. On the side of the vehicle, she could make out the last letters IFF that weren't blocked by the car in the next slot. Someone was in the driver's seat.

'Sir, there's a sheriff's vehicle here in the same lot. Might be Deputy Steele's. Someone's behind the wheel.'

'Or it could be his replacement. Give me a minute.'

She heard the ding of an elevator then his end of the phone line sounded like a wind tunnel.

Maggie dropped back into her car seat and waited and watched. The driver hadn't moved. His head was down, chin tucked. Hat tilted. From this angle it looked as if he might be reading something.

Another ding and Cunningham said, 'Are you still with me, Agent O'Dell?'

'I'm here.'

'Damn it! He's not in his chair.'

Cunningham sounded out of breath.

'Where is he?' he asked, but it was mumbled, and Maggie realized he wasn't asking her.

Someone close-by answered.

'Steele's not here, Agent O'Dell. The nurse said he left in a hurry. Shortly after Dr Patterson and I left the room.'

'So this could be him down in the sheriff's vehicle?'

'I need to stay here with Katie. Approach with caution, Agent O'Dell.'

Again she was surprised by the urgency in his tone.

'Sir, are you saying you believe Deputy Steele could be dangerous?'

'All I know for sure is that Steele left his post without being relieved. He's tired, he's exhausted. Could be he just needed a break. Maybe he was called away on a family emergency. Just be careful, Agent O'Dell. No matter what's going on with Steele, we know we have a killer still on the loose.'

'Understood.'

'Call me as soon as you've made contact with the deputy.'

'Yes, sir.'

And she clicked off. The driver behind the wheel hadn't moved. Maybe he was asleep. Cunningham was right. Steele could just be exhausted.

She stepped out and closed her door as softly as possible. Her fingers reached into her jacket and unsnapped her holster. She took the long way around so she could approach from the back of his vehicle. She kept on the right side, intending to use his blind spot to her advantage. Although she realized this could backfire on her. Was it smart to sneak up on an armed deputy who was already exhausted?

The thought made her slowly slide her revolver from its holster. She glanced around. Minutes ago there were employees coming and going. Now there was no one. She held the revolver down at her side. Twenty more feet and she'd be at the passenger window. It looked like he still hadn't lifted his head.

She needed to slow down. Her pulse raced and her palms were sweaty.

The deputy looked like he was napping. She wasn't sure if it would be safer to announce her approach. Again, she realized that a startled law officer might instinctively grab for his weapon.

A few more steps.

She felt a trickle of sweat slide down her back. The rain had stopped but now she felt a few drops starting again. She relaxed her stance and continued to hold her gun down by her side, out of sight. She decided to walk around the hood of the vehicle, giving the driver the chance to see her. As she passed by the passenger window her eyes darted inside along the empty seat, the console, the dashboard. The deputy's hands were in his lap. His hat was lowered over his forehead and most of his eyes.

He definitely looked like he was asleep.

She'd need to wake him without startling him into reactive mode.

She moved slowly around the hood of the cruiser. Her hand gripped her weapon. She kept her eyes on him but let them dart around. There was a stretch of woods at the far end of the parking lot. In the opposite direction were rows and rows of vehicles.

There was something on top of the hood. Something small. Square. White. She tried to ignore it.

'Deputy Steele,' she called out as she came around the hood.

He didn't move.

Now at the driver's door, she tapped gently on the window. Nothing.

She knocked with her knuckles.

This time, when he didn't even stir, she felt her heartbeat start to pound.

This was not good.

She grabbed the handle with her left hand, her revolver still clutched in her right. In one quick motion she yanked the door open.

She smelled the blood before she saw it. The vehicle reeked with the metallic scent. She kept the gun pointed at him as she stretched to see inside the backseat. She reached in and gave the deputy's hat a gentle push.

As the hat slid off, his head lolled back. Deputy Steele's throat had been slashed. The front of his shirt was soaked with blood. She didn't need to check his pulse.

Maggie stepped back just when her phone started vibrating in her pocket. She grabbed it, but still kept her revolver at her side. Her eyes darted all around her. Whoever did this might still be here somewhere. Was that possible?

'O'Dell?' It was Cunningham.

She realized she had clicked her phone on but hadn't answered.

'Deputy Steele is dead.'

'What did you say?'

'His throat's been slashed.'

She closed the car door. Her eyes checked between the rows of vehicles. She had her revolver in one hand and the phone in the other.

'I'm coming down,' Cunningham told her. She could hear him tell someone else to call security. 'Stay on the line with me and be careful, Agent O'Dell. He could still be in the area.'

But she was already down on her knees looking under the vehicles. If someone were sneaking away, Maggie might be able to see his feet.

Satisfied there was no one close-by, she got back up. Then

she noticed the object on the hood of the cruiser. Earlier she had ignored it. Now she could tell it was a foam container. The type used for takeout food. The raindrops were more frequent. Several splattered the container, and Maggie could see that rain wasn't the only thing running down one side.

There was blood. Her stomach took a dive.

'He left something,' she told Cunningham. 'I'm guessing Steele's throat isn't the only thing he cut.'

30

'He was here!' Katie told Gwen.

The girl's wide eyes darted around the room. Her lower lip trembled. Gwen sat on the edge of the bed, and Katie grabbed her hand, gripping it tightly, the fingers like claws trying to hang on.

She was sleeping when Gwen and Cunningham had left a second time. The doctor on staff insisted that Katie needed to rest. The same nurse offered to sit with her. Yes, she would call immediately if anything changed.

Cunningham was headed back to the cafeteria for more coffee. He'd just convinced Gwen to go home for a few hours. She desperately wanted to get out of the pantyhose and heels. The exhaustion from being up all night was starting to take a toll that no amount of coffee could revive. But just as they had gotten down to the hospital lobby, Agent O'Dell called.

Now all Gwen knew was that the deputy standing guard had left his post unannounced. And something was going on down in the hospital parking lot. Gwen had seen a flicker of panic in Cunningham's eyes before he left. Two hospital security guards were outside Katie's room. The nurse had left to get instructions from the doctor. And now Katie seemed convinced that someone had been 'here.'

'What do you mean, Katie? Who was here?'

'The man who hurt my daddy.'

'In your dreams?'

'No, in this room. I saw him.'

The terror in her eyes was real but Gwen wasn't sure if the girl had been dreaming. Perhaps the drugs caused some side effects. Despite the chaos outside the hospital and the changing of the guards outside the door, there had not been anyone else in Katie's room.

'He was standing in the doorway,' she said, pointing at the now closed door. 'He was looking in. I saw him. I swear I saw him.'

'Okay, sweetie, I believe you.' Gwen pulled the girl against her, hugging her as best she could without disturbing the IV lines. She held her close even as she asked, 'Tell me what he looked like.'

'It's hard to say.'

'He can't hurt you. We won't let him.'

She pulled the girl away to meet her eyes.

'Just do your best, okay? Describe him to me.'

'I couldn't see his face.'

Gwen realized it must have been a dream. She can see him, but his face would be in shadows.

Then Katie added, 'It was hard to see his face with that hat on.'

'He wore a hat?'

'Yes. And he had it on when he hurt my daddy.'

'What kind of a hat?'

But Gwen already knew.

'The big round ones like police wear.'

Before Gwen could ask another question there was a knock. Katie's eyes went wide and flew to the door. The hospital security man with the friendly demeanor and wrestler's build suddenly filled the space. There was a woman standing behind him, impatiently trying to peek around.

'Dr Patterson, there's someone here—'

Gwen saw the resemblance in the woman's face even as Katie squealed, 'Grandma!'

31

Cunningham caught himself clenching his teeth, biting back his anger. His jaw was clamped so tight he was sure it contributed to the pounding in his head. He didn't like being broadsided, and that was exactly how he was feeling. Like this killer had slammed into him when he wasn't looking.

Hell, not just slammed into him. Knocked him completely off his feet.

He already had two perimeters in place. The wider one encompassed the entire employee parking lot on this side of the hospital. Local law enforcement and hospital security managed it. No one – absolutely no one – was allowed to cross without Cunningham's permission. The narrower perimeter formed around the police cruiser and spanned out enough for the CSU techs to work. Keith Ganza had brought only two with him to help process the vehicle. Stan Wenhoff was on his way to take care of Steele's body.

Cunningham stood about twenty feet away. His eyes scanned a steady loop around the controlled chaos. He'd sent Agents O'Dell, Turner and Delaney to check out anything and anyone in the parking lot and surrounding areas. He saw Agent Turner on hands and knees searching under a row of vehicles. Delaney was in front of the hospital talking to a couple of employees in blue scrubs.

Where the hell was O'Dell?

He turned a full circle before he caught a glimpse of her

across the street. The main entrance and a busy highway were in the other direction. Agent O'Dell had crossed a quiet street to another parking lot. This one belonged to set of red brick apartments. He could see her head swivel up, looking for cameras on the light poles. Then she'd look back down examining the insides of parked cars.

Cunningham put his hands on his hips and fought back a smile. This is what she did best. She was already thinking like the killer. Where would he park if he wanted to escape with little notice? Probably not the busy hospital lot. But an apartment complex where most residents were at work in the middle of the day would provide a perfect spot.

He fought back regret that Agent O'Dell was the one to find Deputy Steele. Especially after yesterday. First day in the field and she had witnessed one of the most vicious murders even he had seen in years. And now this. But today she didn't flinch at the sight of another bloody takeout container. Of course, they hadn't opened it yet. Cunningham was leaving that to Ganza.

O'Dell had good instincts. She saw things that others dismissed. Cunningham still wasn't convinced that her special talents would transfer easily to the field. On the academic side he knew she could teach other law enforcement officers what to look for, how to process and piece together bits of evidence that might ordinarily be viewed as insignificant. Already she was doing that with the long distance cases.

And for every case she was working on, he had two dozen more requests, specifically for her. He'd gotten comfortable keeping her busy with those. But there was the rub – *he'd* gotten comfortable. This wasn't about him. Phenoms like O'Dell belonged in the field. That's where they shined. It became a passion, not unlike an addiction. At some point, photos of the crime scenes weren't enough. There would be a need to walk where the killer had walked; to see everything that the victim saw for the last time; and to smell, feel and hear all of it. He knew this because twenty-five years ago he was exactly like her.

'A.D. Cunningham,' Ganza called from behind him.

Cunningham turned. Ganza was at the hood of the police cruiser with the open takeout container. His techs wore windbreakers. Ganza wore a hip-length lab coat that used to be white but was now a dingy gray, probably from too many washings with blue jeans. He had on purple latex gloves and offered Cunningham a pair. He also pointed to a box of shoe covers and Cunningham didn't hesitate to do as the man asked.

'There's another note,' Ganza told him.

'In the container?'

'Yeah. You know he left a speeding ticket in the one you guys found yesterday.'

Cunningham nodded and drew closer, pushing up his glasses. Ganza pulled the container forward and set it at an angle for Cunningham to see clearly inside.

'By the way,' Ganza told him. 'It's a toe.' But this was not what Ganza had called him over to see. 'Left foot. Big toe. I don't think it's his.'

'What do you mean? You don't think it's Deputy Steele's?'

'The smeared blood is probably his. And Wenhoff will make the determination. It's too cold to be his.'

'Cold?'

'As in ice cold.'

'I don't understand. Are you saying he left someone else's toe?'

'Yeah, I think so. Feels like he had it on ice,' Ganza said, but he was more interested in getting to the piece of paper he held between a pair forceps. 'He folded this up and tucked it neatly underneath.'

Cunningham could see the creased lines. Ganza had eased it open just enough to read but it wasn't enough for Cunningham to be able to read.

Ganza glanced around. Nobody except his techs was in earshot and even they were crawling around inside the vehicle. Ganza kept his wire-rimmed glasses at the end of his nose and held up the paper to accommodate his sightline.

'Block print. Almost looks like a child's. It says, "Dear pretty FBI agent. Hopefully my work will soon fascinate you instead of make you sick."'

Cunningham wasn't sure he heard him correctly. He asked Ganza to read it again.

This time when he finished, Cunningham could feel Ganza's eyes on him.

'The bastard was there watching us yesterday.'

32

The stand of trees along the corner of the parking lot was deeper than Maggie realized. She entered from the back and made her way through the tall pines. She could hear traffic but couldn't see it. She hiked for some distance before she saw the hospital, and then only slices of it through the branches.

If the killer had left this way, no one would have seen him. In fact, he could have watched from somewhere behind a cluster of trees and probably not be visible from the parking lot.

Maggie started looking for the police cruiser as she walked. As soon as she got a first glimpse she slowed her pace. She kept her eyes moving, scanning the ground, searching for anything out of place. Pine needles and cones crunched underfoot. There were no freshly broken twigs or branches that she could see. No mud for footprints.

The incline leveled and now from where she stood she had a view of Ganza and his team packing up their gear. Her eyes darted along the ground, and she almost missed something small and metallic amongst the pine needles. She pulled out a plastic evidence bag from her jacket pocket and bent down.

It was a foil gum wrapper, folded over a wad of discarded gum. She pinched it gently by the corner using the inside of the plastic bag so she didn't touch it with her fingers. No guarantee this was the killer's. Still she sealed it and put it in her pocket. As far as she could see there was no other litter. Maybe the area was too remote for a lunch break stroll and certainly not a convenient cut through.

By the time Maggie made it back to the hospital, the police cruiser was being towed out of the lot. Cunningham's perimeters were being dismantled. She saw him just as he was turning. He gestured for her to meet him inside the hospital, pointing to a side entrance.

'Anything?' he asked when he joined her.

'Found this up in the trees.' She showed him the plastic encased gum wrapper and shrugged. 'Looks fresh. The gum was still soft. But it might be nothing.'

Cunningham walked to the entryway, craning his neck to see the stand of trees.

'You think he could have been watching from up there?'

'Hard to say. But there would have been a great view of the police cruiser. On the other side of the trees is another parking lot for a couple of apartment buildings. Nobody around this time of day.'

She watched him scrape a hand over his jaw ending with a quick shove at the bridge of his glasses.

'I've asked everyone to meet back at Quantico in two hours. Could be a late night. Get yourself something to eat. I'm going to check on Katie one more time.' He started to leave then stopped and turned. 'And Agent O'Dell, watch your back.'

Maggie checked the time then searched for a vending machine. Food could wait but she'd grab a Diet Pepsi for now. She found one off the lobby. Instead of backtracking and finding the side entrance she and Cunningham had used, she made the mistake of heading out the front entrance of the hospital. As soon as she turned the corner she walked right into the middle of a dozen reporters and TV cameras. She tried to casually pass through, except her FBI windbreaker gave her away.

'Any information about the dead officer?'

'Has he been identified?'

They didn't even bother to ask if she was on the case. Of course she was on the case. Why hadn't she thought to take off her windbreaker? Suddenly she was surrounded with microphones stuck out in front of her and tape recorders pushed within inches of her face.

'I'm not authorized to give any comments,' she said, impressed at how official she sounded.

'What about the little girl?'

'Is the officer's death related?'

'Can you at least identify her?'

'No, I can't,' Maggie said as she tried to politely step between the reporters who blocked her. She knew two of the cameras pointed at her were rolling. Cunningham wouldn't want her to be rude. Boring or mediocre rarely made the evening news. Rude or angry would certainly be picked up even if she didn't provide any details.

'Is it true the people in that trailer were tortured before they were murdered?'

She pretended to not hear the question. How the hell did they already know about that?

She reached out with one hand to try to make a space for herself. The short dark-haired man, who had asked the question, didn't budge, and now he shoved the microphone up closer to her mouth. Maggie gently pushed it away. This time she led with her shoulder.

From behind her she heard a woman call out, 'Was the little girl tortured too?'

Then someone else added, 'Is it true she was gang raped?'

Maggie had managed to move only a foot or two at the most

but now she stopped and turned around. Reminded herself to keep calm and cool.

'It really doesn't help matters for anyone to speculate,' she said. 'When we know something, I'm sure we'll let you know.'

'Don't you think the public deserves to know right now whether there's some dangerous killer running around?'

It was the short guy again, with the microphone. This time he didn't stick it in her face, but he held it up to catch her comment.

All of them waited for her response. The crowd had gone quiet, waiting, TV cameras rolling, tape recorders dangling from outstretched arms.

'I don't have the authority from the FBI or the victims' family to discuss any of the details. While you're waiting for someone to provide more information, I would hope that all of you would have the decency to understand this little girl deserves some privacy. And so does the family of the law enforcement officer.'

That wasn't what they expected to hear. But no one challenged her. Maggie turned to leave and this time several of the reporters moved out of her way. She was proud of herself. They could have caught her off guard. She had to bite her tongue to not correct the speculations they were tossing out, but now she understood they had lobbed the questions – even the ridiculous ones – in the hopes of making her want to correct the record.

Before she got to her car she saw that the mass of reporters had already forgotten her. She glanced up and searched the third floor then did a double take. Cunningham was standing at the window of what must be Katie's room. He was looking down, and despite being three stories up she could see him frowning at her.

33

'It's sad, isn't it?' Rita Burke pointed her chin at the corner television while she set down a tray of empty pilsners.

Drew Nilsen only shrugged. He didn't even bother to look at the screen. Just last week his aloofness drove Rita crazy. Now that she had decided he was dating material she didn't mind. Instead, she saw his brooding silence as sexy. He didn't have time for the news.

When he came in late this afternoon his hair was still wet, and he smelled so good, like he had just stepped out of the shower. The only reason he was stuck bartending was so he could attend culinary school during the day. She liked how he looked in the tight, black T-shirts he wore, hinting at the six-pack abs. The hem of his shirt was tucked neatly into his blue jeans. She liked the way those fit him, too, hinting at more lean muscles and a nice bulge.

She wiped her forehead with the back of her hand as she handed off her drink and grill orders. The back kitchen was heating up the place again as the trendy bar and restaurant filled with another packed evening crowd. They were right on the courtyard of Atlas Walk in the upscale Virginia Gateway Mall. Just off Interstate 66, every night seemed to be a mixture of tourists, travelers and locals. The place got crowded fast and they couldn't open the doors to the outdoor patio seating because of the rain.

But who was she fooling? The crowded bar and the

gourmet burgers on the hot grill weren't the only reason for the heat crawling through her body. It was ole blue eyes in his tight jeans. He had the prettiest blue eyes she'd ever seen. Sometimes they were almost turquoise, and when he looked at her it felt like he could see deep down inside her. She could feel the electricity just thinking about it.

He was probably too young for her, but Rita knew she didn't look her age. People were always shocked when they discovered she had a sixteen-year-old daughter. In public together, they often got mistaken for sisters. Thankfully her daughter, Carly, thought it was cool and funny instead of weird or creepy. They were each other's best friend, and that in itself was enough reward for putting her life on hold to raise Carly all by herself. However, Rita realized all those years of putting off dating and sex contributed to the heat she was feeling lately.

She tried to get her mind off Drew, so she focused on the television while she waited for him to finish preparing her next round of drinks. She read the closed captions that crawled along the bottom of the screen. Nothing new from earlier. Just a rehash of what they already reported. The little girl was found at a bloody crime scene. Somewhere in rural Virginia. A double-wide trailer on a secluded acreage. The girl was still hospitalized.

Rita had been obsessed with the news story since hearing about it on the radio. The girl – who they were calling Jane Doe, because her name and identity had not yet been released – was the lone survivor of what sounded like a bloody rampage. A man and woman had been murdered inside the trailer. Another man was found dead in the river. Unconfirmed reports claimed he was shot, but the victims inside the trailer had been tortured and stabbed to death.

And now this poor little girl was left alone. Probably her entire family had been murdered. No one knew what kind of injuries she'd suffered. According to the closed captions, the little girl wasn't talking and who could blame her.

Rita glanced over to the kitchen counter to see if her order was ready. Drew was finishing the tray of drinks. Then she noticed the new guy leaning on his mop back in the corner where a customer had spilled a beer. His name was Morgan but someone said he liked to be called by his initials, J.P.

Give me a break.

It sounded like a made-up name. J.P. Morgan? He looked like an ordinary guy, but there was something about his eyes. She didn't like the way his eyes wouldn't meet hers, but didn't hesitate to navigate the length of her body.

He had stopped his cleaning to watch the television. Of course he had. A reporter was trying to talk to a pretty woman in an FBI jacket as she came out of the hospital. Rita glanced at Drew to check her order and found him staring at her now.

Oh great! Of course he'd catch her watching the new guy. She tipped her head toward Morgan and rolled her eyes.

Thankfully, Drew smiled. He brought the tray of drinks, handing it to her over the bar without saying a word. Then he winked at her, and damn it, her knees actually wobbled.

34

QUANTICO

For the second time in as many days A.D. Cunningham had asked Maggie to stop by his office before their taskforce meeting. She had half a dozen messages from Detective Hogan and a couple of other law enforcement officers wanting updates on their case files. Was Cunningham going to tell her she wouldn't be on this taskforce? That she needed to get back to her other cases?

Before she got to his office she saw him at the other end of the hallway. He was carrying five large pizza boxes and trying to open the conference room door.

'I've got it,' Maggie called out.

'Agent O'Dell,' he said, stepping back and letting her help him. 'I hope I didn't keep you waiting?'

'No, I just got here.'

He set the boxes on the table, pushed up his glasses and gestured for her to come in.

'Go ahead and close the door.'

His shirtsleeves were rolled up in careful folds and his tie was loosened but she noticed his collar was still buttoned and his hair was neatly combed. This was as undone as Cunningham allowed his agents to see him.

He took a plastic bag from his trouser pocket but he didn't look at it. Nor did he hand it to her.

'There's something I wanted to tell you before the others arrive.'

She braced herself. Would she argue with him? Try to convince him she could handle her cases *and* be on the taskforce? Why take her to the crime scene if he hadn't intended for her to, at least, be a part of that case?

'Keith Ganza found this earlier.' He lifted the plastic bag, and she could see there was a creased piece of paper with block printing inside. 'It was in the takeout container. The one on Deputy Steele's vehicle.'

He handed it to her now.

DEAR PRETTY FBI AGENT.

HOPEFULLY MY WORK WILL SOON FASCINATE YOU

INSTEAD OF MAKE YOU SICK.

Without looking up at Cunningham, she said, 'He was there?'

'Apparently.'

When she glanced up she saw that he was studying her, watching for her reaction. She wasn't sure what he expected. Truthfully, she wasn't surprised the killer had been watching the double-wide trailer. During her drive back from DC, she wondered if he had been up in that stand of trees, overlooking the hospital parking lot.

'What else was in the container?' she asked.

'The big toe from a left foot.'

Now she stared at him as though she hadn't heard correctly.

'A toe?'

'Yes.'

'Not Deputy Steele's,' she said with certainty.

'What makes you say that?' He wanted to know.

'Two days ago Agent Turner and I attended an autopsy of a victim who was missing her big toe from her left foot.'

'Is that the woman who was found in Devil's Backbone?'

'Yes.'

But he didn't seem to know about the specifics. Would he be upset that Turner had taken her to the autopsy?

Cunningham rubbed at his jaw, and she could see his exhaustion though he tried to hide it. He crossed his arms, the plastic bag dangling from his left hand.

'I don't think the spleen we found in the trailer was from any of the victims inside the trailer,' she told him.

'Did Stan Wenhoff tell you that?'

'No. Just a gut feeling.'

'And what does your gut tell you about this note, Agent O'Dell?'

'He liked my reaction to his container.'

Cunningham was examining her, again, as if he were looking for a crack in the veneer. She didn't flinch. She didn't want to give him an excuse to exclude her.

Then he finally nodded and said, 'Let's hope it's that simple.'

35

QUANTICO

Maggie guessed Agent Turner was on his third slice of pizza by the time she had managed her first bite. Her appetite had taken a nosedive. The note bothered her more than she was willing to admit. Not only had the killer been watching but also he'd been pleased to see her emptying her stomach because of his 'work.' It wasn't unusual for a serial killer to want credit for his method or handiwork as if he were an artist or a performer. It was however, a bit nauseating to be singled out.

Cunningham had already started marking his signature whiteboard with lines and bullet points, ready to fill them in. When Dr Gwen Patterson walked into the conference room he stopped and turned. Maggie wondered if she was the only one who caught the look Cunningham and Gwen exchanged.

Maybe she was mistaken. She did tend to overanalyze everything these days. She glanced around the table to see if anyone else had noticed. Agent Turner mumbled a greeting over a mouthful. Delaney stood and nodded to the doctor, asking how Katie was. Keith Ganza continued to jot notes on a yellow legal pad.

From what Maggie knew, Dr Patterson ... Gwen. She needed to remember that she preferred to be called Gwen. The doctor had asked her to do so the last time they had briefly worked together. From what Maggie knew, Gwen had been with Katie at the hospital all last night and most of today. Other than a hint of exhaustion under her eyes, the woman looked good – always very stylish – impeccably dressed in designer slacks, a knit sweater and leather pumps with two-inch heels. Her jewelry was expensive but simple and tasteful – watch, bracelet, necklace, all gold. Her strawberry-blond hair was swept back to reveal diamond studs in her earlobes.

Maggie went to great lengths to not stand out from her male counterparts. She chose blazers that draped rather than shaped, with straight-leg trousers and flat leather shoes. The male agents wore a watch and maybe a simple wedding band, so that's what Maggie did. Now she folded her hands together, suddenly reminded that her only valuable piece of jewelry was missing, most likely at the bottom of a cold and murky river.

'We have an active killer, folks.' Cunningham started the meeting. 'Katie is being moved to a more secure facility while she recovers. At this point we must still consider her a potential victim of this killer. Agent Delaney was able to track down the girl's grandmother. Her father's name was Daniel Tanner. He was Louis Tanner's brother.' He looked at Delaney. 'Anything else you can tell us?'

'The grandmother's Lucille Tanner. She was pretty shook up. I didn't want to push her too much. She just lost both her sons. I'm checking on Katie tomorrow after they transfer her. I figure I can talk more to Mrs Tanner at that time.'

Maggie knew Delaney's 'talking' skills as a trained nego-tiator had coaxed a jumper off the ledge of a high-rise just a few months ago. Last year, he convinced a bank robber into releasing all three of his hostages. If Lucille Tanner had any information that could answer why her sons were murdered, Delaney would get it.

Cunningham gestured to Keith Ganza who stood at the other end of the table.

'I'm going to have Ganza update us. There are a lot of strange pieces to this one.'

Cunningham took his place alongside the whiteboard, ready to fill it while Ganza shuffled files and photographs.

'Lets start with the double-wide trailer.' He seemed to wait for Cunningham to mark the top of each of his lists.

Cunningham had divided the board into three columns. Now he wrote:

Double-wide   Cruiser   DBSF

Maggie realized he was separating the evidence and information according to each crime scene, and he was considering Devil's Backbone State Forest as one of the scenes.

Ganza continued, 'Inside the takeout container was a human spleen. It was placed on top of a piece of pie. Pie à la mode, to be more specific. I now have confirmation from Stan Wenhoff that the spleen did *not* belong to any of the victims inside the trailer nor did it belong to the victim pulled from the river.'

'So it was brought to the scene?'

Maggie noticed Turner put down a slice of pizza as he asked the question.

'That's correct,' Ganza said, glancing at them over the wire-rimmed glasses at the end of his nose while he read his notes. 'Under the piecrust I found a portion of a speeding ticket. It was issued to Louis Tanner the week before and signed by Deputy Steele.'

'I thought Sheriff Geller and Steele told us they didn't know the occupants of the trailer,' Delaney said.

'It's possible Deputy Steele may not have known Louis Tanner,' Maggie suggested.

'That's what I thought, too,' Ganza said as he tossed a plastic evidence bag across the table for them to take a look at. 'This note was found in the trouser pocket of Deputy Steele.'

The paper had been crumpled but immediately, Maggie recognized the same block styled print. It looked similar to the note Cunningham had shown her earlier.

The note read:

I SAW WHAT YOU DID AT THE TRAILER.
MEET ME IN THE PARKING LOT AT
YOUR CRUISER.

'Son of a bitch!' Turner said dragging the phrase out and ending it with a whistle.

36

QUANTICO

'So Deputy Steele was involved in the murders?' Maggie asked. Cunningham hadn't shared *this* note with her. 'He made it sound like he'd glanced inside the trailer before we all got there, but that was all.' Then she remembered something else. 'Steele asked me if I thought the girl had seen anything.'

'But he also looked surprised when I mentioned the piece of pie,' Turner said.

'You told Deputy Steele about the container?' Cunningham wasn't happy.

'Sheriff's department called us in. Usually we share information. Is that not the case?'

'Not this time.' Cunningham pursed his lips and crossed his arms, emphasizing that was the end of the subject for now. Then he nodded for Ganza to continue.

'Okay, so we know this killer was watching all of you when you were at the scene.'

Ganza added another plastic bag with the second note. Maggie recognized it as the one Cunningham had shown her earlier.

'There was another takeout container today on the hood of Deputy Steele's police cruiser. This note was left inside.'

Maggie watched as Gwen carefully handled the bags, reading both notes and comparing them before she passed them on to Turner and Delaney. She glanced up at Cunningham then at Maggie. She held Maggie's eyes as if looking for a reaction to being singled out. Maggie thought she saw more concern in the psychiatrist's eyes than examination, but it still made her uncomfortable. It was Maggie who looked away first.

'It's unusual for a serial killer to leave a note, isn't it?' Gwen asked. 'This guy's left two?'

'Three,' Ganza said, 'if you consider the speeding ticket a type of note.'

'It's unusual,' Maggie said, 'but certainly not unheard of. David Berkowitz was the first to call himself Son of Sam in a note he left at one of his crime scenes. The Unabomber actually sent a 35,000-word manifesto to the *New York Times* and *Washington Post*. You can go back as far as Jack the Ripper, who taunted police through letters. In fact, one of those letters included part of a kidney that he claimed he'd taken from one of his victims. In that same letter he wrote, "Catch me when you can." The Beltway Snipers left a note on the back of a tarot card – the Death card; so yes, I think we need to consider the speeding ticket. He was trying to tell us Steele was involved.'

Turner was looking at her, nodding and grinning. 'You're like a walking encyclopedia about serial killers. I love how you can remember all that crap.'

'Okay, let's back up,' Delaney said. 'So this note does make it sound like Deputy Steele was involved in the murders at the trailer.'

'Not just involved,' Ganza said. 'It makes it sound like Steele killed Louis and Beth Tanner. Possibly Katie's father as well.'

'And takeout guy watched him.' Turner pointed to the container Ganza had brought – it was also wrapped inside an evidence bag. 'We need a different name for him. I don't like

Takeout Guy. You didn't tell us yet. What was in that second container?'

'A toe,' Ganza told him.

Maggie saw Turner's eyes go wide and then dart across the table to meet hers.

'Big toe,' she told him. 'Left foot.' To Ganza, she asked. 'It's not Steele's, is it?'

Ganza shook his head.

'Is it a woman's?'

'Yes. And it was ice cold. He must have had it in a cooler.'

'For how long?' she asked.

'Excuse me?'

'How long could he have had it on ice? Is there any way to know how long ago he extracted it from his victim?'

'I know where you're going with this, Agent O'Dell. I've already got Stan Wenhoff doing a DNA comparison to see if the toe belongs to the woman who was found in Devil's Backbone.'

'Wait,' Gwen held up her hands as if surrendering after a round of pivoting her head back and forth from one agent to another to Ganza. 'What woman in Devil's Backbone? You know that state forest isn't open to the public?'

'Agent Turner and I attended an autopsy a few days ago.' Maggie tried to remember what day it had been. She had told Cunningham it was two days ago, but that didn't sound right. So much had happened since then. 'The victim's body was found by a park worker. She was dehydrated. Lots of scratches and insect bites all over her body. Wenhoff believes she might have been dropped in the park and had to survive on her own for days, maybe a week. Possibly longer.'

'But she was alive when he left her there?'

Maggie nodded.

'That doesn't make sense. Why would he do that?'

'So he could hunt her,' Turner said in a low voice filled with disgust.

'Excuse me?'

Turner nodded at Maggie to continue.

'There was a broken arrow through her left calf. Wenhoff thinks she was shot with a crossbow.'

Gwen shook her head as she ran her fingers through her hair. 'Just when I thought I'd heard it all.' She scratched notes in her small leather portfolio as she asked, 'What was the cause of death?'

'He hadn't yet confirmed that when we were there,' Maggie said, looking to Turner. Technically it was his and Delaney's case. She had only been a tagalong, so she hadn't gotten any official updates.

'Strangulation,' Turner provided.

'And the toe. I'm hoping it was taken post mortem?' Gwen asked.

'Yeah, he did say that. But come on, that's still some kind of freak, taking a toe,' Turner said. Then he looked at Ganza. 'So this guy goes around cutting off pieces of his victims and collecting them in takeout containers.'

'I think you may have just found our nickname for him,' Delaney said. 'The Collector.'

37

'Is it possible Deputy Steele and the Collector worked together?' Delaney asked.

Maggie felt all eyes on her.

'It's rare for serial killers to work together,' she said. 'But again, just like the notes, it's not unheard of. It depends on what the evidence supports.'

She deferred to Ganza who scrunched his eyebrows together considering this. Then he shook his head. 'If they were working together the Collector wouldn't need to leave Steele a note telling him he saw what he did.'

'What if he saw Steele shoot Daniel Tanner?' Turner suggested. 'But the Collector was the one who killed Louis and Beth? Katie's father was shot, but the other two had their throats slashed, just like Steele ended up. Serial killers don't usually change up weapons.'

'If the woman from Devil's Backbone is one of the Collector's victims that would mean he used a crossbow then eventually strangled her,' Maggie reminded him, playing the devil's advocate.

Turner grinned at her. 'I bet you can tell us a bunch of killers who used different weapons.'

She felt the beginning blush of embarrassment. Turner said this as a compliment, but she wasn't sure if he was teasing or flirting. For all her knowledge and insight into human behavior, those two behaviors baffled her.

'Just for the sake of argument,' Gwen said. 'Let's say the two men were both responsible. What would that look like? Which came first? And why would both Steele and the Collector choose the Tanners if they weren't planning this together? Seems too complicated that two different men – one who appears to be completely oblivious of the other's presence – would target the same family.'

'What do we know about Steele?' Delaney asked.

'I've tried to talk to Sheriff Geller,' Cunningham said. 'Of course, he's devastated about his deputy. But I have to say, even at the crime scene I suspected there was something he wasn't sharing with us.'

'Steele was wearing an ankle holster at the time of his death,' Ganza told them. 'That gun and his service revolver are being tested. We should know if one of his weapons shot Katie's father.'

Cunningham added 'ballistic report' to his whiteboard. Maggie noticed that while they had been discussing Steele's and the Collector's roles in the murders, Cunningham had been filling in his columns.

Double-wide	Cruiser	Devil's Backbone
Tanners (3)	Steele	Identity???
(2) throats slashed	(1) throat slashed	(1) crossbow/ strangled
(1) shot in back	note in pocket	arrow in left calf
takeout container (spleen/ticket)	takeout container (toe from DBST?)	toe missing ballistic report

'There is something else,' Gwen said. She put aside her pen and rested her hands on the tabletop. 'Katie told me that the man who shot her father was there at the hospital.'

'She saw him?' Delaney asked.

'She thinks he looked into her room. At first I thought she might have dreamed it. But then she said he was wearing his hat just like he was when he shot her father. A big hat like the police officers wear.'

'Do you think she'd recognize him from a photo line-up?' Delaney suggested.

'We can definitely try it.'

'She's never mentioned a second man.' Cunningham added. 'Agent Delaney, find out what you can about the victims and any possible connection to Deputy Steele. I think we might find that Occam's razor applies. The answer to any given problem is often the simplest explanation.'

But he didn't offer what he believed that explanation might be. Other than sharing his instincts about Sheriff Geller, Cunningham didn't interject his opinion. He didn't want his agents manipulating the facts to fit their boss's preconceived notion, and Maggie respected that about him.

'Agent Turner,' Cunningham continued, 'Identify the female victim who was found in Devil's Backbone. Who was she? Where did she live? Where did she work? How long has she been missing?'

'You got it.'

'Agent O'Dell, I need you to tell us who the Collector is.' His eyes stayed on Maggie's. 'He's killed before. Somehow he's managed to do it under the radar. He's calculating enough to kill in the middle of the afternoon, in a public place.'

Maggie nodded.

'Dr Patterson, I'm hoping you'll be available to Agent O'Dell?'

'Of course.'

Gwen smiled at Maggie, and immediately Maggie wanted

to protest. Instead, she remembered the look the two had exchanged earlier. At the very least, Cunningham and Gwen were old and dear friends and turning down the psychiatrist's help would definitely be frowned upon.

'Also, Gwen can you accompany Agent Delaney when he does the photo line-up with Katie.'

'I'll be checking on her tomorrow morning. Perhaps we could do it then?'

'That works,' Delaney told her.

Satisfied, Cunningham said, 'There's one other thing.' He turned to Ganza. 'Go ahead and tell them what else you discovered.'

'Deputy Steele's index finger was cut off. His right hand. My team searched the entire vehicle and the surrounding area. We didn't find it.'

He waited for that to sink in before he added, 'It was his trigger finger.'

38

Saturday

Ever since he saw her on TV last night, Stucky couldn't stop thinking about the pretty FBI lady. Actually she'd dominated his thoughts ever since he watched her outside the double-wide trailer, down on her hands and knees paying homage to his handiwork. And now thanks to the news reporters he had a name to go along with her: Special Agent Maggie O'Dell.

He'd been disappointed that she hadn't opened the container he'd left on the hood of asshole's cruiser. He wanted to watch her face when she read the note. Instead, some guy in a ratty-ass lab coat with a stringy ponytail did the honors. He poked and prodded Stucky's precious work with gloves, forceps and absolutely no expression on his face. It was emasculating and anticlimactic when that masterpiece should have elicited orgasmic awe.

He decided he'd give her a second chance. And as soon as he got off work he started looking for the contents of his next package.

He'd learned long ago that he required very little sleep. Back in the days when he was writing computer code, he could work straight through the night. Sometimes two nights, chugging down Mountain Dews and eating bologna sandwiches. The excitement of the finished product propelled his energy.

Some of the earliest video games he created were still his

favorites because they were born out of his long sleepless dedication and passion. Never mind that they also made him filthy rich. However, it didn't take long for him to feel confined by the limits of his imagination. The video games allowed him to control his rages, but once he experienced and smelled blood and felt it on his hands, there was nothing in virtual reality that even came close.

He blamed his father. All these years later and sometimes Stucky felt like the bastard was standing right next to him, whispering to him: 'Cut deeper. Go ahead, see what it feels like.'

Of course, his father was talking about game birds and deer. It wasn't enough to kill them and cut off their heads. He wanted to watch his son slice open their prey. See the steam leave the body. Feel the blood on his hands. He insisted Stucky remove the guts while they were still warm and as his father pointed out each disgusting organ.

Then he'd always say what a good job his 'little man' had done.

God, he hated that term! Little man.

Stucky wondered what his father would think of him today. Would he be proud or shocked? Sometimes he regretted killing the bastard, just so he could make him watch now.

As soon as his shift ended he'd gone to his apartment to grab a few things. He didn't bother to change his appearance except for a couple of small details. It really wouldn't matter whether or not this next quarry could identify him.

Some of the bars in the area stayed open until 2:00 a.m. Stucky had done his homework when he moved to the area. There were fifty-two colleges within a fifty-mile radius. On a Friday night – actually a Saturday morning – it'd almost be too easy to pick off an inebriated coed. Were they even called coeds anymore? He rarely sank to the level of targeting college students. They didn't present much challenge especially the ones who stayed out drinking till 2:00 a.m. But this time he simply needed an easy kill.

He left his car at his apartment and walked the five blocks. The cast on his arm made his skin itch and the sling rubbed against the back of his neck. He'd placed the cast all the way down to his fingers so no one could see the syringe clutched in his hand. In his other hand was a small lunch cooler.

He chose the bar at the end of the mall where the other businesses had been shuttered up for the night hours ago. Under the shadows of a tree and from across the street, he watched a group of young women exit the bar. Their sing-song goodbyes and giggles, along with their skips and staggers, made them perfect targets. Except there were too many of them. He had almost discounted the group and was ready to move on, when three of the young women got into the same car, and as they drove off, they waved to the fourth as she continued to the far edge of the parking lot.

Stucky didn't want to startle her. She was fumbling with her keys when he crossed the street behind her. He weaved in between the vehicles and found a shiny black Lexus SUV to stand beside.

'Hey, excuse me,' he called out to the woman who was now only a couple cars away.

She looked up and around before she realized he was speaking to her. He made sure the arm cast was turned toward her and instantly he saw her eyes dart down to it.

'I have a flat tire,' he told her, walking around to the back of the Lexus and motioning to the other side of the vehicle – the side she'd never be able to see. All the while he kept an eye on the entrance to the bar.

'My wife used the tire jack last and she left it in our garage.' He waited for the word 'wife' to sink in. 'Do you think I could borrow yours?'

He stayed by the vehicle waiting for her to think of him as weak, helpless and stranded. She looked too young to be drinking age and the extra makeup, tight clothes and over-stylized hair made her look even more like a teenager playing dress-up.

'Can you help me out? I'll even pay you twenty bucks.' Then he shrugged his shoulder where the sling was and added, 'It's just been a really bad day.'

That made her smile.

'Can you even change a tire with your arm like that?'

'Hey, it'll be less painful than waking up my wife.'

Now she laughed. She was fumbling with the key fob again. She popped the trunk just as he came up beside her. His eyes scanned the parking lot. No one was around and he noticed a large Suburban was parked on the other side of her small sedan, blocking anyone's view from the bar.

'I don't know much about my jack,' she said as she bent over the lip of the trunk.

He stabbed the needle into the back of her arm. She didn't even see it. She batted at the prick as if an insect had stung her. He grabbed the keys dangling from her fingertips and gave her a slight shove. That's all it took for her to tumble into her trunk bed. Her eyes stared up at him in disbelief as he slammed it shut.

He adjusted the car's seat as if it belonged to him. Took time to reset the side mirrors and the rearview mirror. The cast came off after undoing a series of snaps and one buckle. He sent it to the floor of the passenger side where he placed his cooler. With one swoop he snatched up all the lipsticks and bottles of girl goop and tossed them into the glove compartment. Before he closed it he grabbed the strand of beads hanging from the rearview mirror and tossed it inside.

He needed to stop at his car and pick up the rest of his things. On the way he'd get ice for the cooler. The whole time, he listened carefully.

Nothing. Not a shuffle or a whimper. This one wouldn't be kicking out the taillights.

Girls! He shook his head. Too immature. Too easy.

He reminded himself that the real prize would be a pretty FBI agent, and he started the car.

39

DEVIL'S BACKBONE STATE FOREST

Susan Fuller had spent another day walking around in circles. And again, after hours of watching the shed from up on the rocks and from behind the trees, she returned.

Earlier she had spent hours investigating a new trail she stumbled upon. This one was so overgrown in parts that she was worried it would end abruptly, and she would be lost in the middle of the forest. The sky still bulged with thick gray clouds, making it impossible for her to get a sense of direction. If only she could see the sunrise she'd know which way was east. She had convinced herself that it would make a difference, but she knew for a fact it wouldn't tell her how to get out of this godforsaken forest.

Twice she had slipped on the mud and the wet underbrush, knocking her off her feet and sending her into a rollercoaster slide. She had slammed her wounded knee against the rocks and added new bruises. Her fingernails were broken to the quick from grabbing onto tree roots and clawing her way back up a ravine. She felt like she had trekked miles and still she hadn't seen a glimpse of another person or another cabin or even a road. She couldn't hear a hint of traffic. No jets flew overhead.

Where the hell was she?

As much as she hated the thought, the shed had become her sanctuary. She became anxious when she didn't think she could find her way back. And she found herself relieved at the sight of the ramshackle structure. It provided warmth and shelter from the rain as well as food and more bottled water than she could carry.

This time before she lay down to sleep she dragged tree branches, twigs and vines and piled them up in front of the door. She hoped the crunch and snap of him removing them would wake her and give her warning. On her day's journey she had found an excellent long branch, heavy at one end and tapered at the other. In her hands it felt like the perfect baseball bat. She made sure it was always close to her. Now as she slept, it was clutched against her.

She was starting to feel a false sense of security. Maybe he had forgotten about her. What if he'd been in a car accident? That actually made her smile despite what it meant about her ever being found. Again and again, she told herself that tomorrow she would venture out farther and she would find a trail – perhaps a road. How wonderful that would be.

For some reason she thought about her mother. It had been almost a year since she had passed away. The cancer didn't give them a chance to say a proper goodbye. The diagnosis came and three weeks later it was over. Susan still couldn't believe her mom was gone. She had dug in to her classes, studying and working nonstop. Her mother was so proud of her going to culinary school. She would have loved the little pastry shop where Susan had landed the job of head chef.

She was still so angry with God. But as she lay on the dirty, thin mattress listening to the night birds, Susan did something she hadn't done since her mother's diagnosis. She prayed.

40

Maggie woke to a sound she didn't recognize. A bang followed by a clink – metal against metal.

Last night she had gotten home late. She had slid into their king-size bed without interrupting Greg's soft snores. Now through the window blinds she could see the gray sky with the first light of morning. The other side of the bed was already empty.

She glanced at the digital alarm clock. 6:45 a.m.

Not unusual for Greg to be up and gone by seven. She'd slept hard last night. No dreams about her father interrupting. No wonder she didn't hear Greg in the shower or getting dressed.

Another bang-clink, tap-tap, clink.

It sounded like it was coming from inside the apartment.

This time Maggie grabbed at her nightstand drawer. She had her Smith & Wesson in her hand before she rolled out of the bed. On tiptoes, she headed toward the sound. The bedroom was down a narrow hallway interrupted by a door to a half bath. The hallway opened to the living room and kitchen. The only thing that separated those two rooms was a long counter with four barstools.

The noise had stopped. Maggie stayed in the hallway. She slowed her breathing, and steadied her fingers on her weapon. Then she leaned forward just enough to glance in at the kitchen. The first thing she saw was a white foam takeout container on the counter, and her pulse began to race.

The next bang-clank made her jump.

Her palms were already slippery with sweat. She readjusted her grip. The sound was coming from the kitchen but she couldn't see anything. It was close to the floor, hidden by the counter.

She eyed the container. No blood dripping down the sides from what she could see. She slid her body around the corner then glanced at her feet. She looked for the floorboards that she knew would creak, and she sidestepped them.

The banging was more constant now and she took advantage of it drowning out her approach. She led with her revolver and rushed the last steps around the counter and into the kitchen.

Greg lay sprawled half under the sink. When he saw her, he started and smacked his head against the cabinet.

'Geez, Maggie! What the hell?'

Now she could see the wrench in his hand. There were pieces of pipe scattered around the tiled floor next to him.

'I thought you'd left for work. I heard a weird sound.'

She turned around to the takeout container. Now on this side of the counter she saw a discarded bag next to it with the logo of Greg's favorite pastry shop.

'You know, Maggie, one of these days you're going to shoot me. This is just one more reason to leave that stupid job.'

That stupid job that she loved.

But she didn't say anything. Instead she placed the revolver on the counter, pointing it safely away from her husband.

'What are you doing?' she finally asked him.

He crawled to his feet and wiped his hands on a towel already grimy from his efforts.

'I'm taking apart the pipes under the sink.'

'I can see that, but why?' She opened the refrigerator and grabbed a carton of orange juice and poured herself a glass. She started sipping, waiting for her pulse to return to normal.

'Why do you think? I'm hoping I can retrieve your ring.'

Maggie almost choked on her orange juice. Thankfully, he was more interested in cleaning his wrench and hands than he was in her reaction. She tried to remember the last time she had seen him with a tool. Quite honestly, she didn't know he even owned any tools.

'Sometimes stuff gets caught in the elbow,' he said.

That was true. She'd heard Ganza plenty of times talking about how killers thought they could flush evidence down the drain and it would get stuck in the pipes.

'Aren't you going into work today?'

'It's Saturday.'

She felt a twinge of guilt. He was going to end up spending a good portion of his day under the sink. She needed to tell him the truth.

'I still can't believe how irresponsible you can be sometimes.' He was shaking his head at her now. Hands clean, he reached for the pastry container, grabbed his cup of coffee and headed for the living room.

Yesterday he'd fixed her breakfast. This morning he hadn't even picked up an extra pastry for her. If he was this upset about her losing her wedding ring down the kitchen drain, how angry would he be to hear that it was actually at the bottom of a river? And that she lost it while trying to pull a floater from the cold water? She'd never hear the end of how she needed to quit that stupid job until he finally made her quit that stupid job.

Either way, whether the ring went down the drain or to the bottom of the river, there would be no salvaging it. Maggie poured more orange juice, picked up her Smith & Wesson and retreated down the hallway to their bedroom. Thankfully, she needed to get to work.

41

Gwen had handpicked this facility for Katie, and Cunningham had simply nodded and made it happen. As she pulled up to the building she was thinking that professionally she could get him to agree to just about anything. He respected her expertise that much. Personally? She had no idea where she stood. Although over the last thirty-six hours she had never felt closer to him.

He still insisted on having an agent on the grounds 24/7, and after what happened in the hospital parking lot, Gwen agreed. The place had tight security and was a locked facility. She had trusted it with her most secretive and public clients that included congressmen and one general. But there was a difference in protecting against reporters or paparazzi and murderous madmen.

The rooms were small suites that included a private area for Katie's grandmother. But when Gwen knocked and opened the door she was surprised to find only Agent Delaney. Katie was sitting up in bed. All the IVs were gone. She was concentrating on sucking at the straw of what looked like a chocolate milk shake. Both she and Delaney looked up at Gwen and smiled.

'What did I interrupt?'

'He tells funny stories,' the girl told her and rolled her eyes at Delaney, but she was obviously enjoying his company. 'Mr Delaney brought me a chocolate shake.'

Gwen was amazed how quickly the girl had gotten attached to him. She watched Katie's eyes and how intently they tracked Delaney even as he got up and fetched a chair for Gwen. In the many hours she had spent with Katie at the hospital she hadn't been able to accomplish this sort of bond. Perhaps Katie was transferring her longing and affection for her father onto Delaney. Or perhaps Gwen was a tad jealous. As a psychiatrist she knew both were probably a little bit true.

Gwen noticed that Delaney had a briefcase at his feet leaning against the side of the chair. He caught her eyes and nodded. So he had been successful in getting a least one good photo of Deputy Steele without his hat. She knew he'd include photos of others, maybe even suspects in other crimes. Either way, they'd soon find out whether or not Katie would recognize Steele or simply remembered his hat.

'Is your grandmother here today?' Gwen asked.

Katie nodded, but it was Delaney who answered. 'Lucille went to get herself some coffee. I mentioned that you and I wanted to talk to Katie this morning and then we'd talk with her.'

'Did your husband come with you?' Katie asked.

'My husband? You mean Mr Cunningham?'

Katie nodded again as she slurped up the last of her shake, holding the cup in two hands and tilting it until the straw gurgled with more air than milkshake.

'Oh sweetie, we're not married,' Gwen told her and knew immediately that it was too late to control the blush that started at the base of her neck. She glanced at Delaney. He simply smiled and shrugged as if to say, 'That's just kids.' Which only made Gwen want to get on with their business.

'Katie, do you remember me telling you yesterday why we were moving you here?'

'Because it's prettier.'

This was going to be harder than Gwen expected.

'That's true, it is prettier. But that's not exactly what I said. Do you remember?'

The girl's head bobbed again, and Gwen tried to hide her frustration. She reminded herself that any response was a positive sign. She heard Delaney pull the briefcase up into his lap and immediately he had Katie's attention. When Gwen glanced at him, he caught her eyes and silently asked her permission. She gave him a slight nod.

'I have some pictures inside my case,' he told Katie as he snapped it open. 'Remember I told you I'm trying to catch the bad guy?'

Katie's hands dropped. The straw came out of her mouth. But her eyes didn't leave Delaney and the briefcase.

'I think I know who he is but I need to be sure. Would it be okay if you looked at my pictures and tell me if you see him?'

Gwen scooted closer to the bedside and without even looking in Gwen's direction, Katie's hand reached out for hers. It was wet and sticky and Gwen held on tight.

As Delaney pulled out the photos, the girl looked up at Gwen and said, 'We're gonna find the bad guy.'

'That's right. But if you feel sick or scared at any time we'll stop, okay?'

Delaney slid the rolling tray over Katie's bed so he could place the photographs in front of her. Then he began setting them out one at a time, side by side with a couple of seconds in between.

'Try not to think too hard,' Gwen told the girl when she noticed her brow furrowing. 'Just look. This isn't a test. There's no wrong or—'

'That's him,' Katie said with a tinge of excitement, almost as if they were playing a game and she was relieved that it was easier than she thought it would be.

Gwen had been watching Katie's face but now she glanced down at the photo she was pointing to. It was Deputy Steele's photo. Without his hat. He was dressed in a blue polo shirt and he was smiling. But did she recognize him as the man who shot her father, or did she simply recognize him as the man outside her hospital room?

Delaney must have been thinking the same thing because he asked, 'Are you sure?'

Now she started looking at the other photos. Her lip quivered. She wasn't sure and she wanted to please Delaney.

'He looked into my room,' she said, so softly Gwen found herself leaning forward.

'So you saw him at the hospital?'

'Yes.'

'But is this the man you saw outside your uncle's trailer?'

She stared at the photo and Gwen could see tears starting to well up in her eyes.

'I don't know for sure,' she finally said, her lower lip quivering, her little fingers digging into Gwen's hand.

'It's okay,' Gwen told her. She gestured for Delaney to pick up the photos. 'It's okay if you don't remember.'

'But how will you get the bad guy?' she asked Delaney.

'Don't worry, we will,' he reassured her. He moved the tray away from the bed and he patted her on the back. Just at that moment there was a gentle tap at the door.

'How's it going in here?' The girl's grandmother came in and she was holding a stuffed brown dog. 'Grandpa brought your doggy.'

Katie's eyes brightened and her hand flew away from Gwen's as she reached for the stuffed animal. Gwen met Delaney at the door.

'We'll be right back,' she told Katie and her grandmother, but the girl's attention had left them.

Gwen and Delaney walked side by side down the hallway before either of them spoke. Finally they turned the corner and found an area across from the reception desk where there was no one else.

'She might never remember the events of that day,' Gwen said. 'I don't think she even remembers walking around inside the trailer, although Cunningham said she had blood on the soles of her feet when you found her.'

'And there were footprints on the carpet. Small. Bare feet.'

'Truthfully, it no longer matters whether or not she can identify Deputy Steele. And she hasn't mentioned a second man.'

'I'll speak with her grandmother. Maybe she'll know something we don't.'

'I'm going to recommend some therapy for Katie. Dr Anderson is better equipped to work with traumatized children.'

'So you're done with her? That's it?'

She checked his eyes. He made it sound like an accusation. Like she was abandoning Katie.

'I'll still see her and I'll still be a consultant for her therapy, but as far as getting any more information from her, I don't think we can wait. Right now the best thing you and I can do for Katie is to find this second killer. Because we won't be able to protect her forever.'

42

At the first hint of dawn, Susan had climbed up into one of her hiding places. The huge oak tree overlooked the shed. Three lower branches provided steps up to a V where she practically was invisible inside the canopy of leaves. She could sit comfortably – or as comfortable as possible in a tree with a bum knee and way too many bruises.

Today she didn't have the energy to leave her sanctuary. Which she realized was ironic. She had told herself the last two nights – was it two nights or three – that she'd returned to the shed to rest so that she would have enough strength the next day to go out and find a path out of this place. And already she had decided to stay put. But staying put did not mean giving up. She'd even dragged her new weapon up into the tree. Somehow she had convinced herself to conserve her energy for when the crazy man returned.

Now she was beginning to wonder if he'd ever come back. She hadn't thought about what would happen when she ran out of food. Water would be easier. She'd already taken the brand new bucket he'd left for her port-a-potty and used it to catch rainwater. Going to the bathroom in the woods was no big deal. It was more important to have fresh rainwater to bathe with and drink.

At first she wasn't sure he meant to leave the bag of food. But then she realized bringing anything to this shed was not an easy task. He wanted her to eat and keep up her strength and that realization brought a new wave of fear. He wanted her to be strong for whatever he had planned for her. But what if she saw him first. Was there a way for her to blindside him?

The sun continued to stay behind the clouds. There had been no rain . . . yet. Susan could hear the low rumble of thunder in the distance. She leaned her head against the bark. The sounds of the forest and the approaching storm lulled her. So much so, that she didn't pay attention when she heard another rumble. Only this one was not thunder.

She jerked up, straining to hear.

Was that an engine?

Muted and low, the sound was coming from the other side of the rock wall that towered behind the rear of the shed. That was the only section she hadn't attempted because the rocks looked impossible to scale. But that was before she started climbing trees. Now from her perch she tried to calculate the risk.

She listened, this time holding her breath. She was annoyed that her thumping heartbeat interfered. Yes, it was definitely an engine. Was it him? Should she wait? Stay hidden? She needed the element of surprise on her side.

What if it wasn't him? What if it was someone else?

It didn't take her long to decide. She scrambled down the tree hauling her batting ram with her. But when she got to the foot of the rock wall she stood there looking up. It towered at least twenty-feet high. There were some scrubs growing between the cracks but most of them were up higher. Still, she examined the surface for footholds.

What was the risk? So she climbed up to meet him. What did it matter? Deep down she knew she wouldn't win the eventual battle. He looked old and vulnerable but he had proven to be very strong and cunning. Even if she were able to surprise

him and hit him from behind, she'd still need to find a way
out of here.

Susan tossed aside the branch she had considered her best
weapon. There was no way she could climb and hold on to it.
She ignored the pain in her knee and the aches in her body.
She started searching for a place to step and found a protru-
sion of rock. She lifted herself up then looked for another and
another. Soon she reached the shrubs and discovered they
were strong enough to grab onto.

She pushed and pulled her body, stretching and leaning inch
by inch. She was breathing so hard when she reached the top
that she couldn't hear over her own gasps for breath. She laid
her body flat against the grassy patch and lifted her head to
make sure she was alone.

Then she heard a car door slam, and Susan realized that
she might have made a mistake. Suddenly she longed for the
safety of the shed. She kept herself pressed into the grass. The
engine was running but the sound was still muted. That's
when she realized that there was a rock wall on this side, too.
The noises she heard were coming from down below.

She crawled until she came to the ledge of the other side.
The tall grass would hopefully be enough to keep her hidden.
She peeked over the edge.

There was a road.

Oh my God! There was a road!

She tamped down her excitement and tried to stay quiet.
This side of the rock wall was almost higher than the other.
She could see a man walking to the back of the car. He opened
the trunk of the small sedan and bent over it like he was going
to remove something.

He looked nothing like the man she remembered. This

one didn't walk with a limp. He stood straight and tall, not hunched over. He was leaner. Definitely no paunch. And he was younger.

No, this couldn't be the same man. Should she wave to him? Call out and get his attention? He pulled and lifted a great bulk up and out of the trunk just as she started to crawl to her feet.

Then she saw an arm slide down from out of the bundle, and Susan dropped to her belly.

43

Cunningham had asked Maggie to come up with a profile for the Collector. He wanted her to tell him who this killer was. But right now they had nothing but a few pieces of evidence. And in one case, literally only a piece of a victim.

She had spent the morning back at the hospital parking lot. The only outdoor cameras focused on the emergency entrance and the lobby. There were none in the parking lot, just as she had remembered. She'd driven the streets surrounding the hospital looking for businesses – especially banks with ATMs – that might capture the parked police cruiser from another angle.

Nothing.

Next she drove back to the double-wide trailer, but she didn't pull into the driveway. Instead, she found a dirt path that led into the trees overlooking the Tanners' property. She left her vehicle at the entrance, just off the main road. She kept to the grass, trying not to step anywhere close to the deep tire ruts, still brimming with rainwater. Someone had been here in recent days and driven up this road in the mud.

She found footprints where he had gotten out of his vehicle. Carefully, she followed where he had trekked into the trees. There was no way of knowing if this was the Collector. There was, however, an excellent view of the double-wide. She stood under the tree where the footprints ended.

The Collector told Steele that he saw what the deputy had

done at the trailer. From up here he might have watched Steele shoot Daniel Tanner in the back, although it was difficult to see the riverbank. Maybe with binoculars. However, he wouldn't have seen what took place inside the trailer. Even with binoculars, the curtains in the windows would have made it almost impossible to see beyond them.

Why were you watching?

Did he know the Tanners? Did he know Deputy Steele?

After much thought, Maggie believed Deputy Steele had murdered all three of the Tanners. That whole crime scene – in Maggie's view – was too messy for someone like the Collector. It was too amateurish for someone who could remove spleens, fingers and toes and manage to pull off a murder in a hospital parking lot in the middle of the day. It was too quick and sloppy for a man who was willing to wait patiently to shoot his prey with a crossbow.

What happened in the double-wide trailer was a result of anger, passion or revenge. There was almost a frantic, blind rage to the way Louis Tanner was strung up and then stabbed.

She remembered, again, how Deputy Steele seemed overly concerned about whether the girl could have seen anything from her hiding place in the cellar. Never once had he asked if she was going to be okay. Yet he had been quick to volunteer to guard her. He may have done so with the intention of killing her, too.

As Maggie left the pasture road and drove to Quantico, she remembered thinking Steele was a bit cocky that day when discussing how gruesome the inside of the trailer had been. Especially for a guy who claimed he hadn't seen anything except a quick look from the doorway. But he appeared genuinely surprised about the takeout container.

Why was the Collector there? Now she was convinced that he had been watching from that pasture road up in the trees. He must have seen Steele shoot Daniel Tanner in the back. And after it was all over? Did he come down from his hiding place to get a better look?

Was he shocked to see what Steele had done?

No, Maggie thought it was more likely that he was impressed. So much so, he wanted to add to the crime scene. Not only add to it, but telegraph who the murderer was by inserting the speeding ticket with Steele's signature.

Wait a minute.

If he wanted to leave a clue for law enforcement about who the murderer was, that would mean the Collector knew Deputy Steele by name. Otherwise how would he know that the signature on the ticket matched the man he saw shooting Daniel Tanner?

That threw off her theory of a random case of voyeurism.

Was it possible the Collector had also gotten a traffic ticket from the deputy? She'd need to check and see if Sheriff Gellar could provide copies, but it seemed like a long shot. They didn't have a name or a vehicle. How would they possibly identify the Collector even if he had been issued a ticket by Steele?

One step forward, two steps back.

And there was still another hole in her theory – what kind of killer just happens to travel around with a spleen?

According to Ganza the woman's toe had been on ice. Maggie could list half a dozen killers who kept pieces of their victims in their refrigerator or freezer, but she couldn't think of a single one who traveled with body parts on ice.

She made a mental note to herself: he travels with a small

cooler. Perhaps he has a job where he needs to take his own lunch or needs to put other things on ice.

She had already added voyeur to her profile of the Collector. Not only had he watched Steele from his hiding place up in the trees overlooking the Tanners' property, he had been watching when they were processing the crime scene. He'd told them as much in his note. How else would he have known that Maggie had vomited outside the trailer?

And despite no concrete evidence, Maggie suspected he had been watching the hospital parking lot. What fun would there be to leave takeout containers filled with shocking contents if he wasn't close by to watch the reactions? He had admitted this in his note as well.

She was pulling onto the road to Quantico when her phone rang.

'This is Maggie O'Dell.'

'Margaret O'Dell?'

'Yes.'

'Your mother is Kathleen O'Dell. Is that correct?'

Maggie pulled off onto the side of the road.

'Who is this?'

'I'm Dr Philip Lawrence with St Mary's Hospital in Richmond. Your mother was brought in last night.'

'Is she ... okay?' She hated how her voice sounded, small and so much like that twelve-year-old version of herself.

'As well as you can expect for a woman who tried to commit suicide.'

44

During the hour and a half drive Maggie tried to keep her mind focused on the case at hand. Takeout containers and killers were preferable to dredging up images of her childhood. But of course, it didn't work.

Maggie and her mother had mourned the loss of Maggie's father in very different ways. While Maggie scavenged for every memento and tried to surround herself with anything and everything to hold onto his presence, her mother wanted to remove herself from every last remnant of their previous life. Within months of her father's funeral her mother had packed them up and moved halfway across the country from Green Bay, Wisconsin, to Richmond, Virginia.

There was no explanation, and Maggie learned quickly that she wasn't to expect one.

Her father had been such integral part of her life that for weeks, maybe months after his death, Maggie would wake in the middle of the night gasping for air. She couldn't breathe. She couldn't move. Years later she recognized these fits as panic attacks. But for a twelve-year-old girl, who'd lost her father and who couldn't rely on her mother, her night terrors kept her awake. She read until she couldn't keep her eyes open and even then, she slept with the lights on.

Her mother, on the other hand, appeared determined to bury the memory of her husband. Her first attempts were with alcohol. Maggie couldn't begin to count the times she'd helped her mother up their apartment steps and then helped her into bed. She'd make herself soup and a grilled cheese, do her homework and wait anxiously for the light of the next day. Too many times she got herself up and ready for school while her mother slept off her hangover. Then Maggie would come home to an empty house. Around eight or nine o'clock at night, the process would start all over again.

In hindsight, those days were not so bad. Maggie quickly learned that being alone was safer. The worse was yet to come. Her mother started bringing home an array of men she'd met at her favorite watering hole. Maggie's first introduction to sexual advances came from the drunken strangers touching her, fondling, groping her in the most intimate and inappropriate ways. One even slammed her small body against the wall of their living room where he trapped her, writhing against her until her mother finally told him to stop. But that incident still didn't stop her mother and the endless parade.

Her mother's first attempt at suicide took place on a night she had brought home one of her regulars. The cowardly bastard panicked and left Maggie to call 911.

After all these years, Greg was the only person she had confided in about her childhood. For all his faults, he was kind and gentle when it came to physical intimacy. He knew and he understood how difficult it was for Maggie. He never pushed her.

That her mother had attempted suicide yet again was not a surprise, although it had been several years since the last. That she had asked to see Maggie was also not a surprise. Their pattern had long ago been established. Her mother broke herself into little pieces then depended on her daughter to put her back together again.

*

A nurse directed Maggie to the fourth floor, but asked her to take a seat in a visitor's lounge. Dr Lawrence had requested to talk to her before she could see her mother.

'Ms O'Dell.' The doctor startled her after almost an hour's wait.

'Yes.'

'I'm Dr Lawrence.'

The deep voice didn't look like it belonged to the small, young man standing in the door to the lounge. He looked no older than Maggie. His head was shaved and he wore a close-cropped beard. He offered what seemed like a large hand for such a small man, but the handshake was soft, gripping only the ends of her fingers. Then he sat on the arm of the chair across from Maggie, and she couldn't help thinking it was an old trick of a short man – a way to maintain his authority by placing himself higher than her so she had to look up to him.

'I'm hoping you can give me some information, some insight.'

'Of course. Although I don't know how much help I can be. I haven't seen my mother for a few months.'

He frowned at her as he took a miniature notebook and pen from his jacket pocket. 'I thought Kathleen mentioned that you live in the Richmond area?'

'About forty minutes away.'

He wrote this down, and Maggie wondered how *this* information would aid him in treating her mother.

'What was it this time?' she asked.

'Excuse me?'

'The last time she took an overdose of Valium and washed it down with Johnnie Walker.'

From his look of surprise Maggie knew her mother had, of course, failed to mention any of this to her new doctor.

'So this was her second attempt at suicide?'

He started writing again.

'Not even close.'

'Excuse me?'

'This is her fifth. I missed one of them when I was in college.'

He was staring at her now. But Maggie could see something in his eyes that wasn't disbelief so much as indignation.

'And yet you don't keep tabs on her.'

There it was.

Her mother had a way of placing responsibility on anyone and everyone except herself. Maggie knew this because even as a young girl she'd been the recipient of her mother's blame.

'There's never been anything I could do or say that made a difference or stopped her,' she found herself explaining. Immediately, she wanted to kick herself. None of this was her fault and offering any kind of explanation only gave credence to her mother's wrongful claims.

'She's still your mother,' Dr Lawrence told her.

Maggie wanted to tell him exactly what kind of mother Kathleen O'Dell had been. But instead she said, 'What information can I give you that might actually help?'

45

DEVIL'S BACKBONE STATE FOREST

Susan had no idea how long she lay in the grass on top of the rock ledge. At first she was shaking so badly she thought for sure he could hear her teeth chattering in fear. She bit back the whimpers that came without warning. Her only salvation was the increasing rumble of the approaching thunderstorm.

But even after she heard the car drive off she didn't trust that he was gone. She imagined him waiting for her. She could almost feel him watching. Somehow she found the courage to move. Perhaps it was the lightning. It had gotten so dark she wasn't sure if it was afternoon or evening.

Still, she stayed low. She belly-crawled, using her elbows to pull herself through the grass and continuing when the grass gave way to hard rock, scraping her skin raw.

She discovered a gouge where the ledge stepped up and joined another. She might not have noticed it if she wasn't on her belly. It was partially hidden behind a scraggly shrub that dared to grow out from a crack in the rock. There was just enough space for Susan to wedge herself inside. She pushed her back against the cool, hard surface and tucked her knees up to her chest.

She hadn't been there long when the rain began and now she missed the warmth of the shed. She was probably being ridiculous. Paranoid. What if she was wrong about what she saw? Did she even know what she had seen? Maybe there was a perfectly good explanation for the man to be carrying an unconscious woman into the forest.

Whatever the reason, he was gone now. And he had been for some time. What was keeping her from making her way down to the road and following it? It was her one chance at escape. But she had no way of knowing how long that road was. The thought of being stranded in the middle of the night in the dark forest made her start to shiver again.

All she could think about was sliding back down the rock wall and snuggling up on the dirty, old mattress inside the shed. She was hungry and thirsty. How many hours had she spent up here? Was she really prepared to spend the night? Because there was no way she could maneuver down either side in the dark without possibly falling and breaking her neck.

The rain came down harder now, forming puddles at the opening of her little cave. There was still enough light. She decided she'd crawl out. She could watch the shed to make sure he wasn't there. From the top of the rock ledge she would be able to see if he was anywhere near. But she needed to do it while there was still some light.

Just as she reached to grab onto the shrub and pull herself out, she heard a crunch. It wasn't the thunder. She snatched her hand back and shoved herself back until the rock was stabbing into her lower back.

Through the leaves of the scraggly shrub she saw hiking boots.

He was here. And he was less than six feet away from her.

46

It was nightfall by the time Maggie left the hospital. The thunderstorms kept to the north, but clouds still clogged the sky. She longed to see a sunset, stars – anything but clouds. Outside, the air was warm and fragrant, a mixture of gardenias and impending rain, unlike her mother's hospital room that reeked of disinfectants and selfish desperation.

'I think it may have been a call for help,' the young Dr Lawrence had told Maggie before he allowed her to enter her mother's room. He said it as though his diagnosis was unique and original, as if Maggie had never heard anything similar before in regards to her mother's many attempts to end her life. By now, Maggie thought she had heard it all.

But there was something her mother said just as she drifted off into an exhausted sleep. It stuck with Maggie, and she couldn't shake it from her mind. Her mother had looked up at her, eyelids struggling to stay open and she mumbled, 'The darkness is starting to suffocate me.'

'What do you mean?' Maggie had asked, but her mother's eyes closed, and soon her breathing took on the slow deep rhythm of sleep.

Usually her mother denied she made any sort of attempt to end her life. The overdoses were, of course, mistakes. Miscalculations. She couldn't remember what the doctors told her. And yes, maybe she'd had too much to drink. She was flippant and sometimes belligerent if pressed.

At some point her mother became the boy who cried wolf, and for Maggie's own sanity, she started to treat each 'cry' after that point as a false alarm. But this – 'the darkness is starting to suffocate me' – *this* was new. And it was unsettling in a way Maggie couldn't explain. It made her sit down and take her mother's hand.

She knew her mother's misery had prompted Maggie to study psychology. In the beginning Maggie had been looking for an explanation. Something, anything to give reason to the woman's self-destruction. And perhaps give Maggie some relief. Take her off the hook, because she did feel guilty. And she did blame herself. *She* wasn't enough reason for her mother to stop. She wasn't enough reason for her mother to live.

As a child, Maggie didn't understand why she felt responsible for her mother's actions. They had reversed roles and Maggie became the caretaker when her mother's drunken stupors resulted in entire lost weekends.

Her father had left them both. Not just her mother. Maggie missed him, too, a physical ache so real and so painful that every night in bed she'd clutch her knees to her chest and rock herself to sleep. What Maggie's mother never seemed to understand was that she had lost only a husband. Maggie had lost a father … and her mother.

Maggie decided to drive home instead of all the way back to Quantico. Home was forty minutes away. Quantico was an hour and half. Surprisingly, she was disappointed when she found the apartment dark and empty. Greg had left her yet another note; their new standard for communicating with one another.

Went out for drinks with Les and Sophie.
Join us if you want. We'll be at Hannigan's.

Les and Sophie had moved in down the hall almost a year ago, and they were perfectly nice. Sophie always politely asked how Maggie's day was, although Maggie knew neither she nor Les would want to hear the gruesome details. The last time they had gone out for drinks the couple had sided with Greg when he told them about the 'excellent opportunity' in his law firm for a claims investigator.

'Oh, doesn't that sound lovely? You two could work together.' Sophie had put her hands together in a silent clap. 'And you probably wouldn't need to carry a gun.'

Now Maggie stood in front of the open refrigerator, regretting that she hadn't picked up dinner when her phone began to ring.

'This is Maggie O'Dell.'

'Girl, where you be?'

It was Agent Turner and she instantly smiled at his poor attempt at slang.

'I just got home.'

'Oh. Sorry. Am I interrupting anything?'

'Just my regrets of not having a pizza already delivered.'

He laughed. She was starting to enjoy hearing his deep baritone laugh.

'You live anywhere close to Fredericksburg?'

'About twenty minutes away.'

'Wanna meet me at Vinny's Italian Grill? Best pizza in town. The pie and the brews are on me.'

She hesitated. Sometimes she wasn't sure if Turner was flirting with her. He knew she was married. But she'd also seen him flirt shamelessly – and harmlessly – with a lot of women. Her pause must have lasted too long.

'I promise it'll be worth your while, O'Dell. I've got lots of good stuff to share. Our boy, the Collector, has been bussssy.'

It was business. Of course, it was business. She couldn't decide if she was relieved or disappointed. She was exhausted. Ordeals with her mother always left her drained even when she wasn't the one wiping up the vomit and dialing 911.

'I'm on my way.'

She left Greg a note.

The crowded streets and restaurants reminded Maggie that it was Saturday night. Vinny's surprised her. It was old style Italian with checkered table clothes and Tiffany lamps hanging from the ceiling. She imagined Turner preferring more trendy eateries like Ollie's, the burger place they'd eaten at the other night.

He waved at her from a table clear in the back corner. She was pleased to see Delaney. Gwen was there, too. Okay, so it was a taskforce meeting. She was relieved and welcomed the chance to fill her mind with details that didn't include her childhood or her mother. Was it wrong that these were the people she preferred to spend a Saturday evening with, instead of her husband and perfectly nice neighbors?

She glanced over her shoulder as she weaved her way through the crowded restaurant, checking to see if Cunningham was here, too.

'Our little party got bigger after I hung up,' Turner told her as if he owed her an explanation.

Delaney stood and pulled out a chair for Maggie. Ordinarily she didn't want to be treated differently than her male colleagues. Tonight, she simply thanked him.

Turner poured beer from a pitcher into a pilsner glass in front of her. And before she scooted all the way to the table, he was leaning over to her.

'I just spent the day in Richmond,' he said.

For some reason his admission made her stomach sink until she decided she was not going to tell them that she had spent the afternoon in Richmond as well.

He glanced around the restaurant and leaned in closer to Maggie.

'Stan Wenhoff had a lot to tell me. First off, I have a name to go with the toe.'

Delaney rolled his eyes and looked a bit embarrassed. 'Come on, Preston. Do you have no manners?'

'I am stating facts. Does it matter if we talk about them before we eat or after?'

'Who is she?' Maggie asked.

'Name's Paige Barnett, twenty-seven years old, single.' He pulled a small notebook from the jacket hanging on the back of his chair. 'From Gainesville. Worked at a place called The Runner's Shop. I think it's in that Gateway Mall area. She didn't show up for work on Monday.'

'Monday? As in this past Monday? Stan made it sound like she had been stranded in the forest for maybe a week. When was the last time anyone's seen her?'

'Hey, I'm just telling you what the good officers in Prince William County have documented. I haven't had the chance to talk with all these folks yet.'

'Did the report list where or how she was taken?'

'They found her vehicle in Conway Robinson State Forest. Sounds like there's a small lot at the trailheads.'

'Where is that?'

'It's off Route 29, pretty much in the middle of the Gainesville area.'

'So about an hour away from Devil's Backbone State Forest.'

'Her sister, Lydia Barnett, filed a missing person's report. I've seen a copy of that. She mentioned that Paige liked to run in the park. But the sister lives down in Fort Lauderdale, and she didn't file the report until last weekend.

'I'm guessing Paige Barnett is like thousands of single people who live alone and don't have a significant other.' Turner continued. 'They check in with friends and family but oftentimes not on a daily basis, so it might be a couple days, maybe even a week for anyone to realize that their single friend or family member's not just blowing them off but might actually have gone missing.'

Maggie knew that was true. If she and Greg didn't leave notes for each other, one of them could go missing for a few days without the other realizing it.

'Stan literally just verified her identity this afternoon,' Turner said. 'And that's not all. Our good buddy, Stan, had another body to identify. This one was found just outside Richmond. Shallow grave somewhere in the woods. Remember that councilwoman who went missing?'

'From Boston?'

'Yeah, that's the one.'

'She ended up down here?' Maggie asked.

'That's not even the weirdest part of this,' Turner said.

It was obvious that Delaney and Gwen had already heard this news because Turner was keeping his voice down and talking directly to Maggie while they sipped their beers and sat back.

'Stan did the autopsy,' he continued. 'And guess what?'

'She had an arrow in her?' Maggie asked.

'Nope, no arrow. But she was missing something. The killer removed her spleen.'

47

FREDRICKSBURG, VIRGINIA

'Where were the woods located?' Maggie wanted to know.

The pizza had arrived, and she practically elbowed Turner out of the way to grab a slice. She was starving.

'I tell you we found the body that might be a match for our spleen à la mode and you want directions?' He was shaking his head at her.

'What are you thinking, Maggie?' Delaney asked.

'How many driving hours is it from Richmond to Boston?'

'I used to drive from New York to the District,' Gwen offered. 'It's about four hours. To Boston is another four, maybe four and a half.'

'And it's almost two hours from DC to Richmond,' Turner said. 'So nine or ten hours. That's a long drive with a dead body in your trunk.'

'Tells us our boy doesn't mind picking up and moving to a whole new area,' Delaney said.

'Boston to Richmond is a straight shot on Interstate 95,' Maggie told them. 'I went back out to the Tanners' property this morning. It's just off Interstate 66.'

'So he also likes to stick to the interstate.' Turner gestured for the waiter. Over three crowded tables he got the man's attention, pointed to the pitcher of beer and raised two fingers. The waiter nodded. 'Are you saying the Collector might have stumbled onto the Tanners just as crap was hitting the proverbial fan?'

'That I'm not sure about, but I did find tire tracks on a dirt pasture road that runs parallel to their property. Found footprints to a perfect view of the place.'

Turner did his whistle then asked Delaney, 'You said Lucille Tanner had quite a bit to say?'

Delaney tugged at his collar. Nine o'clock on a Saturday night and he was still wearing a tie.

'Gwen and I talked to her after we did the photo line-up with Katie.'

'Did she identify Deputy Steele?' Maggie asked.

Delaney glanced at Gwen, letting her answer.

'She picked out Steele but she wasn't certain if she remembered him from the hospital or from the crime scene.' Gwen ran fingers through her hair and let out a long sigh. 'She might never remember details from that day. At this point, it's not going to help us to wait, especially if she didn't see the Collector.'

'Lucille Tanner told us her daughter-in-law was having an affair,' Delaney said.

'Whoa! I didn't see that one coming,' Turner said.

'Her son, Louis seemed convinced the guy was in law enforcement,' Delaney continued. 'According to Lucille, her son gave Beth a choice and she chose Louis. After that he started getting harassed by a cop. Speeding tickets. Parking tickets. Once, he was stopped for a taillight that was out. She said the taillight looked like it had been kicked in by someone.'

'But he never gave his mother a name,' Gwen added.

'That actually makes sense,' Maggie said. 'Considering the condition Louis Tanner's body was in. What about Daniel and Katie?'

'They were trying out a new boat,' Gwen said.

'They may have been on the river when Steele arrived,' Delaney suggested. 'When they were coming back to the double-wide Daniel must have suspected something wasn't right. Katie told me, all her father said was to hide in the cellar and not to come out until he came for her.'

No one said the obvious. Daniel Tanner never came back for her.

'The way I see it, Steele comes out of the double-wide,' Delaney said. 'He's surprised to see someone outside. Daniel takes off running. Steele can't stop him without shooting him.'

'I think that's the part the Collector might have seen,' Maggie told them.

The waiter arrived with two pitchers of beer and everyone went silent.

'Your second pie should be out in a few minutes. I'll go grab it.' And he was gone.

'Still doesn't make sense how the Collector just happened to come along,' Turner finally said after refilling their glasses. 'Yeah, I get that it's right off Interstate 66 but that exit doesn't lead to diddley-squat. There's an exit with gas and eats right before that one if he needed to take a piss – oh, pardon my French, Dr Patterson.'

Maggie wanted to smile, pleased that he hadn't included her in his pardon.

If the missing Boston councilwoman was one of the Collector's victims that certainly widened his region. But as far as the Tanners went, there wasn't anything new that Maggie hadn't already suspected. She asked Turner if he'd mind if she talked to Paige Barnett's employer and maybe even the sister in Florida. He was going to track down her vehicle and take a look at her apartment.

By the time Maggie left, she was glad she had joined them. The pizza was delicious and getting her mind back on the case, and off her mother, was exactly what she needed.

It was after midnight when she crawled into bed. She thought Greg was fast asleep. His back was turned to her.

'I'm sorry about your mom,' he said without moving, his voice groggy with sleep.

She had told him in her note about spending the afternoon in Richmond.

'Me too.'

'You know it's not your fault,' he told her.

'I know.'

As she rolled over to stare out the window into the dark night, she remembered her mother's words again: 'The darkness is starting to suffocate me.'

Despite all of Maggie's studies, her advanced degrees and training, she still felt like that twelve-year-old girl who wasn't enough to fill her mother's void. Even now, she had no idea how to help her. And how could she, when she hadn't mastered how to fill her own void?

What Maggie had learned was how to construct barricades, so that no one could leave her, no one could abandon her. And the way that she did that was making sure that no one could matter enough to ever hurt her, ever again.

48

Sunday

Maggie gave up on sleep. In her dreams she was back in Green Bay, Wisconsin, helping her mother pack up their things. Only Maggie wasn't a little girl. She was grown. The house didn't look anything like the one they had lived in. It was small and dark and smelled bad. Boxes surrounded them. They didn't speak to each other while they packed. But instead of boxes, her mother just kept handing her one takeout container after another.

Finally around 3:00 a.m. Maggie crawled out of bed and quietly gathered her running gear in the dark, so she wouldn't wake Greg. By five o'clock she'd run two miles under the light of street lamps with her shoulder holster under the baggy sweatshirt. By 6:30 a.m. she was on the road after she'd showered and changed into jeans and a T-shirt. Her shoulder holster was back in place, snug against her body and hidden under her FBI windbreaker. She'd left another note for Greg, keeping it ambiguous enough that he might think she'd be spending most of her day with her mother. At the moment she was headed in the other direction toward Quantico.

The guard at the security hut shook his head at her. Pete was used to seeing her early on weekend mornings.

'You're getting as bad as your boss,' he said.

'He's here?'

'Beat you by—' He checked his wristwatch. 'Twenty-two minutes.'

She handed him a hot coffee with cream, no sugar and a fresh glazed donut. His weathered face managed a grin and his 'thank you' was a bob of his head accompanied by a mumbled, 'You are too good to me.'

When she got off the elevator she thought about stopping by Cunningham's office. Instead, she headed in the other direction to her own. She needed to do several computer searches. One on ViCAP. Days ago she had searched and gotten a hit. At the time it didn't seem to fit, because it was too far away. Massachusetts, not Virginia. A brown paper bag was left near the restrooms at a rest area or a truck stop off Interstate 95. It had been flagged as a possible prank. She checked and there were no stolen or missing body parts reported from organ donor organizations. Now she wanted the details.

She requested the file that included two photos. The brown paper bag had no markings, no logos. It could have come from any grocer. Inside was plastic bag of melting ice and on top was another plastic bag with what looked like a bloody glob that was later identified as a human lung.

She downloaded the information including the photos and as she waited, she sat back in her desk chair.

Was it the Collector's handiwork? Had he advanced from a simple brown paper bag to a takeout container? Days ago when she first saw the entry she'd discounted it. But Councilwoman Brenda Carson and her missing spleen had changed Maggie's mind.

She checked the date on the report. The brown paper bag had been discovered three months ago. If it was the Collector he might have been living in the Boston area. Serial killers often stayed close to home, finding comfort in the familiarity of their surroundings.

Something made him move.

What would cause him to pull up roots and leave a hunting ground? Could it have been the national attention that the missing councilwoman had garnered? Suddenly his familiar surroundings would have been under a microscope, swarming with investigators.

He moved south but still kept to Interstate 95. Now Maggie wondered how many other women had gone missing along the I-95 corridor close to Boston? She did another computer search. This one was for missing persons, narrowing it down to within one hundred miles of Boston. She downloaded that list, too.

Then she started printing copies of anything and everything she could about Paige Barnett, the woman whose autopsy she had attended last week. The woman with the broken arrow in her leg who Stan Wenhoff believed had been left to fend for herself in Devil's Backbone State Forest. The Collector had taken her severed toe, kept it on ice then put it in a takeout container and strategically placed it on the hood of Deputy Steele's police cruiser.

Other than the missing person's report filed by Paige's sister, Lydia Barnett of Fort Lauderdale, Florida, there wasn't much more. Maggie found and made a copy of the woman's driver's license. It was issued by the state of Florida and listed Paige's address as the same as Lydia's. So the woman had moved recently. She was twenty-seven years old. She was attractive with long dark hair and an infectious smile as she posed for the DMV. None of that was apparent during the autopsy. Maggie remembered how battered her face was, her hair a tangled and matted mess. Even her sister wouldn't have been able to identify her.

Turner had told Maggie last night that he would check out Paige's apartment, so somehow he had a local address. Maggie jotted down directions for the The Runner's Shop in Gainesville's upscale Gateway Mall. Although she'd never stopped at the shopping center before, she guessed it was about forty minutes away. Still, she brought up a map.

Look at that, she thought to herself. The Gateway Mall was just off Interstate 66.

49

GAINSVILLE, VIRGINIA

Rita had heard the Sunday lunch crowds were crazy, but this was her first time working one. Usually she took the evening shifts. Still crazy, but bigger tips. Rita liked to call the restaurant business organized chaos. And already she could add that the Sunday lunchers were fussy and demanding.

'This isn't at all what I expected,' an older woman told Rita when she delivered her chicken sandwich.

She wanted to tell the woman it looked exactly like the photo on the menu, but instead, she asked if there was something else she could bring her.

'Would you like to see the menu again?' Rita asked.

Sunday also brought families with kids – pouty, noisy, disruptive and picky kids. One of them had already spilled an entire glass of soda, and J.P. Morgan didn't look happy about cleaning it up. Rita had asked to be on the patio where the smaller, bistro-sized tables accommodated only two or three people, which eliminated her having to deal with the little monsters. But her customers were still needy and persistent.

One gentleman waved her down for a salad fork. He had a fork, but it was a dinner fork. He needed a salad fork. And then there was the well-dressed couple at the table near the far end of the patio. A table they had requested for privacy's sake.

They hadn't ordered yet, but were on their second basket of bread. Rita tried to ignore their gestures for a third.

She longed for just a few minutes to feed her news addiction. On her way to and from the kitchen her eyes scanned the captions streaming on the bottom of the television screen. Earlier this morning she learned that the little girl – the lone survivor of the brutal murders in Warren County – had been moved from the hospital to an undisclosed location.

Undisclosed. That sounded ominous.

Rita wondered what that meant. Did they believe the girl was still at risk from whoever murdered her family?

But the big news this morning was that a body had been found in a shallow grave outside of Richmond. They'd identified it as the councilwoman from Boston, Brenda Carson. The woman's photo had been plastered all over the news since she went missing. She was only thirty-four, just two years younger than Rita. She'd ended up a long way from home, and Rita thought that was saddest part of the story. But the whole thing was intriguing. It was probably good that she was working the lunch shift or she would have wasted her entire Sunday glued to the television.

Rita's biggest complaint about working the Sunday lunch was that she'd miss working with Drew that evening. Her daughter, Carly, had her very first art show opening. Actually it wasn't Carly's show. Four of her sculptures were included with five other artists. But all the others were adults. Carly was the only teenager. Of course, her daughter hated it when Rita fussed over her. Rita was just so proud, and of course, she wouldn't miss this event for all the Drew Nilsens in the world.

Still, she considered telling Drew about it, inviting him to drop by the gallery. It was only a block away on the other side of the Gateway Mall's courtyard. There was a reception with wine and hors d'oeuvres. It started before his shift. Maybe he could swing by. She had planned the invitation in her mind for days and had it down pat, making sure she chose words that sounded cool and casual.

No big deal. Drop by if you want. She could hear it in her head.

She'd mention that she heard Chef Luigi from Aperto's was doing the food. After all, Drew was going to culinary school. He'd appreciate checking out another chef's specialties, wouldn't he? Her daughter Carly loved going to other art shows to check out other artists' works. It couldn't be that much different?

But Rita had chickened out and didn't ask him last night. She figured she had one more chance. She knew he sometimes stopped by early on Sundays to pick up his check. So through all the waving hands and come-hither gestures from her customers, she kept an eye out for Drew.

Just then, Rita heard a crash behind her. So did everyone on the patio.

In the corner by the door one of the busboys had left a wobbling stack of dirty dishes on a table he had started clearing. One of the glasses had tipped from the pile and shattered on the brick patio. And of course, the busboy was nowhere in sight. All eyes darted between the mess and Rita.

'It's okay, folks,' she said, a tray in each hand. 'We'll get it cleaned up.'

For the first time ever Rita was relieved and happy to see J.P. Morgan with his artillery of broom, dustpan and handheld vacuum. She smiled at him and when his eyes met hers, her immediate reaction was, *I'm gonna regret that smile.*

She delivered all her plates to her customers and weaved her way around the tables on her way back to the kitchen. That's when she noticed that the young couple had left after eating two baskets of bread. However, it did look like they left her a tip under a water glass.

But there was something else on the table next to the empty breadbasket. It looked like a white foam takeout container.

50

GAINESVILLE, VIRGINIA

Maggie almost missed the entrance for Conway Robinson State Forest. Her mind was preoccupied. Before she left Quantico she had called her mother's hospital room. She hardly recognized the cheerful voice that answered the phone. Her mother was doing 'just fine,' but thanked Maggie for asking, like it was an ordinary courtesy call. Then she told Maggie that she'd need to call her back because they had just brought her a 'lovely lunch.' She made it sound like Maggie had interrupted her stay at five-star resort. There was no relief in hearing that her mother was back to her old self.

Maggie followed the half circle drive on the edge of the park. It was a narrow curve of cracked asphalt flanked on both sides by tall pines and hardwood trees. The parking space at the top of the half circle had room for about ten cars. Small wooden signs marked the trailheads.

Maggie parked away from the two cars already there. When she got out of her vehicle she was surprised that the busy traffic she had just left on Route 29 could barely be heard as little more than a hum. Other than the two cars, there was no obvious sign of anyone. She stood at the top of each trail to see how far into the forest she could see. But the trails curved and turned. There were no straight shots.

Did he wait for Paige to come back from her run? Or did

he take her before she started? The Collector wouldn't have surprised her down on one of the trails. It'd be too difficult to bring her unconscious body back to this parking space. And he wouldn't have risked being seen.

Maggie remembered the fluorescent orange running shoe Paige Barnett had worn. She probably bought the shoes because they'd be an unnatural color in the middle of the forest. Many of Virginia's forests were open to hunters. A splash of orange could protect a runner from being mistaken as a fleeing deer. Ironically, Paige's orange shoes had made her an easy target for the Collector.

He took her from this spot. But was she a random catch? Had he simply parked here and waited? Something told Maggie there was nothing random in the way the Collector worked.

She pulled a plastic evidence bag from her pocket and gathered a handful of the pebbles that made up the walkway from the parking lot to the trailheads. Then she left.

As she drove to the Gateway Mall, Maggie noted how many miles it was from the state park. This time it took her awhile to find a parking spot, but she finally scored one on the edge of the promenade.

The Runner's Shop, where Paige had worked, was several blocks in the other direction, but Maggie wanted to spend some time walking and getting a feel for the area. Unlike the park, the streets were busy with shoppers. The lunch crowds spilled out onto the outdoor patios.

The shopping center had a small-town feeling. Storefronts were brick with lots of glass windows for browsing and there were pavers for sidewalks. Hanging from street lamps were colorful banners. Potted plants and a floating ball sculpture decorated the courtyard. Shop windows advertised specials, and she could smell the wonderful aromas from the restaurant grills.

She walked by a pastry shop and took in the scent of fresh baked bread. She had gone almost half a block past it before she backtracked. In The Dessert Stop window was a neon sign with the store's logo. The cheerful lettering circled around a frosted donut with pastel sprinkles. She had seen this logo somewhere recently, but where?

That's when a woman's scream startled her and stopped every shopper. The second scream sent people fleeing in the opposite direction.

Maggie ran toward the scream.

51

'FBI. Don't touch it!'

Maggie yelled at the waitress standing over the takeout container. She held up her badge in one hand while the other stayed inside her jacket on the butt of her revolver. But she could see that someone had already opened the lid.

Still, the woman in the emerald green apron stepped back. Maggie could see she wasn't the one who had screamed. A younger woman sitting close by – close enough to see the bloody glob inside the container – was now being helped away.

'Are you really FBI?' an older man asked from a nearby table. 'Are you filming for a movie or something?'

Maggie saw the waitress's nametag then locked eyes on her. 'Rita, can you please make sure no one touches that?'

The woman nodded.

Maggie rushed back out into the courtyard then turned at the first corner where she could see the closest parking lot. People were still hurrying away. Then she backtracked. She examined faces including those on the street and in the shops looking out the windows and standing in the doorways.

He's here. He has to be. He likes to watch.

Was he surprised to see her? He couldn't have possibly guessed that she would be here.

She looked for ordinary. A regular guy who fitted in. Who belonged. He wouldn't look out of place. Somehow he could disguise himself in such a way that he made everyone look past him. Discount him.

She stopped and did a double take at an elderly man using a cane, trying to hurry along, but then a young girl joined him, taking his hand.

Where are you?

By the time Maggie made it back to the patio a uniformed police officer was arguing with the waitress named Rita.

'Who the hell told you that?' he wanted to know.

'I did,' Maggie said, wishing her pulse would stop racing.

She held out her badge for him while her eyes scanned over the customers and restaurant staff. Most of the customers had left or had moved to the brick courtyard outside the restaurant. Some stayed to watch. The older man who had asked if she was filming a movie, smiled at her when her eyes came to his, as if he was in on her secret.

'What the hell does the FBI have to do with this?'

She glanced at his nametag before she said, 'Officer Vaughn, I'm Special Agent Maggie O'Dell. I just happened to be in the area.'

From the look he gave Maggie, she wouldn't have been surprised if he also asked if she was filming a movie.

'I need you to secure this area as a crime scene,' she told him as she pulled out her cell phone. 'You'll need to call some backup. We'll want to start talking to people before they leave.'

'What? You can't—'

'Yes, actually I can.' And she stared him down until he give in and reached for the radio strapped to his shoulder.

'Rita, can I ask you something?'

'Of course.'

'This was your area today?' Maggie asked, gesturing to the patio.

'Yes. It sure was.'

'Are you the one who opened the container?'

She looked away, embarrassed, then nodded before she said, 'I thought one of the customers had forgotten it, but I knew I hadn't boxed up anything.'

'It's okay,' Maggie assured you. 'We will need to fingerprint you, just to eliminate you from any other prints that might be on the container.'

'Okay.'

'I have to make a phone call then I'd like to talk with you.'

Two other officers were hustling up the promenade. Earlier people had scattered. Now there was a crowd gathering around the restaurant.

Ganza answered on the third ring.

'It's Maggie,' she said. 'I have another container for you to come get.'

She gave him the directions. He was quiet for so long she thought she'd lost the connection.

'Be careful, Maggie. He might still be there.'

Hearing Ganza – Mr Cool – tell her to be careful set her on edge. Her eyes started darting around the faces in the crowd. That's when she saw the security camera on the corner of the building pointing down at the restaurant's patio area. Again, her pulse began to race.

Don't stare at it, she told herself. *Pretend you didn't see it.*

She didn't want the Collector to see that she'd noticed it. And at the same time she wanted to shout, 'Gotcha.'

52

From up close, she was prettier than Stucky expected. At the moment he stood less than twenty feet away. Earlier, when she first rushed through the restaurant and onto the patio, she had actually brushed past him. So close he could smell her scent. Something citrus with coconut. And he caught a glimpse of her eyes. They were caramel brown.

He had been so focused on the container, watching the responses to it, that he didn't immediately notice the woman shoving her way through the crowd. Of course, he recognized Agent Maggie before she pulled out her badge. From that moment on, he found it difficult to restrain his excitement. When she raced back out of the restaurant looking for him it took every ounce of discipline to stop from shouting after her, 'Here I am.'

Now the uniformed officer was making them move back. Two more joined him. Stucky wanted to see Maggie take a good look at his handiwork, but so far she'd only glanced at it like she knew exactly what to expect. But this one was different. He wanted to tell her that. If she'd just read the note, she'd know how different. He longed to see the look on her face when she discovered that he had made a fresh kill just for her.

He liked the way she moved. Within minutes she took charge of the situation. Even the male officers were following her instructions. There was confidence and authority in her words and gestures. It was hard to believe this was the same woman he had witnessed less than a week ago, on her hands and knees, vomiting up her lunch.

Stucky was sure he had contributed to her new strength. Yes, she had him to thank. Little by little she was becoming a worthy adversary. A few more scavenger hunts and she would be ready.

53

Ganza arrived with Turner. Maggie saw them making their way across the crowded promenade. She couldn't help thinking that they looked like an aging rock 'n' roll star and his personal bodyguard. Today on his day off Keith Ganza wasn't wearing his lab coat, just his signature black jeans and a black T-shirt with a white skull across his chest. Agent Turner was parting the crowd in front of Ganza, adding to the perception that he was leading the way for a celebrity.

Ganza set his forensic case on a chair next to the table with the container and got to work without a word.

'Girl, you do keep finding messes,' Turner said to Maggie.

She turned her back to the crowd behind them and whispered, 'I think we got him this time.'

'What are you talking about?'

'Try not to look and be obvious,' she kept her voice low. 'Up on corner of the building, right behind you is a security camera. The restaurant's owner is pulling up the feed.'

'You know these types of cameras are notoriously awful.'

'It's pointing down almost exactly on the table,' she told him.

'The Collector is smarter than that. He had to know there was a camera.'

'Maybe not. Come on.' She tugged on his elbow. 'He should have it ready for us. He has the monitor in his office.'

She led Turner between the tables. The crowd inside the

restaurant parted for them. Turner followed her past the kitchen and down a hallway. She knocked on the office door but didn't wait for a reply. Maggie thought Henry Gibson looked more like a high-priced lawyer in Greg's law firm than the owner of a bar and restaurant. His close-cropped hair was silver at the temples. He was handsome, tall and lean and wore a polo shirt with chinos.

'I have it for you, Agent O'Dell,' he said, standing up from his desk. He had been polite and almost overly cooperative.

'Mr Gibson, this is Agent Turner.'

He came around his desk to shake Turner's hand. Then he pointed back to the monitor. 'It's pretty easy to work. Buttons are down below. Play, rewind, pause. Sorry, no zoom. There's also no sound, but I set it up for five minutes before that poor woman starts to scream. She's in the upper left part of the screen. You'll see her put her hand to her mouth. Unfortunately the camera's angle only captures a corner of the table.'

'Is this your only camera?'

'Yes. I actually had it installed because we had a few patio customers walking off without paying their bill.'

'But there's a wrought iron fence around the patio.'

'I put that in at the same time as the camera. Can I get you two something to drink? Something to eat?'

Maggie caught Turner's face lighting up, and she wanted to roll her eyes.

'I'm fine,' she said as she settled down in Mr Gibson's chair and hit PLAY.

'Only if it's not too much trouble,' Turner said.

'It'll give my staff something to do while they're waiting. How do you like your burger?'

'Any way you bring it to me will be fantastic. Thanks.'

As soon as the office door closed Maggie said, 'Really, you're hungry?'

'I haven't had lunch.'

He came around the desk and kneeled down beside her. His bulk filled the small space. Even on his knees he was eye-level with her.

'What is that?' he asked as he sniffed the air. 'Coconut?'

'Excuse me?'

'Shampoo?'

This time she did roll her eyes at him.

'What? A guy can't compliment a woman on how she smells?' But he turned toward the monitor and said, 'These cameras are usually too grainy. But this one is pretty good quality.'

Maggie fast-forwarded until she saw the woman put her hands to her mouth. She stopped and pushed REWIND. Then she hit PLAY again. The corner of the table was empty though she could see there were other items on the other side – flatware, the edge of a glass and what she knew was the bottom of a basket. Earlier, out on the patio, she had already taken note of the contents on the table and their proximity to the takeout container.

She thought she had rewound the tape too far when there was a flurry of customers getting up and walking in between the camera and the table. When they cleared out of the way the foam container was there.

'There it is,' Turner pointed, and she stopped the tape. 'That happens awfully quick. Almost as if he knows exactly where the camera is.'

Once again, Maggie pushed REWIND then hit PLAY. At

the first sign of someone coming into the screen, she pressed PAUSE. She found the button that would show them frame-by-frame. It was excruciatingly slow. There was a flurry of arms and elbows, a large purse. Then she saw the container in a narrow space, a small triangle created between people. She hit PAUSE.

'I wish we could zoom in,' she said.

Turner leaned in so close he was pressing against her arm that controlled he buttons.

'I can see his fingers.' He gestured at the screen. 'He's holding it between his thumb and index finger. Right there.'

'We've got his prints.' She tried not to get excited. Perfect prints meant absolutely nothing if the Collector had never been fingerprinted before.

'That's all we see of him,' Turner sounded like they were finished.

There was one more thing Maggie wanted to check. She started the tape again, frame-by-frame. The open triangle moved and they could no longer see the container but when it moved, something else filled it. She caught a glimpse of what he was wearing, and although she could only see a piece of it, she recognized the restaurant's logo on the dark colored fabric.

'He was wearing an apron.'

'What's that?'

'The staff all wear aprons with the restaurant's logo,' she said, using her index to finger to point it out. 'Emerald green ones, with white logos imprinted on them. Aprons that in black and white would show up looking like that.'

54

QUANTICO

Assistant Director Cunningham stood at the windows of the cafeteria looking down into the woods. The place was empty. The kitchen was shuttered on Sundays but he couldn't stand another minute being down in the Behavioral Science Unit, six stories below ground level.

He had never shared with anyone how much he hated not having an office with a window. How much he wanted – no, how much he needed to see the outside. He didn't mind if the sky was hidden behind clouds. His agents and even his administrative assistant, Anita, had all gotten used to him taking lunch at his desk every day after he went for his daily run. They believed he ran for health purposes but truthfully it was more about his sanity. How could he be there for his agents if he couldn't control his own idiosyncrasies?

And now Cunningham worried he may have jeopardized Agent O'Dell's safety by not taking her off this case as soon as the Collector singled her out.

Keith Ganza had told him about Agent O'Dell finding what she believed might be another container left by the madman. She had been checking out the shopping center where Paige Barnett worked when she heard a scream coming from one of the restaurant's patio areas.

The container showing up in the same vicinity as one of the

victims worked meant that O'Dell might have stumbled upon the Collector's stalking grounds. But Cunningham hated that O'Dell had been the one to make the discovery. He couldn't help wondering if the Collector had planned it that way. And this fact infuriated Cunningham, so much so, that he found himself pacing the length of the cafeteria and then the hallways and walkways.

He considered putting on his running gear and taking to the trails to stomp off some of the anger, but he needed to stay in contact with Ganza, and cell phone reception out in the forest was spotty at best.

Earlier in his office he had made a pot of coffee, and now he gulped down the dregs at the bottom of his travel mug. His stomach already churned from too much caffeine and not enough food. He was contemplating his choices in the vending machines when his phone rang.

'This is Cunningham.'

'It's definitely our boy's work,' Ganza told him.

His stomach knotted up despite the churning.

'What did he leave this time?'

'Looks like a kidney.'

'And a note?' Cunningham asked with his jaw already clenched.

'Yup. He was kind enough to put this one in plastic so it wouldn't get soaked.'

'What do you mean, wouldn't get soaked?'

'This one's a bloody mess,' Ganza said in a low voice that told Cunningham he was still on the scene and didn't want to be overheard.

'Is O'Dell right there with you? Has she seen it?'

'She's with Turner. There's a camera. They're going over the video feed to see if it might have caught sight of him.'

'Can you read it to me?'

'Sure, hold on a minute.'

He could hear a soft thump of the phone being put down then a crinkle like paper being unfolded.

Ganza was back, his voice low, almost a whisper. '"Dear Agent Maggie. I hope you appreciate the finesse and freshness."'

Cunningham winced. The Collector knew her name.

That exchange with reporters outside the hospital had made all the cable news channels. They had no other information so they looped that stupid segment over and over. But there was something that made things worse. The other containers had body parts taken from previous victims days, maybe weeks, before. He'd even kept Paige Barnett's toe on ice. If these words meant what Cunningham suspected, the Collector had made a fresh kill just for Agent O'Dell.

'He even spelled finesse correctly,' Ganza said. 'And I have to tell you, although it looks like a glob, there was some precision cutting. Stan's the expert, so I don't want to speak out of turn, but I'm guessing he used a scalpel, and he's pretty damn good with it.'

'How soon are you able to get the container to Stan?'

'I'm packing up now. Turner and Maggie want to talk to the owner and the staff after they finish watching the video.'

'Any chance we have fingerprints this time?'

'He was awfully careful with the other two containers. And a waitress opened this one up.'

'You're kidding?' Cunningham said.

'Maggie already had me take her prints so we can discount them. She might have smeared any others, but I should be able to tell you later today.'

They had barely ended the call when Cunningham's phone started to ring again. He figured Ganza had another concern.

'This is Cunningham.'

'Director Kyle Cunningham?'

He didn't recognize the baritone voice. 'Yes, that's correct.'

'My name's Fred Olson. Sheriff Olson. I'm over here in Shenandoah County. I know Stan Wenhoff's working with you folks on that woman we found in Devil's Backbone State Forest.'

'Yes, that's right.'

'Well, we got another one.'

55

GATEWAY MALL, GAINSVILLE

Maggie watched Turner use his charm to talk with the staff of Gibson's Restaurant and Pub. Delaney was usually the negotiator and interviewer, but Turner was doing a good job, getting the staff to recall details and information they may have otherwise not realized was important.

Maggie had asked to talk to Rita, the waitress. The woman was waiting for her at a bistro table in the corner of the patio. The police officers had managed to disperse the crowds and maintain a perimeter, so only Keith Ganza was left and it looked like he was packing up to leave. Maggie gestured to Rita that she'd only be a minute as she stopped to talk to Ganza.

'Turner and I reviewed the restaurant video footage. We saw him touch the corner of the box,' she told him. 'It looked like the front left corner.'

'Okay,' he nodded and his ponytail bobbed. His eyeglasses were at the tip of his nose and he pushed them up as he continued packing up.

She noticed that he wasn't looking at her. Maybe even going out of his way to avoid meeting her eyes. Then it hit her, and her knees felt a bit wobbly as she said to him, 'There was another note.'

'Yup.' He finally glanced up as he was stuffing the evidence bags into his duffle. 'Don't let this asshole get to you, Maggie.

He wants attention. Don't let him have it. If we lift prints, we might know who the bastard is by the end of today.'

She wanted to ask to see the note, but he had already packed it, and he was right. She didn't need the Collector in her head right now. Instead, she needed to find out who the hell he was. Besides, Rita was waiting.

Maggie guessed that the waitress was in her early thirties. She was attractive with short brown hair, dark eyes and a friendly face.

'It looked like a bloody piece of raw meat,' Rita said. 'Is that what it is?'

'We won't really know until we get it back to the forensic lab and run some tests.'

She didn't want to tell the woman, but Maggie already suspected that it was a human kidney.

'Wait a minute,' Rita said. 'I recognize you now. It's been nagging at me where I might have seen you before. You were on the news.'

Maggie stopped from grimacing.

'You're on that case with the little girl who survived her family being murdered. Is this connected to that case?'

'I don't know.'

'Sure, I understand. You probably can't talk about it.'

'Were you the only waitress working the patio for lunch?' Maggie didn't want to get sidetracked.

'Yes.'

'So no other employees would be out here?' She and Turner had agreed that they needed to ask the questions without making the staff realize they suspected one of them.

'It's busy for Sunday lunches. We have table bussers and sometimes runners.'

'Runners?'

'Someone who takes the food from the kitchen to the table if I get behind. Mr Gibson doesn't like a hot plate sitting on the kitchen throughway.'

'So you wouldn't have been the only staff member on the patio?'

'No.' Rita looked uncomfortable as she glanced around. 'You obviously saw something on the camera video that makes you think it's one of us who left the container?'

Pretty and smart. Maggie knew she wouldn't get far with Rita if she wasn't straight with her. And one of these staff members had to have seen the Collector.

'To be honest, it's difficult to see anything on the video feed. The camera didn't catch much.' She figured there was no harm in divulging that much. 'I thought I got a glimpse of an apron. Is it possible that someone could have come into the restaurant, put on an apron, placed the takeout container on the table and then left?'

Rita thought about this for a few seconds then shook her head. 'One of us would have noticed a stranger with our apron on.'

'How about an ex-employee?'

'Again, one of us would have noticed. We're a pretty tight-knit group. Except—' and she stopped herself.

'What is it?'

'Well, there is this new clean-up guy. But it's nothing. I mean he hasn't done anything wrong. It's just . . . well, it's just a feeling.'

Maggie's phone interrupted them.

'This is Maggie O'Dell.'

'Agent O'Dell, are you still in Gainesville?'

It was Cunningham.

'Yes. We're talking with some of the restaurant staff.'

'I'll talk to Agent Turner about finishing up. I need you somewhere else. A woman was found in Devil's Backbone State Forest.'

Maggie stood and walked away from the table, turning her back to Rita. She shouldn't have been surprised, and yet she felt a sick feeling coming over her.

'Let me guess,' Maggie said, 'She's missing a kidney.'

'No, as far as I know she's not missing anything. She's alive.'

56

WARREN MEMORIAL HOSPITAL

Gwen watched Cunningham present his badge to the ER nurse in front of him. He gestured back at Gwen and still the woman – a stocky, gray-haired veteran – didn't look impressed. Gwen imagined the nurse already had her fill of officials making requests and demands. Warren County's Sheriff Geller and Shenandoah County's Sheriff Olson were already stalking the small area that constituted the guest lounge for the emergency and trauma center.

'I'm sure you understand . . .'

Gwen heard bits and pieces of the conversation. Cunningham could be polite even when sounding authoritarian. But this time he had met his match. It was obvious this woman ran this ER/trauma center. At least she did on this Sunday evening.

'And I'm sure you understand that this patient has the right to be examined in peace and quiet.'

'Of course,' Cunningham said. 'But Dr Patterson is a psychiatrist and she may be able—'

'Excuse me, but I couldn't care less if she was Mother Teresa. Nobody's bothering this patient until she's been examined and treated. It's my understanding that she is not suspected of committing a crime.'

'On the contrary, we believe she's been a victim. My only

concern is to protect her and future victims. I can't do that unless I can talk to her and find out—'

The woman waved her hand at him to stop, and Cunningham did so in mid-sentence. Then she pointed to the lounge. Without another word she disappeared behind the steel door that led to the examination rooms. Gwen could see the nurse through the small window, hesitating, waiting for the door's lock to click.

Gwen sat down in one of the plastic chairs and let the men pace the floor. Cunningham caught her eyes and looked apologetic. She simply shrugged and smiled. She let him talk to the sheriffs while she pretended to be interested in the local news on the small television attached to the wall.

Gwen had just gotten home from Sunday lunch with a friend when Cunningham had called her. This time, at least, she wasn't just enticed by a long drive in the country with him – tempting as that sounded. She wanted to meet the woman who had survived being taken by the Collector.

The double doors to the outside hissed open and Maggie O'Dell rushed in, stopping short when she saw Cunningham and the two sheriffs. She was dressed in jeans and an FBI windbreaker. Gwen's eyes stayed on the television screen. The men were taking turns telling Agent O'Dell pieces of the story. Sheriff Olson's voice boomed no matter what level he attempted.

'Scared the hell out of the park worker. He said she looked like a ghost stumbling out of the forest.'

Suddenly the men went silent just as the trauma nurse came back. She paid no attention to them and went behind the desk to the computer monitor.

O'Dell said something to Cunningham then left him and

approached the nurse. On the local news they were talking about a festival in Front Royal, and whether the rain would stop long enough. Gwen glanced to see O'Dell tell the nurse something then she pulled what looked like a Polaroid photo from her jacket pocket. She showed it to the nurse. To Gwen's surprise, the nurse stood back up, came around the desk and gestured to her and Maggie to follow.

'Just the women,' the nurse said. And she swiped a card to unlock the steel door.

Maggie held it open and waited for Gwen while the nurse continued to march up the sterile hallway.

Gwen leaned in and whispered to Maggie, 'What in the world did you show her?'

Maggie handed the square Polaroid to Gwen. It must have been the latest takeout container with a bloody glob inside.

57

Susan wished they'd just let her go home. She kept telling the doctor and the nurses that she was fine. No, she hadn't been sexually assaulted. And no, she couldn't tell them what day it was.

She knew she looked awful. She had caught a glimpse of her reflection in the glass door when they brought her in. Susan hardly recognized the wild-eyed woman with medusa hair and mud-caked clothes.

But what about all the bruises?

Yes, she knew they covered a good portion of her body. And yes, her knee hurt. But she was fine. She was out of that godforsaken forest. And no, she wasn't crying because she was in pain. She was crying because she was finally free.

Could she just please go home?

The doctor had left, and Susan was looking around for her clothes. Maybe she could leave. How hard could that be? She'd made it out of the forest, why not out of this emergency ward? Surely it wasn't locked down. She studied the IV stand and heart monitor, following the tubes and cords to where they connected to her. The needle wouldn't be that difficult to remove. Then she remembered the injections her captor had plunged into her arms.

She pushed it out of her mind.

It was over. She just needed to get home.

That's when the nurse with the gunmetal hair and the constant scowl peeked into the room again.

Susan closed her eyes. The nurse was probably looking for the doctor. She'd shut the door and leave when she didn't see him. But she stayed in the doorway, and she said to Susan, 'There're a couple of FBI women who'd like to ask you a few questions. Would that be okay with you?'

Susan jerked and sat up. 'Are they looking for that other woman?'

'What other woman?' the nurse asked as her eyes widened.

Susan realized she hadn't told any of the hospital staff. How could she? They hadn't given her a single chance. But she did tell that park worker. And the sheriff. She was certain she'd told him.

'Yes, I'll talk to them.'

The smaller of the two was older with chin-length strawberry-blond hair. She was dressed in slacks and what looked like a designer blouse. The younger woman had short auburn hair and looked more like an FBI agent. Her windbreaker even said so.

'Thanks for talking with us, Susan. I'm Maggie O'Dell and this is Gwen Patterson.'

The examination room was small, and both women had no choice but to stand right beside her bed.

'I don't even know if she was still alive,' Susan told them.

'Excuse me?' The FBI agent seemed confused.

'Isn't that why you're here? I told the sheriff I saw the man taking a woman out of the trunk of a car. It was that road that I followed. It wasn't far from the shed.'

The women exchanged a glance.

Then the one named Maggie said, 'I think we need you to start from the beginning.'

Susan told them about going to work early in the morning. She could no longer remember what day that was. She was a pastry chef, she told them. Recently promoted to head pastry chef at The Dessert Shop in Gainesville.

'At the Gateway Mall?' Maggie asked.

'Yes. The only part of the job I dislike is going in when it's still dark.'

She continued to tell them how she saw a man struggling with his groceries. She thought he must live in her apartment complex.

'Did he give you his name?' Maggie asked.

'No,' Susan said, now slightly embarrassed at how easily she had been tricked.

She told them how she opened the trunk of her car for him to set the grocery bags inside and suddenly felt the sting in her arm. How her entire body felt paralyzed. How strong the man was when he looked so fragile.

Susan stopped. She looked up and met Maggie's eyes. 'He's done this to more women than just two, hasn't he?'

'Yes. Yes, he has. But you're going to help us stop him from doing it to any other women.'

Susan nodded and crossed her arms, suddenly cold. The woman named Gwen pulled the blanket up.

'Is there anything we can do for you, Susan?'

She knew Gwen meant right at the moment, to make her more comfortable. Get her a glass of water. Something to eat perhaps. But Susan still asked, 'When we finish talking can you please take me home? I'd give anything to sleep in my own bed tonight.'

58

'Do you think the other woman is still alive?' Maggie asked Cunningham.

They had settled into a corner booth at a little diner not far from the hospital. The sign on the door said they were open only until 8:00 p.m. on Sundays but their waitress had already told them if she could get their order to the cook in the next fifteen minutes they were welcome to stay past closing.

'Sheriff Olson has had his men in the forest for several hours.' Cunningham pushed up his glasses and rubbed at his eyes. 'He's bringing in a K9 unit tomorrow morning. He says there're a lot of ravines and steep bluffs to fall and get hurt. Were you able to get a physical description of the man?'

Maggie waited for the waitress to set a Diet Pepsi in front of her and coffees for Cunningham and Gwen.

'Susan said the man in the forest, the one taking the body out of the car trunk, looked different than the man who took her. He was tall, lean, and young. The man she helped was older, a bit overweight, hunched over. He was struggling to carry a couple of grocery bags. She felt bad for him.'

Cunningham raised his eyebrows and glanced from Maggie to Gwen. 'Are we back to thinking there might be two killers?'

Maggie shook her head and noticed that Gwen was doing the same.

'He injected her with something that paralyzed her,' Maggie told him. 'And he ended up being stronger than she imagined. I think the different descriptions support the theory that he changes his appearance. He had to be at the restaurant today or somewhere on the courtyard. I must have missed him by minutes, and yet I couldn't see him. And here's the thing.' She leaned her elbows on the table. 'None of the restaurant staff noticed him either. According to the video – and granted, we only saw a slice of him – he was wearing one of their aprons with the restaurant's logo when he put the container on the table.'

Cunningham sat up. 'You think it's possible he works there?'

'The waitress – the one who opened the container – she said there's a new janitor working for the restaurant. She called him the 'clean-up guy.' She admitted it was just a feeling but that he seemed a bit odd.'

'That doesn't sound right,' Gwen said. 'If the Collector blends in so well that you missed him then he wouldn't choose a disguise that makes him seem odd, would he?'

'Rita said it was just a feeling she had. He might not appear odd to anyone else. Being a clean-up guy or janitor fits with the idea of blending in. Nobody would notice him. Turner said he'd check him out. The guy goes by J.P. Morgan.'

'Now that sounds about right,' Cunningham said. 'I can see him using strange names, like a code or an inside joke. Something to thumb his nose at authorities.'

Cunningham's phone started to ring and he dug it out of his pocket. 'I have to take this. It's probably the transport team.' He slid out of the booth and walked to the front of the diner before answering.

'I'm glad you were able to convince him to let her go home,' Maggie told Gwen.

Back at the hospital Gwen had promised Susan that she'd find a way to get her home and in her own bed tonight. Initially, Cunningham didn't like the idea until Gwen reminded him how difficult it had been securing Katie Tanner in her hospital room. Now the girl was in a lockdown facility where her grandmother could comfortably stay with her, and she was safe from the Collector.

Maggie had heard Gwen's argument for Susan to return to her apartment. Finally Cunningham had relented, but only if Susan agreed to have a security detail with her at all times, at least for the next week. If and when the Collector realized the woman had escaped the forest, all he'd need to do is return to her apartment complex and wait for a chance to finish her off. But at the same time, Cunningham recognized that it might be an opportunity to catch the bastard.

The waitress delivered their food while Cunningham paced the sidewalk outside with the phone pressed to his face. Maggie glanced back at him through the window, trying to gauge his mood. He seemed wound tight, the tension obvious in his clenched jaw and brisk pace up and down the sidewalk.

'He's worried about you,' Gwen said over a forkful of salad.

'Me?' It caught Maggie completely off guard. Maybe she'd heard her wrong.

'The notes. On our drive here, he told me about the latest one.'

It occurred to Maggie that she still didn't know what it said.

'You know as well as I do from all the other cases you've

worked,' Gwen continued. 'It's never a good sign when a killer chooses to get personal with an individual law enforcement officer.'

Maggie didn't want to remind Gwen that most of the other cases she'd worked on had been long distant cases. Maybe that's why she didn't feel threatened by the Collector's notes. Disgusted? Yes. And a bit anxious. Lots of serial killers liked attention. As long as he wanted her attention, he most likely wouldn't harm her.

Besides, Maggie didn't like feeling psychoanalyzed by Cunningham's independent psychiatrist. And now Maggie wondered if he had asked Gwen to talk to her about it. She felt a flicker of anger.

She looked to see Cunningham still pacing, still talking outside.

'So what's the deal with you two?' she asked Gwen, knowing she had absolutely no right to ask. 'Is there something going on?'

Gwen didn't look fazed in the least. She reached across the table for the pepper as she said, 'I have no idea. But if you figure it out, please let me know.'

Maggie stared at her, looking to see if she meant the comment to be snide or sarcastic. Gwen met her eyes and added, 'He's married. So nothing's going on. But do I wish there was?' She glanced over Maggie's shoulder to the front of the diner where Cunningham was. Then back to Maggie's eyes, 'Yes, sometimes I do.'

Gwen went back to her salad. Maggie realized what it meant for someone like Gwen to let her guard down and confide such an intimate and personal vulnerability. She didn't know how to respond.

Just then her phone rang, saving her. Or so she had thought, until she answered.

'Ms O'Dell, this is Dr Lawrence. I'm ready to discharge your mother. She said you'd probably want to pick her up.'

Maggie closed her eyes, and when she opened them Gwen was staring at her, worried creases at the corners of her eyes.

'Actually Dr Lawrence, I'm on a case about two hours away.'

Silence. She told herself not to fill it. Wait for him.

'Well, that's unfortunate. Is there another family member available?'

'I'll need to call you back.' She hung up.

'Are you okay?' Gwen asked. Her concern was genuine.

'My mother tried to kill herself Friday night.'

'Oh God, Maggie, I didn't know.'

'This isn't the first time. She's been practicing since I was twelve.'

'Is she okay?'

'Oh yes. She's ready to go home and pretend like nothing happened. She told her doctor that I'd be picking her up.' Maggie pushed her hair behind her ears and let out a frustrated sigh.

'Are you okay?' Gwen asked. She reached across the table and put her hand on Maggie's.

'She really knows how to push my buttons.'

Now Gwen smiled. 'Of course she does. She helped install them.'

59

THE MUSE ART GALLERY, GAINESVILLE

Rita still didn't want to believe that what she had seen in that takeout container could be human. All she had told her daughter was that someone had left something disgusting to shock people.

'That's kind of what artists do all the time,' Carly told her.

Rita realized how grown up her daughter had become. And tonight she certainly looked older and simply fantastic in a body-fitting shift dress with a chic belt and hipster ankle boots. Her long blond hair was smooth and silky. But it still made Rita uncomfortable watching men ogle her sixteen-year-old daughter.

Carly's sculptures were gorgeous abstracts and even Rita could appreciate the delicate carvings and soft curves. She'd watched Carly start with a thick slab of what looked like gray mud and transform it into something elegant, so Rita knew how much work went into each piece. Carly said it was all about visualizing the creature inside the clay and setting it free. The girl was passionate about her art and carried around her kit with all the sharp, pointy and smoothing tools like she was a medical doctor making house calls.

Rita helped herself to a second glass of complimentary wine, but she still had no appetite. She smiled when she saw Drew standing by the hors d'oeuvres table as if viewing one of the gallery's masterpieces. *He* looked like a masterpiece in his tight-fitting black jeans and T-shirt. She shook her head and sipped her wine, tonight letting herself enjoy the heat he raised inside of her.

Earlier when she introduced Carly to him, Drew had said they looked like sisters ... 'beautiful sisters'. He was more talkative tonight, and she wondered if it was just the excitement of the day. A crisis could bring out the best in people and bring them together. Mr Gibson had closed the restaurant early, and Rita was pleased to see some of the staff had come over to the gallery. Of course, free food and drinks was always a good bet to entice people. But she was surprised to see Mr Gibson.

Drew brought her a small plate of appetizers and she thanked him, despite the scent of shrimp and the sight of blood-red salsa churning up her stomach. So he wouldn't notice, she tried to focus their attention somewhere other than the food.

'It was nice of Mr Gibson to close early,' she said.

Drew shrugged. 'He's probably used to that sort of thing.'

'What do you mean?'

'I just mean crisis management. Controlling the PR stuff. He owns about a dozen other restaurants and pubs.'

'Today was still pretty unusual.'

'Remember that councilwoman that disappeared?'

'Sure, I remember. They found her body outside of Richmond.' Of course, Rita remembered. She was a news junkie. She had hoped he would have noticed that by now. But she wasn't sure what the woman had to do with the events of the day.

'She was taken from a parking lot in Boston,' he said. 'I think they found her car still parked by the restaurant.'

'Okay, sure. I do remember that.'

'The restaurant in Boston,' Drew said. 'It's one of Gibson's.'

60

'Is it possible he left the prints on purpose?' Maggie asked Ganza.

She had brought all her files to his lab and set up shop at the counter where he kept a second computer. But she ignored his ergonomic barstool with hydraulic lift to adjust the height. This morning she needed to pace as she worked. Last night she had told Gwen Patterson that she didn't feel threatened by the Collector. But when Ganza showed her the last note addressing her as 'Agent Maggie,' she was surprised at the shiver that slid down her back.

It didn't help her tension level that she had driven to Richmond in the early morning hours after very little sleep. Dr Lawrence had agreed to wait until morning to discharge her mother, but only if her daughter was there to sign the papers and pick her up.

'I guess that means you're responsible for me, Mag-pie,' her mother had said with a faux cheerfulness that passed right by the discharge nurse.

Mag-pie was her father's nickname for Maggie, and hearing her mother use it felt like fingernails on a chalkboard.

Getting her mother settled and comfortable back in her own apartment and her own bed had thrown Maggie behind schedule. That's the reason she packed up her files and headed upstairs to Ganza's lab. But deep down, she knew the real reason was that she didn't want to be alone.

Now she was glad that their usual back and forth was keeping her engaged. She didn't want to think about how she had found a bottle of Valium in of her mother's favorite hiding place at the back of the silverware drawer. Maggie had slipped the bottle into her pocket before she left, but she suspected her mother had others hidden.

'I deal in facts,' Keith Ganza was telling her now, and she had already forgotten what they were talking about. 'It's your job to figure out intent. Have we gotten any hits yet on those prints?'

The prints. Of course – the fingerprints.

Other than the waitress's fingerprints, Ganza had been able to find a thumb and an index finger on the container. It helped that Maggie and Turner had been able to see on the video where the Collector had held the corner. Ganza had entered the two latent fingerprints into the Integrated Automated Fingerprint Identification System (IAFIS) last night.

'Nothing yet,' she told him. 'He might not be in the system.'

'Or he had someone else put the container on the table for him.'

Maggie's head jerked up from the computer screen. She hadn't thought of that.

'You mean someone who worked at the restaurant? But wouldn't that person tell us once he or she discovered what was inside the container?'

'With the cops and FBI crawling all over the place?' Ganza shook his head. 'I come from an era where we learned that you never admit anything to cops.'

She didn't want to believe that Ganza could be right. That would certainly explain the apron. She'd need to talk to Turner. He'd interviewed the staff members, including J.P. Morgan, the new janitor. Turner would have been looking for stories that didn't add up or possible lies and cover-ups. They were trained to look for tells in the body language of suspects and even witnesses.

'I have a team bringing in Susan Fuller's car,' Ganza said.

'Where did they find it?'

'The parking space she always uses at her apartment complex. I guess she saw it last night when they were taking her home.'

Maggie shouldn't have been surprised. Police had found Paige Barnett's car in the parking space at the trailheads of Conway Robinson State Forest. Right where Maggie suspected she had left it while she went for a run.

'So he uses the victim's own vehicle,' Maggie said, and she hated to admit that it was really quite ingenious. 'Blood, hair, saliva, pieces of fabric – nothing connected to the victim would ever show up in his vehicle, especially if he took a change of clothing.'

'He wouldn't need to wipe his prints away inside the vehicles,' Ganza said. 'Why bother? If the investigators found the victim's car right where she disappeared, they'd have no reason to believe it was used in the apprehension.'

And they might never have known except for Susan Fuller surviving and finding her own car back at her apartment complex.

'Susan said he injected her with something that paralyzed her,' Maggie told Ganza. 'How easy would it be for him to get his hands on a drug like Succinylcholine or Ketamine?'

'You can get your hands on just about anything these days if you know how to go about it. It's interesting that he'd use something more than good old chloroform. Ketamine's become popular as a recreational drug. Believe it or not, there are some people who like that out-of-body feeling. But too much, and it can be dangerous. Tends to cause blackouts. If he's going to shove them into the trunk, why does he need to totally incapacitate them?'

'My gut instinct is because he can. Someone shoves you into your trunk, you're scared, but you still might try to fight. Someone injects you with something that paralyzes you – that feeling of not being able to move a single muscle is terrifying. I think he likes terrifying them, just like he enjoys shocking people with his takeout containers.'

'Evil bastard, huh?'

'Did you see Cunningham's memo this morning?' she asked.

'I try not to read my emails before lunch.'

'We have a prime opportunity to catch the Collector tomorrow,' she told him. 'It'd be nice if I had some idea of what he looks like.' She went back to the computer and started tapping in her password to access IAFIS.

'What exactly happens tomorrow?' Ganza asked.

'All three of the Tanner family are being buried. I'm hoping the Collector won't be able to stay away.'

And just at that moment Maggie saw on the computer screen that she had a hit. The system had found the Collector's fingerprints.

61

Ganza had pulled up a stool alongside Maggie. He had gotten a brown paper bag with his lunch out of the refrigerator and brought it to the counter like he was getting ready for dinner and a show. Without asking, he placed each half of his sandwich on paper towels and slid one of the halves to Maggie. He'd also brought her a cold can of Diet Pepsi.

'What's this?' she asked.

'Tuna salad on rye.'

Maggie knew Ganza kept plastic evidence bags in the same refrigerator. She also knew he was a deeply private professional and that this gesture of sharing his precious lunch was a huge token of trust and friendship.

Maggie popped the tab on the soda then took a bite of the sandwich. Her right index finger tapped and scrolled down the computer page.

'Looks like he was never charged, but they did fingerprint him.'

'Any photos?'

'No. But this was ten years ago. I don't recognize the county in Massachusetts.' She took another bite of the sandwich. It was good, really good. 'I never think of putting tuna salad on rye.' She kept reading the computer screen but out of the corner of her eye she could see Ganza smile.

'What was he *almost* charged with?'

'Something to do with his father's boat. Not much here. All

they have is a name – Albert Stucky – and his address at that time. Maybe I can find a driver's license.'

She downloaded the scant information available at IAFSI then started doing another search.

'State of Massachusetts hasn't issued him a new license in ten years. He was twenty-one, six foot and weighed one hundred seventy pounds. The licenses weren't digitized back then, so no photo.'

She continued searching other records. There was no marriage license, no property or home ownership. She was going to need to dig deeper.

'He probably doesn't go by his real name,' Ganza said. 'Hell, he may have not been Albert Stucky for the last ten years. Guy like this, he likes controlling the risks. I bet he's been off the radar for a while. You know he didn't just start killing. As bloody as that mess looked in the last container, that kidney was extracted with some precision. Same with Barnett's toe and Deputy Steele's finger. This guy has been perfecting his handiwork for a while now.'

Maggie stepped back from the computer and rubbed at her eyes. She was functioning on too little sleep. Whatever hope and excitement that came with those two fingerprints quickly evaporated. Even knowing the Collector's real name brought her no closer to knowing who the hell he was. Or what he looked like.

Susan Fuller's description of the man she saw in the forest taking the woman out of the trunk was probably the truest description they had. Tall, lean, young. But Susan wasn't even sure what color his hair was because of the shadows, and because she was hiding.

Maggie looked over at Ganza. Now finished with lunch, he was back to work.

'I've got nothing,' she said, trying not to sound as exasperated as she felt.

'Right now he's been calling the shots,' Ganza said. 'He's been leaving for us what he wants us to find. Sooner or later we'll have something he didn't mean to let us see. Like Susan Fuller.'

'That's true. Maybe you'll find something inside her car.'

'And maybe you'll get lucky tomorrow,' Ganza told her.

She raised her eyebrow at him not following what he meant.

'At the funeral. So far, he's had control over the playing field – the Gateway Mall, the parking lots, the victims' cars. Even luring Deputy Steele to his own police cruiser. Not to mention full run of Devil's Backbone State Forest. If he shows up tomorrow, he might be out of his element. He may trip himself up.'

'Or he might not even show up.'

'There is always that,' Ganza shrugged.

62

The sky was indigo blue with only wisps for clouds. Maggie couldn't help thinking it a cruel irony. After a week filled with dark and stormy skies, the sun had arrived just in time for them to bury Katie Tanner's family.

Maggie had volunteered – perhaps a bit too anxiously – to skip the church service so she could be one of the surveillance details at the cemetery. Funerals reminded her too much of her father's.

All she had to do was walk inside a Catholic church, get a sniff of the incense, and without effort or will, revert back to her twelve-year-old self. All those emotions that she worked so hard to bury came bubbling to the surface. There wasn't a day that she didn't think about her father, that she didn't miss him, even though he'd been gone now for over fifteen years.

Maggie believed being out at the cemetery wouldn't trigger those memories as easily. She was outside, able to breathe in fresh air. She could pace, let the sunshine stave off the dark thoughts. She was wrong. The waiting was too long and she couldn't stop the memories.

Maggie could see him lying in the huge mahogany casket, wearing that brown suit she had never seen him in before. She always remembered the crinkle of plastic under his clothes, his mummy-wrapped hands tucked down at his sides. His hair was all wrong, combed in a way he would never have worn it.

Maggie had reached her small hand up over the edge of the smooth, shiny wood and the satin bedding. She needed to brush his hair off to the side, off his forehead. Only her fingertips jerked back after revealing the blistered skin, patched up. The mortician had attempted to paint over the burned flesh and salvage what pieces of skin that were still there. But despite her fear, she had to rearrange his hair. She had to put it back to the way he always liked to wear it, the way she remembered it. She needed her last image of him to be one she recognized. It was a small, silly thing, but it had made her feel better.

The sight of her father haunted her childhood dreams and they still came to her when she least expected. Even the smells came back to her, that nauseating scent mixed with the perfume the mortician had used in the hopes of masking the burned flesh.

That smell. There was nothing close to or worse than the smell of burned flesh.

Maggie could smell it now as if it were sifting through the fresh countryside air.

The cemetery was almost three miles outside of the small town of Jasper. She could tell that at one time there had been a country church here, too. Only the foundation was left. That was on the other side of the road. Up here on the hill she could see how the tombstones lined up in even rows. All around her were rolling meadows dotted by stands of trees. On the horizon, vibrant green met blue. It was breathtakingly beautiful and she couldn't help think the view was wasted on the dead.

From where Maggie stood she could finally see the mile-long procession of vehicles snaking their way along the only road to the cemetery. The two-lane blacktop came to a dead end at the entrance providing a dirt path for the line of vehicles to loop around and head back out. For now they were slowly and patiently lining up, pulling bumper to bumper to park on the side of the road that went nowhere else.

Inside her earbud she heard Delaney checking in. She tried not to look for him. He wore jeans, a flannel shirt and hiking boots. He wandered back and forth from the pickup truck parked on the cemetery grounds. The stenciled logo on the vehicle's door made him look like the guy responsible for the grave. The guy no one really wanted to notice, let alone acknowledge.

The parade of mourners got out of their vehicles and two-by-two walked along the narrow path from the road to the gravesite. Cunningham and Gwen blended in with their black attire and their heads bent. The path was challenging enough that Cunningham offered his arm to Gwen, and Maggie couldn't help noticing that they looked good together. Like they belonged together. For the first time she could understand why Gwen might be confused.

Back on the road, she saw Turner standing solemnly as he held open the limousine door and helped family members out. Making him and Maggie funeral home employees had been a smart move especially since Turner was the only black person here. He'd have to be part of the employed entourage.

Lucille Tanner had insisted on two things: firstly, that Katie not be here. She wanted her to rest and heal. Maggie had been impressed that her grandmother recognized that there were other ways of grieving than to put the young girl through this traditional mourning.

Mrs Tanner's second insistence was that the sheriff and his deputies stay away. Cunningham willingly relented, in part because he wanted to keep a low profile. He didn't want to spook the funeral attendees any more than he wanted to spook the Collector. He was able to make his agents – and even Gwen – fit in.

Of course, Maggie knew they might not fool the Collector. But even if he suspected that the FBI was here, he wouldn't necessarily know which friends or family or funeral home workers were actually agents who were there watching him.

It wasn't unusual for killers to show up at the scene of the crime or at one of their victims' funeral. Berkowitz – better known as Son of Sam – spent his early life of crime as an arsonist. He'd start fires in New York City then wedge himself amongst the spectators watching the first responders. He even admitted to masturbating while he watched.

The Collector was interested in watching, but only to see the responses to his handiwork. Maggie wasn't sure if there was anything here at the funeral that would intrigue him. Yet just last week he had been interested enough to park on a muddy pasture road, hide in the trees and possibly watch Daniel Tanner gunned down by Deputy Steele.

Yesterday Ganza had told her that the ballistic report did confirm that the gun Steele had strapped to his ankle was most likely the one used to shoot Daniel Tanner in the back. Not only that, but the gun's serial number had been filed off.

Maggie had to admit, she still didn't understand if there was a connection between Steele and the Collector. Were they old friends? Acquaintances? There was no way the Collector had randomly stumbled upon that scene at the double-wide trailer. Steele or the Tanners had caught his attention. But would it be enough for him to show up here, today? If he did, Maggie was convinced it would be out at the cemetery, where he couldn't easily be fingered or, more importantly, where he was less likely to be trapped.

But now as she studied the last trail of mourners gathering under the tent and those staying at the fringes, she became frustrated and anxious. Knowing his real name – Albert Stucky – had produced nothing more. And unless he panicked and made some mistake, there was no way for them to identify who he was.

Unless they could see past his disguise.

As Maggie stood back in position, she saw no one observing her, glancing her way. If the Collector had come today just to watch 'Agent Maggie,' it would hopefully take him some time to find her. She had taken a page out of his playbook. Today she was dressed in the royal blue boxy blazers like the other funeral home employees. She wore black-framed glasses, a short blond wig and a body suit that added almost twenty pounds to her torso giving her a stocky build that even changed the way she walked.

She scanned faces and gestures and postures. As she looked for him, in her mind she taunted him. *Two can play at this game.*

63

Stucky decided the only piece of clothing he'd be able to wear from the delivery driver was the bright orange ballcap. The guy was too small and unfortunately he had bled out on the bright orange company T-shirt.

Not a big deal.

The logo on the ballcap matched the one on the T-shirt. How many people even noticed what the delivery guy was wearing when he was handing them a beautiful bouquet of flowers? In fact, how many people paid attention to the driver, period?

He had stuffed the man's body into a trash bag and shoved it to the back of the white sprinter van. The vehicle was refrigerated and loaded with flowers ready for delivery. *Good timing.* They wouldn't expect the driver to get back to the store for hours. Perhaps even the whole afternoon. He'd have plenty of time. When he was finished he'd leave and wipe everything down – hell, why even bother. He'd just leave the van parked along a street in the residential area where he'd hijacked the guy. Then he'd walk away. His own car was parked in an apartment complex lot where no one would notice its presence.

Stucky shook his head at how easy it had been. He'd actually gotten the idea two days ago when he was driving and doing one of his look-n-sees, searching for potential prey. This same florist, same van – different driver – had been making a delivery in the middle of the day. That driver had been taller. Stucky could have worn his T-shirt.

What he noticed was how the guy had left the engine running and the vehicle unlocked. Of course, he left it running – refrigerated cargo. In a quiet residential area where most of the occupants were at work, why not leave it unlocked? Not like anyone would come along and steal flowers. Or at least the company didn't believe that was a risk.

So imagine the surprise on the driver's face this morning when he slid back into the driver's seat and glanced up into the rearview mirror. The first thing the guy noticed was that the door to the back had been left open. Before he could unbuckle his seatbelt to get up and close it, a cool sharp blade slid across his throat.

But that was Stucky's one mistake. Despite his expertise with a scalpel, the blood had messed up the front of the man's T-shirt, making the logo look like an abstract splash of wildflowers.

He smiled to himself. Maybe no one would have noticed. There was so much color inside and outside. The van was wrapped in giant yellow sunflowers and orange roses with the logo smack-dab in the middle. It was probably the most garish disguise Stucky had ever used. But he was pleased with himself. This would work just fine.

64

Delaney had donned a blue blazer and joined Turner and Maggie. Although at the moment, Maggie had lost site of Turner.

The cemetery had been a bust. If the Collector had attended, he was probably long gone now, laughing about how he fooled them all. But that didn't seem right to Maggie. Why bother to come and just watch? He would have wanted them to know he had been there. He would have left something. That was part of the game, after all, wasn't it?

Now as she scanned the church's reception hall, checking and rechecking the one entrance and two exits, she wondered if there was any way he could come in and leave without them noticing. The large banquet-sized room was filled with rows of long tables and folding chairs. It was a tight squeeze to weave between the crowd made up of Tanner family and friends either getting seated or still waiting in line to load their plates with thick slices of ham, scallop potatoes and home-made biscuits.

Small children raced back and forth. Maggie saw two little boys hiding underneath one of the tables while another peeked out from dozens of bouquets lined up close to the wall.

At one end of the room was a long counter that separated

the kitchen. Maggie remembered this from her own experience growing up in Green Bay. Her father made sure they went to church every Sunday and were a part of the church community. If a parishioner her father knew passed away, they attended the funeral. Maggie didn't think he was a deeply religious man, but he respected and honored tradition and ritual. Like with the medallion he'd given her. Certainly he didn't believe it would protect her from evil.

Did he? She needed to stop. She didn't want to think about him again for fear her memories would loop back to his funeral.

She did remember how the women from the church prepared the funeral meal for the family's guests. And though the family bought the meat, potatoes and bread, there was always a smorgasbord of food that the church community contributed. One glance and Maggie could see the line of covered dishes of various salads, cake plates, pans of brownies and cookies as well as several different kinds of pies. Lids, plastic and foil wrap were pulled off and the dishes placed on the counter for the long line of funeral attendees to add to their already overflowing plates.

'Take a look,' Delaney said as he pointed with his chin.

That's when she realized they had failed. None of them believed the Collector, Albert Stucky, would dare to venture into this crowd and risk being trapped. It was the last proof she needed when she saw Turner smiling and chatting over the open counter that separated the women in the kitchen. His plate was filled with meat, potatoes, salads and two biscuits topping the pile.

She saw Cunningham and Gwen now. They were seated at a table with Lucille Tanner and her husband. Children of various ages surrounded the grandparents. A teenaged boy who looked enamored with Gwen had monopolized her attention, but she was listening and smiling.

'I was so sure he'd show up,' Maggie said. She wanted to scratch up under the wig. It was more uncomfortable than the body suit.

'Not your fault.' Delaney told her.

'Is it possible he was at the church?'

Delaney shook his head. 'Cunningham doesn't think so. And he and Dr Patterson got there early. Although—' He stopped and his eyes surveyed the tables surrounding Lucille Tanner's. 'He pointed out that there's a visiting priest no one seems to know. And now I don't see him.'

Maggie's pulse ticked up a beat. Why hadn't she thought of that? A priest would be the perfect disguise. How could anyone do a quick check? If he showed up, said he knew one of the deceased and found it in his heart to be here, who would question him?

'What did he look like?' she asked Delaney.

'Tall, fit, dark hair, dark eyes. He was dressed in black – trousers, blazer, shirt and the white collar. He actually looked like a priest.'

They stayed where they were, both of them studying the banquet hall with easy, smooth pivots. That's when Maggie saw it on the end of the long counter where all the potluck dishes were lined up. She knew it hadn't been there ten minutes ago.

'He's here.'

65

Maggie tucked her hand inside her jacket and snapped loose her revolver.

'You see him?' Delaney kept his voice low, but she saw him reaching for his weapon, too.

'The takeout container at the far end of the counter,' she told him without looking at it. Her eyes were scanning over anyone and everyone who was standing or walking the room. 'I'm positive it wasn't there ten minutes ago.'

'Damn,' Delaney whispered. He toggled the microphone that was tucked inside the cuff of his shirt and rubbed his jaw as he spoke into his sleeve. 'He left a package. Far east side of food counter.'

Maggie saw Cunningham's chin move up just slightly, and his eyes started searching the tables around him. He excused himself and stood up. Then he headed toward the lobby where the restrooms were. Across the room at the far exit – one of only two – Maggie noticed Turner push the door open, and he slipped outside.

'We need to get that container before someone accidentally picks it up,' Delaney said.

'I'll get it.'

'You sure?'

'It's my reaction he wants to see. Just watch for him,' Maggie said. 'I don't think he'll leave until I open it.'

She was surprised to find her knees a bit unsteady. Moments

ago the scent of salty ham and cheesy potatoes made her mouth water. Now that same smell started to nauseate her. As she got to the counter she could see that something was written on the top of the foam container. A ballpoint pen had indented the foam's surface. Was he carving his notes to her on the outside this time? But as she got closer she saw it was LUCILLE TANNER written in block letters not unlike the printing he used for his notes.

And Maggie's stomach did start to churn.

What gruesome body part had the Collector left for this poor woman? Hadn't she been through enough? For God's sake, she just buried her two sons and daughter-in-law.

'That's for Lucille,' a woman on the other side of the counter told Maggie when she noticed her. She was small woman, slumped shoulders and the kitchen apron she wore came all the way down to her knees. 'We saved her a piece a pie.'

'Pie?' Maggie hoped her face didn't show the panic that was galloping in her chest.

'Someone brought a sour cream and raisin one. That's Lucille's all-time favorite. Poor thing's not much hungry right now. The girls and I sliced her a piece to make sure she had some to take home with her.'

'Do you mind if I take it for her?' Maggie said, trying to sound like a courteous funeral home employee instead of a frantic FBI agent. 'I'm packing up some other things for her.'

'Oh, sure,' the woman said, without a hint of suspicious. 'Let me grab a small box for you in case it melts or leaks a bit.'

If only she knew the irony of her words. Maggie picked up the container using the palms of her hands, one on each side. The woman looked at her like she was being a bit overly cautious but she set the box down on the counter. Maggie put the container inside and thanked her. Then she headed out the other exit.

Turner saw her come out, and when he noticed the container his head swiveled in every direction.

'Lets use the back of the SUV,' he told her, and he led the way.

There was no one in this parking lot back behind the church. The main lot was on the opposite side and faced the entrance.

Turner had the tailgate down and a plastic evidence bag laid out in place. He handed her a pair of latex gloves as his eyes continued to search all around them.

'You want me to open it right here?' she asked.

He raised his cuff to his mouth and said, 'Back parking lot. We've got it in the SUV. Okay to open?'

Through her own earbud she heard Cunningham's firm, one-word reply, 'Yes.'

She knew he and Delaney were still watching for the Collector. Was he moving into position where he could see them, but not be seen? Was it possible he was already out here inside one of the vehicles?

She couldn't think about that right now. Her fingers were actually shaking as she eased the tab out of its slot. She let the top of the container spring back.

'What is that?' Turner asked.

'Sour cream and raisin pie.'

And that was all that was in the container. Just a piece of pie.

66

Stucky waited in line at the security gate. He'd watched how this worked. The guard would ask to see the driver's license and want the name of the person he or she was there to see. Then he'd check the name against an approved list. If things matched up, he raised the gate. But service vehicles were usually waved through.

Seemed like a system just asking to be busted.

Stucky pulled the ballcap down low over his brow like he was serious about making the delivery and getting back on the road. Two more cars.

He thought about Agent Maggie. He had managed to bring her to his stalking grounds. Just the idea excited him. But he also knew the risk was tilting out of his favor. It was best to tie up loose ends. Maybe move things a bit south. He'd used the Richmond area when he first moved down to Virginia. It was an hour away in the wrong direction. That would make it over two hours to get to Devil's Backbone. He didn't like spending that much time on the road. But it might be necessary if he wanted to remain unpredictable enough to lure the pretty agent into a trap.

Stucky imagined what it would be like to drop her in the middle of the forest. He was certain she'd provide him with a challenge like no other. But at the same time, it reminded him that he hadn't been able to find Susan Fuller his last trip out. He'd dumped the college girl and had an extra hour to go hunting, but he couldn't find her. He could tell she had been staying close to the shed. Most of them did. It was like a security blanket.

Provisions were eaten. Bottled water was almost gone. She'd even rigged the bucket he'd left under the roofline to gather rainwater. But he couldn't find her anywhere. She'd probably fallen into one of the ravines and broken her neck.

That's what happened to that ridiculous spandex girl he had taken from the fitness center parking lot. She looked fit and trim, long-legged with a nice shape that she obviously had worked many hours to acquire. But put her in an isolated forest and she went apeshit on him. He'd barely gotten one arrow off when she panicked and ran while looking for him over her shoulder. Her head was pivoting in every direction except down at her feet.

Stupid bitch. And what a waste of his time and effort.

Now he was up. It was his turn. He pulled up to the guard, but before he came to a full stop the guy gestured for him to go on through the gate.

So easy. And he had to keep from smiling.

Next was the locked front door, but he'd seen how this worked, too.

He parked and filled his arms, one large vase and two smaller ones. He had to use his elbow to push the intercom button, and as he did, he looked up into the security camera. Without a word the lock clicked open and a young woman pulled the door open.

'Oh wow! Those are so pretty.' She stood out of his way as she shoved the door until it hit the wall. 'Have you been here before?'

'Nope. I sure have not.'

'I can take the smaller ones.'

He let her the bouquets while he shifted the large vase, pretending it was incredibly heavy.

'Do you remember the name?' she asked, trying to look for a card inside the ones she carried, but not surprised to find none.

'All of them are for Tanner.'

'Oh sure,' and she started leading him down the hallway. 'Poor thing. Her father's funeral is today. That's probably what all these are for.'

'Probably,' he said politely, without asserting any interest.

'Here we are,' and she knocked on the door before she eased it open. 'Hi Katie, we have some beautiful flowers for you.'

And just like that she held the door open for Stucky. She found a spot for him to set the large vase down while she positioned the smaller ones on tabletops. The space surprised him. Other than the bed there was a sitting area and two other doors. One was open to another bedroom. The other was probably a bathroom.

The little girl smiled at him and clapped her hands together, pleased with the gifts as if they had come directly from him.

'Thank you so much!' she told him.

He just nodded.

As the woman led him out of the Katie's room he asked if there was a bathroom he could use before he hit the road. And she pointed to a door at the end of Katie's hallway. He kept from shaking his head as he fingered the syringe in his jacket pocket. She was so tiny, smaller than he expected. The double dose he'd prepared was almost overkill.

Too easy.

And to make matters more ridiculous, he noticed that after using the bathroom no one would even see him duck back into Katie Tanner's room.

67

Maggie had never seen Cunningham so angry. And frustrated. She was more determined that ever to find out everything she could about Albert Stucky.

She had holed up in her office since she returned from the funeral. In just a few hours she'd managed to turn the small area into a mess. Stacks of files littered the surface of her desk. Her disguise from the day sat in a heap on her only chair. With the wig and glasses on top, it looked like a melted version of her earlier self. She had changed into blue jeans and a University of Virginia T-shirt. And now she was printing and sorting every scrap of information she could find. She was even jotting down notes on her own whiteboard.

When her phone rang she grabbed it before the second ring. 'This is Maggie O'Dell.'

'Agent O'Dell, hello. This is Michael Hogan.'

The name didn't register. And then it did, and a wave of guilt washed over her.

'Detective Hogan, I'm so sorry I haven't gotten back to you.'

'I'm glad to catch you. I know it's after five there, but I just wanted to make sure you received the package I sent.'

'Yes, I did.' And she tried to calculate how long ago that was. It seemed like months, but she knew, in fact, it was just last week. Still, a week with a killer on the loose could mean a lifetime for the officers working the case. She knew that all too well right now.

'I'm so sorry, Detective Hogan,' she apologized again. 'We have an active killer here as well that's been tying up too much time.'

'Understand completely. I was just hoping that your fresh eyes might see something we're missing.'

'Of course,' she said. 'I did look at the photos and the medical examiner's report. Has there been anything new since you sent the package?'

'No, and that's the frustrating thing. It's like he packed up and moved across the country. But I know that serial killers stay close to familiar territories, so is he just laying low?'

'Actually they don't all stay put,' Maggie told him, and in her mind she was already accessing a list. 'Richard Ramirez, the Night Stalker, moved from LA to San Francisco when he realized the media and police in LA had a solid description of him from a couple of survivors. Ted Bundy murdered in several states. Six, I believe. Then you have someone like Donald Henry Gaskins. He drove along the coastal areas in the south. Gaskins stopped killing for a short period, but only because he was in prison.'

Hogan was quiet and Maggie realized that sometimes she went overboard on what others considered trivial.

'I think the point is,' she filled in his silence, 'what we've found is that killers with a high psychopathy and high IQs tend to be more mobile. They're more organized. The planning and anticipation provide a level of satisfaction and gratification. They also tend to be the ones who want desperately to share just how smart and organized they are.'

'So what do I do?'

'I'm going to email information on how you can access ViCAP directly. I know it's frustrating but the FBI is working on it so that agencies like yours will have access via the internet. I'll do a search, too, but there may be things you recognize that might not mean anything to me.'

'What kinds of things?'

'Type of victim. MO.'

'You think he's done this before?'

'Just a hunch, but yes. Unfortunately, ViCAP probably won't list any deaths that were listed as accidental drownings, unless they were suspicious enough to be entered into the system.'

'This is a good start. Thank you.'

It was a slap-together, by-the-seat-of-her-pants effort, and Maggie wasn't proud of it. As soon as she ended the call she started hunting for the package he had sent her. She'd put it on top of the mess she had created, and she vowed to slide it in her portfolio before she went home for the day.

But Hogan's case had her thinking of the Collector again. Why hadn't she realized this before? She and Ganza had already determined that he had killed before. The councilwoman whose body was found outside of Richmond was abducted from Boston. His fingerprints were taken in a county in Massachusetts. And the brown paper bag left at a rest area off of I-95 was somewhere close to Boston. Maybe the answers to who Albert Stucky was lay not in what he was doing now but where he had been.

Maggie sat down at her computer and started again. This time she'd do it from scratch. But she'd barely keyed in her searches when a knock at the door interrupted her.

'Come in.'

She glanced up then did a double take when she saw Cunningham. This late in the day and his shirtsleeves were still rolled up in neat and careful folds, his collar buttoned tight and his tie straight.

'I was hoping you might still be here.'

His eyes took in her mess. She realized she was too exhausted to be embarrassed. She saw him glance at her whiteboard – a much smaller version of his whiteboard – and she thought she saw the corner of his lip hitch up just slightly.

'Sheriff Olson's K9 team found something.'

Devil's Backbone. She'd forgotten that the Shenandoah sheriff's department was still looking for the woman that Susan Fuller had seen. The limp body that the Collector had taken out of the trunk. From the look on Cunningham's face, this woman wasn't as lucky as Susan.

'They found the woman's body?'

'Yes. But it's worse than we thought.' He scraped his hand over his jaw. 'They think they found a mass grave.'

68

His father would have called him soft. But what challenge was there in doing a kid?

Stucky parked the florist van in the residential neighbor two blocks from where he'd left his car. Out of habit, he wiped down every surface inside the vehicle that he had touched. He had known for years that tracking his fingerprints to his real identity led only to an old life, a past existence that had no connection to any of his aliases. There were no bank accounts, no properties, no credit cards – nothing. Still, today's failure was one he certainly didn't want attached to Albert Stucky. And that's exactly how he viewed it – a failure.

He had knocked on Katie Tanner's door and walked back into the room.

He asked her if she recognized him.

'You're the man who brought me all the beautiful flowers.'

'Yes, that's right. But do you remember me from anywhere else?'

He watched her eyes while his fingers gripped the syringe inside his pocket. The damned thing was throbbing against his thumb as if it had a heartbeat of its own. The girl stared at him hard. There wasn't a hint of recognition.

Then she asked him, 'Are you a friend of my daddy's?'

That's when it hit Stucky. He realized what must have happened on the Tanner property that day. Katie's father didn't *run away* because he believed he could *get away*. He did it to protect this little girl. A father's unconditional love. Something Stucky had never experienced with his own father.

He told her that he didn't know her father very well, but that he was a brave man.

Then Albert Stucky left.

He walked through the locked security door. Waited for the guard to raise the gate, and he drove away.

He told himself that it was because she didn't recognize him. She posed no threat. But it bothered him that it wasn't the real reason.

By the time he made it back to his small apartment, he barely had enough time to shower and get ready for his shift. There was something brewing deep inside him. The anger that he continually tamped down was smoldering again, pushing its way to the top. Usually a good hunt – a challenging one – kept it at bay.

That's what he needed.

Enough with the watch and see.

The shock value of others discovering his handiwork had become quite boring. It was time to ratchet things up. Move on. He needed to plan and prepare for his next big hunt. Already he felt the claws inside his chest ease off.

Yes, he needed to start laying the groundwork. Then he'd figure out how lure Agent Maggie into his snare.

69

DEVIL'S BACKBONE STATE FOREST

Maggie figured they had two hours before the sun set. Maybe only half of that before the forest started to get dark. But Keith Ganza wanted to get the 'lay of the land,' so he could prepare his team for the next day. A day that promised to be as physically brutal as it would be mentally.

Already Maggie was out of breath, and they had just left the service road – supposedly, the only road into the forest. The rest of the way would be on foot. As they trudged over the rocks, through the mud and between the trees – some places so tight they had to sidestep – Maggie realized how limited they would be as to what gear and equipment they'd be able to carry to the site. At the same time she couldn't imagine how difficult it would be to haul out the bodies.

Sheriff Olson had sent one of his young deputies to guide them, a tall lanky man whose long legs hiked effortlessly so far ahead of Maggie and Ganza that he had to stop every once in a while for them to catch up. Deputy Ryan didn't seem to mind. Instead, he looked excited to be chosen. He took the responsibility seriously and consulted the handheld GPS device, making sure they hadn't strayed off course.

Maggie couldn't believe the Collector had used this path to dispose of his victims. There had to be another.

'Not much farther,' Deputy Ryan called to them as he waited up ahead.

Maggie was surprised that Ganza was right behind her. He was in much better shape than she guessed. Tomorrow might be different with heavy backpacks.

'We need to be careful from this point on,' Deputy Ryan told them. 'They're some drop-off ledges and steep ravines. And we're getting into that shadow time when it's tough to see them until you're right on top of them.'

'Is this the only way in?' Ganza asked as they caught up with the deputy and took a break. 'I can't imagine him hauling a body.'

'This is the path the dog followed.'

Deputy Ryan pointed to another fluorescent orange ribbon tied to a branch at eye level. He'd mentioned the ribbons when they started, and Maggie noticed them along the way, but only because she was looking for them. Otherwise she wasn't sure she'd be able to find them.

'The dog handler said this might have been the guy's shortcut. It was probably the most recent path he used.'

'So there might be another?'

'Sure. We just didn't want to get lost.' He gestured as if to say, take a look around.

'Did you find a shed?' Maggie asked.

'Remember where we parked? It's just down the road and up over that rock wall. Dog found it, too.' He stopped and grinned. 'Of course, the dog didn't climb the wall. But she sure did some scratching at it like maybe the guy had climbed it.'

Maggie thought it felt as though they had been climbing the whole way, a constant incline, steep enough in places that she needed to grab onto tree roots and anything else jutting out of the rock and the dirt. But now they were going down and she saw what Deputy Ryan meant. The shadows were swallowing up any last rays of sunshine that had been filtering in through the trees.

The ground finally leveled a bit and at a patch of scraggly shrubs the young deputy stopped and put his arm out for them to stop, too. On the other side of the shrubs it looked like the ground had cracked open. The ravine was about ten feet across and thirty feet wide, tapering at both edges so that it looked like a gaping mouth. But even looking over the edge, Maggie couldn't see the bottom.

Deputy Ryan grabbed a flashlight from his utility belt as he said, 'Sheriff Olson is working on getting a generator set up. It's tough to see down there. Lots of shadows in the middle of the day, too.'

He flicked on the light and began to sweep down against the dirt and rock wall. He stopped when the stream of light found a white bloated face with a tangle of hair and eyes wide open, staring up at them.

70

STRASBURG, VIRGINIA

Maggie was trying to explain to Greg why she wouldn't be home that night. She had expected to leave a message and was disappointed when he actually answered the phone.

'Sounds like a party,' he said.

The restaurant next to the Fairfield Inn seemed to be a favorite even at ten o'clock on a weeknight. Both were near the junction where Interstate 81 met Interstate 66. It looked like truckers and tourists mixed with locals. Had she known Greg would answer the phone she would have made more of an effort to find a quieter spot.

'It's off the interstate,' she told him. 'Not like we have a lot to choose from.'

She didn't want to tell him about the Collector or anything to do with the case. She knew she'd get a lecture. But he didn't seem to care about any of that. In fact, he didn't ask any questions about the case, or why she would be staying overnight. Instead he launched into a whole other reprimand.

'Your mother called.'

And Maggie's stomach did a flip. 'Is she okay?'

'You'd know if you'd just check in with her.' There was no sympathy in his voice, nothing in his tone that would remind her of the other night when he had told her it wasn't her fault.

She didn't argue. Instead she said, 'You're right. I'll call her in the morning.'

That silenced him. She thought she'd lost the connection. But then, almost as if he had to get the last word in, he said, 'Well, okay then.'

When she put the phone down she noticed Turner watching her from across the table. And she saw genuine sympathy in those warm brown eyes, so much so, that she had to look away.

Turner and Cunningham had arrived before nightfall. They had met Ganza and Maggie at the restaurant just steps away from the hotel. Cunningham had already taken care of getting them rooms. Ganza had called his team and given them a long list of what he wanted them to bring in the morning.

They'd just settled in and both men were anxious to hear what she and Ganza had seen. But Maggie wished she could check into her room, take a hot shower, curl up under the covers. She wanted to block out the memory of that woman's eyes staring up at her. This was nothing like examining crime scene photos. And it was nothing like finding body parts. This woman had been alive, perhaps only days ago. Now her body was broken, probably cut up and thrown into a ravine as if it were garbage.

Was she sacrificed just so the Collector could offer Maggie a fresh kill?

That hadn't occurred to Maggie until this moment, and suddenly the restaurant was much too hot. It felt like the floor was tilting, and she caught herself grabbing onto the table edge. Then she looked to see if anyone had seen her.

No, thank goodness.

Both Cunningham and Turner were listening to Ganza. She

knew Ganza was speaking only because she saw his mouth moving. She couldn't hear him over the wind tunnel in her ears. She reached for her water, half expecting the glass to slide off the table before she could grab it. She took a gulp then slowed down to sips.

Breathe. In and out. Just breathe.

Finally she heard their voices. She scooted her chair in to anchor herself against the table. The room had barely straightened itself when the men were looking at her.

Had they noticed her strange behavior?

No, they didn't look concerned. They were waiting for her answer to a question. Only Maggie never heard the question.

That's when the waitress appeared, drawing their attention. Taking their orders. Letting Turner be charming. Telling them what was good. Reminding them of food and drink. And saving Maggie from admitting that maybe she wasn't okay.

71

GAINSVILLE, VIRGINIA

There was another woman missing. Rita slid the tray with empty glasses onto the counter without taking her eyes off the television in the corner. This one was a college student: Jessica Todd, twenty-one years old from Manassas. She was last seen Friday night having dinner and drinks with her friends at Ollie's Bar and Grill. Her car was found in the parking lot.

Ollie's was literally just up the road. Way too close for comfort.

In the photo they were showing, Jessica looked younger than twenty-one and Rita couldn't help thinking she wasn't that much older than her daughter, Carly.

'You okay?'

Rita jumped, startled because she hadn't heard Drew.

'That poor girl,' she said, pointing at the screen. 'What do you suppose happened to her?'

He glanced up and shrugged like he had no idea who she was talking about even though the girl's photo had been on every news channel. He took the order sheet from her tray of empties and started grabbing bottles and glasses to fill the order.

'You think it's the same guy who took that councilwoman?'

'I thought she was in Boston?' He didn't look up as he added ice to the glasses.

'Remember, she was taken from Boston. You said it was a restaurant parking lot. One of Mr Gibson's.'

'Oh yeah.' But he didn't look interested.

'They found her body someplace down by Richmond.'

Was she the only one who had committed all these details to memory?

Drew had already moved on to pouring the liquor. She liked watching him. His hands moved with such purpose. There was discipline and organization to the way he made the drinks, not just remembering how to layer the liquors like in a Tequila Sunrise. She could see why he wanted to be a chef. He used his fingers the same way as Carly did, both of them committed to creating a masterpiece with each work.

He caught her watching and lifted his hands in mock surrender as he said, 'What? Am I not fast enough?'

But then he smiled. At her. Only her.

The smile was such a rarity that she couldn't stop the blush. Thankfully, he went back to finishing the drinks, and Rita tried to concentrate on something, anything other than that annoying pleasant heat crawling through her body. That's when she saw the small, bald-headed man with a mop and bucket going down the hallway to clean the restrooms.

She turned back to Drew and asked, 'What happened to Morgan?'

Drew shrugged like he didn't know and didn't really care.

Truth was she didn't know what Morgan's schedule was. She was feeling a bit on edge ever since she'd mentioned him to that FBI agent.

Finished with the drinks, Drew set them on her tray, two at a time. He slid it all the way to overlap onto her side, making it easier for her to grab. He was so thoughtful.

But now Rita's mind tried to retrieve what she had told the agent – Maggie O'Dell. She still had her card. Rita had slipped it into her wallet. Was it possible the FBI questioned him, suspected him, just because of what Rita had said? She thought that she'd told Agent O'Dell that it was only her impression. Though she couldn't remember the exact words she'd used.

Rita took the tray. She hoped she hadn't spooked the man. And even more so, she hoped Morgan didn't know she had told the FBI. Who knew what that creepy guy was capable of doing.

She thought about Jessica Todd again, and how close Ollie's was. It would be easy enough to get off the last shift here and be waiting in Ollie's parking lot for an unsuspecting, slightly tipsy college girl.

Rita felt a shiver and shook her head. She needed to stop watching the news.

72

DEVIL'S BACKBONE STATE FOREST
Wednesday

This was the first time Maggie had ever used her go-bag. Usually it sat in the corner of her office back behind the door. Every two or three months she updated or refreshed it. Now she was grateful she had stocked it so thoughtfully despite never using it. She had transferred some of the basics to a day-pack – protein bars, ChapStick, Vicks VapoRub (which she had added since the Tanners' double-wide), bottles of water, latex gloves, maglite and a lightweight rain jacket that rolled into a neat small tube.

She wore a T-shirt, hiking boots, jeans and a long-sleeve button-down shirt that she left unbuttoned with the sleeves rolled up. It had been a rainy summer, unseasonably cool, and though the sun was out, she wouldn't be surprised to have a thunderstorm come rolling over the mountains.

Deputy Ryan, who turned out to be quite the outdoorsman, offered them kerchiefs. He said they were soaked in natural oils and he promised they would ward off mosquitoes and other insects if they tied them around their upper arm or neck.

Maggie had prepared herself for rain, humidity, temperature changes, insects, and the foul smells of decomposition. What she had no way of preparing herself for was how she would respond to what they found down in that ravine. The hellhole that the Collector had chosen as a gravesite for his victims.

Despite her pre-med expertise and her ability to detach emotionally at an autopsy, she already knew from the double-wide trailer experience that there was a massive difference in viewing an autopsy and in recovering a decomposing corpse.

Sheriff Olson had already found a way to have his men haul into the forest a portable generator, fuel to run it and floodlights along with the necessary equipment to set up a pulley system. As Ganza had suggested the night before there was an easier, more beaten-down trail that led to the ravine. However, it was also much longer and circled all the way around, bringing them to the site from the opposite direction.

All of them – Ganza, his two CSU techs, Turner, Cunningham and Maggie – carried an extra pack on their backs with gear. Maggie was surprised that Assistant Director Cunningham had joined them. She suspected this was his way of dealing with the frustration. The Collector had bested them all. But he hadn't counted on them finding this treasure trove of information.

They got to work immediately, setting up a staging area with tarps and constructing a makeshift tent. On this side of the ravine the ground was more level and covered with grass and soft clover instead of all rock. There was an open space with a break in the canopy of trees overhead so that sunlight streamed down in patches instead of slivers of light.

Sheriff Olson's men had also decided it was too steep of a climb to get to the bottom. Standing on the edge and looking down Maggie realized it wasn't that deep. Maybe ten feet. And only one side was rock. The others were dirt. The deputies had lowered a telescoping ladder, securing it at the bottom and the top and giving it enough of an angle for it to function as a ramp, so Ganza and his team could walk up and down carrying their gear without holding onto the rungs of the ladder.

Sunlight filtered in, but Maggie knew it wouldn't stream down to the bottom of the pit. She saw that Ganza and his techs had strapped on headlamps even as the sheriff's men strung the floodlights. They had also slipped on facemasks that they let hang by the elastic around their necks. Now as Ganza looked ready to descend the ladder he handed her a facemask and headlamp. She caught herself swallowing hard. Her mouth and throat were suddenly cotton dry.

This was it.

How best to understand a madman than to view his handiwork. It was what profilers did. Only she had been doing it from the comfort and safety of her cramped office for too many years. It was a lot different than examining the contents of Stucky's takeout containers. Without a body, without eyes staring wide open – like the woman down below – it was much easier to detach from a toe, a kidney or a spleen.

'You ready?' Ganza asked.

Her fingers fumbled in her daypack for the Vicks VapoRub. Maggie hoped her fingers weren't shaking but she couldn't be certain. When she noticed Ganza watching, she offered the small container to him first.

Ganza stroked his mustache and shook his head. 'Stays in my mustache forever. I hate that.'

But he waited for her without a hint of impatience. She appreciated the fact that he had to know she was anxious, and yet he didn't point it out by asking if she was okay.

Finally she told him, 'Let's do this.'

73

Maggie fell back on her forensic training. She tried to concentrate on details. *Observe and examine.* Her eyes adjusted to the dim light. There was actually more space than she imagined. But there were also piles of dirt and debris.

First, they removed the woman's body. Already Maggie realized how much she hated maggots. Up this close she could see them clinging to the soft tissue even as the CSU techs swiped at them. Some fell off as the techs lifted and wedged the corpse onto a medevac basket the sheriff's department had provided. They tightened the rope around her then waited while Cunningham and Turner pulled, engaging the pulley system.

There was only the one corpse out in the open, though Maggie didn't need to look hard to know there were others. They, however, would require some digging. She could see several bones, the white knots gleaming against the black dirt. Ganza's techs got busy filling buckets and sifting thought the dirt. If they found something of interest they hauled their buckets up the ladder where they could filter the contents through screens.

They'd collect trace evidence and pieces of remains. Maggie knew they'd also bag up samples of the soil and any vegetation present. Although the victims were dumped here they probably weren't killed here. Particles still clinging to their clothes or mud on their shoes could sometimes lead investigators to the original crime scenes.

Ganza didn't expect anything from Maggie except to observe and ask questions. They were used to working through puzzles. Still, she helped him clear away branches and wet leaves. Underneath they could see a running shoe and a heap of discarded clothes. It looked like some of the debris had been tossed on top.

'Why bother to hide anything down here?' she asked out loud, not expecting an answer.

She was already trying to figure out why the Collector had tossed the bodies into a ravine in the middle of a state forest that had no public access. This was the same killer who wanted to show off the items he extracted.

'Ordinarily I'd suggest remorse or regret,' Ganza said. 'But we both know serial killers don't feel either.'

'He's careful,' Maggie said. 'He must know that the victim's body, her identity, where she went missing – all of that could leave clues for us to track him. Even the fact that he takes their cars to dump their bodies then returns the vehicle. This is a level of killer that I haven't encountered before.'

'Bundy and Edmund Kemper had high IQs. Usually their arrogance or rage does them in. Maybe we'll get lucky, and that'll happen with this guy.'

Maggie grabbed and pulled off the last branch. She stared at the pile and for the first time since she'd descended into the ravine, she felt cold and clammy and a bit nauseated.

'It's not just a heap of clothes,' she said. 'There's someone in there.'

Ganza bent over and with gloved hands he tried to pick up a piece of spandex that was still connected to tissue and bone. The decomposed flesh had soaked into the clothes, leaving it a hard and crumpled mass. He pried at a piece of torn fabric but it didn't come away clean. He dug in his pack and pulled out a plastic evidence bag, depositing it before continuing.

There was a zipper on what looked like a hip pocket. And she could see the outline of something inside. It was the size of a driver's license. Ganza saw it too and began working carefully to release it.

All this time and trouble the Collector had taken to hide his victims, certain that they would never be found. So sure of himself that he left the woman's driver's license in her pocket.

74

Stucky was anxious and excited. It felt like he was finally back on track. Like he had shaken off that last failure and was ready to hunt.

He filled bags with the basics – more staples that didn't spoil quickly and a few apples and oranges. This time instead of small water bottles he bought jugs of drinking water, pleased with his brilliance. Jugs were less portable. Agent Maggie would have to return to the shed if she got thirsty.

The weather was promising more storms in the next day or two. He hated hunting in the rain but he realized the thunder and lightning provided a psychological fear that even he couldn't compete with. He'd bring her here just in time and let the storm soften her up.

Last week he had discovered where Maggie lived with her husband, Greg Stewart. A corporate lawyer. He had to admit, that surprised him. He also knew where her mother lived. He knew where Maggie liked to do her morning jogs, how early she left for work, and that she wasn't very good at noticing when someone followed her.

He hadn't decided yet how or where he would take her. He had to lure her someplace where he felt comfort. Familiar surroundings for him, but someplace that would take her out of her element. That Conway Robinson State Forest might do just fine. He had snatched that pretty Paige with her fluorescent shoes right at the trailheads. It was quiet there.

He was thinking – dreaming, really – about how he'd do it when he noticed a buzz that didn't belong in the forest. He had just dropped off the groceries and was taking one of his shortcuts up to the bluff that overlooked the creek. He'd planned to do some target practice.

But the sound – it was coming from the direction of the ravine. A low and continuous buzz, almost like an engine. But that was impossible. There were no roads. No official road, except for a service one that park workers used. That was on the other side of the rock wall and definitely not where the sound was coming from.

Stucky changed directions. He hiked the slick incline knowing exactly where to grab and how to set his feet. Half these trails he'd made himself and he could trek them with his eyes closed. He readjusted the weight on his back and continued to climb. The ground turned into rock the higher he went. Pine trees replaced hardwood oaks and chestnuts.

Now he could smell gasoline fumes. His pulse began to race. His breath came faster as anger and panic took turns galloping in his chest.

What the hell was going on?

Just a few more feet. He pushed his legs and rolled his shoulders trying to ignore the ache. He lowered himself to his knees as he came to the ledge. He hid behind the shrubs sticking up out of the rock.

He couldn't believe his eyes. His heart sunk as though he had been betrayed.

This was his special place. His hunting ground. His secret hideout. The one place he could go to where he could control the rage.

Now it was gone to him.

75

Maggie had been standing in place, staying out of the way while Ganza processed the disarticulated pieces of the spandex victim. She avoided touching the walls after one of the CSU techs had found another bone protruding out of the dirt. At first glance the white knot looked an awful lot like a rock.

Now she handed equipment – trowel, various picks, hand shovel – like a surgeon's assistant. She was trying to be helpful, and also trying to *not* watch Ganza. The crunch and squish sounds were unsettling as he pulled away pieces of tissue and bone held together only by fabric.

It wasn't until she accidentally dropped a trowel that she saw the hand. The heel of her hiking boot was inches away. When she realized what it was – that it was fingertips and a palm sticking up through the floor of the ravine – she dropped the trowel again.

She was standing on top of another corpse. One that was buried under a thin layer of soil right beneath her.

Ganza noticed, and that's when he insisted they break for lunch. They'd been at it all morning.

Maggie didn't argue. She was relieved to crawl out into the sunshine and into fresh air. However, there was no escaping the smell. She noticed that immediately. The scent of death permeated her clothes, her hair, her skin and had seeped in through her facemask. But it was the exhaustion that had overtaken her. She was trying so hard to *not* feel, and it was proving to be a draining, if not impossible feat. She was finding it difficult to detach. How could she not be moved by what they were finding?

The mental fatigue made her body feel heavy, like she was wearing weights around her ankles. Her mind kept trying to construct profiles of the victims. The Collector snatched these women up out of their daily routines. Susan Fuller said she had been on her way to work. Paige Barnett was going to start or had just finished jogging. The corpse in the spandex may have been taken from another running trail weeks – *maybe months* – before.

It wasn't until Maggie climbed out of the ravine and saw the tarp, its surface cluttered with bones, that she realized the Collector had been using this burial ground for much longer than she imagined. The sight stopped her, almost took her knees out from under her. They already ached and begged for her to sit. She found a rock in the sunshine and collapsed, hoping the men didn't notice. She fumbled one of her water bottles out of her daypack then sipped water, attempting to quiet the panicked voice in her head.

He's been killing for years. How did we not know?

The deputies had left, scheduled to return whenever the group was ready to pack up for the day. Cunningham and Turner were photographing, bagging and labeling each piece the CSU techs had brought up. While one tarp held bones – along with fragments the techs believed to be bone – the other tarp was littered with broken arrows, bits of fabric, shoes and jewelry, all waiting to be processed.

Now that Ganza and his techs took a break, Cunningham and Turner followed suit.

'How many do you think are buried here, Keith?' Cunningham

asked as he removed his glasses and wiped the sweat from his face.

'It's tough to say. I'll call Wagner. This is his specialty. I'll have him do his magic and piece together whatever he can.' Ganza glanced over at the tarps. 'One thing's for certain, he's been a busy boy.'

Then Cunningham turned to Maggie and asked, 'Is this just a convenient way to dispose of them after he's finished playing his games? Or am I missing something?'

'I don't think he ever expected anyone to find this place. It may have started as a convenience. I think the woman we removed from the top of the pile is the same woman Susan Fuller saw him taking out of the car trunk. *If* that's correct then he brought her body here to dump. I'm guessing Stan Wenhoff will find that one of her kidneys is missing.'

'So you think he took her someplace else to do that?'

Maggie looked to Ganza for reassurance. It was Ganza who answered. 'That kidney was cut out with clean precision. I can't imagine he did that out here. But then I wouldn't have imagined half of what we're finding.'

'I think he brings them here,' Maggie said, 'with the intensions of hunting them like he did with Paige Barnett. And intended to do with Susan. He leaves them untethered in the shed hoping they'll wander off trying to escape. And he watches for them from some hiding place.'

'But Susan Fuller was here for days and she never saw him except when he was carrying the body out of the trunk.'

'She did see him later,' Maggie reminded him. 'She hid up on that rock wall near the service road. She said he walked by several times as though he was searching for her. She spent that night hiding, tucked under a rock ledge.'

'There's at least one more full corpse buried down there,' Ganza said. 'I scooped some of the dirt away from her before I came up. She has a broken arrow through her wrist.' He pointed to several pieces of other arrows they had recovered. 'I think Maggie's right. He brought these women here to hunt. The trophies he took to show off. Not unlike hunters taking the head of a deer and mounting it above their mantle.'

Cunningham didn't look pleased. He was standing in a patch of sunlight and Maggie noticed the creases in his brow. His arms were crossed and he looked deep in thought. Maggie thought she heard something whizz through the air.

Cunningham winced.

It wasn't until he crumpled to his knees that she saw the arrow sticking through his left thigh.

Their combined mission was to pull Cunningham to safety. Maggie and Turner shielded his body as they dragged him behind the rocks. Both agents' eyes searched the bluffs above. But to do so was to look directly into the sun. Maggie saw no movement.

'Would he have a scope?' Turner asked.

She looked for reflections.

'Son of a bitch, that hurts,' Cunningham said.

Maggie felt the urgency thump inside her chest. She'd never seen her boss in pain. She'd never seen him project an ounce of weakness. Cool, calm and collected. That was Cunningham even in the face of frustration and anger. For him to complain that it hurt meant that it was bad.

She took her eyes off the bluff and glanced down. He was bleeding. His fingers, where they gripped the wound, were covered in blood. There was too much blood.

She looked up. Turner had noticed and his eyes were wide. Maggie searched for Ganza. He came around the rocks, crawling on hands and knees, bringing with him a first-aid kit.

'Get the medevac basket,' he told Turner. 'Maggie, find some ropes or cords. Cut them from the pulley if you need to.'

He poked and plucked what he needed from the kit. 'Frank, Josh, cover everything up as best as you can with the extra tarps. Anchor down the edges. As soon as I get him ready we need to get him the hell out of here.'

There were no more whizzing sounds. No movement from above. By now Maggie wondered if the Collector had moved to a lower hiding place. But all she could see were rock and trees so thick she hoped he couldn't possibly send an arrow through them.

'Kyle, you need to talk to me,' Ganza said.

Maggie edged closer to the gear left by the sheriff's department. There was plenty of rope.

'Kyle, did you hear me?'

Maggie blinked hard and took several deep breaths. She needed to ignore Ganza's voice. She knew he was trying to keep Cunningham from going into shock.

So much blood. What if the arrow hit the femoral artery?

'Kyle—'

'I hear you. Stop shouting.'

But Ganza's voice had been barely above a whisper.

Maggie met Turner as he crab-walked back, holding up the medevac basket as a shield. He waited for her. She looped rope over her shoulder and grabbed a few other items from the gear.

'I know that's tight,' Ganza was telling Cunningham as he finished tying a tourniquet. He had also wrapped gauze around the arrow, strapping it down so it didn't move and cause more damage during transport.

While the men moved Cunningham to the medevac basket and secured him, Maggie tried to call Sheriff Olson. Then 911. Reception was spotty. It took four attempts before she stayed connected long enough to let them know what was going on.

Now came the tricky part. Carrying a stretcher through the narrow trail between trees and over rocky inclines that had been challenging one at a time. And all the while watching for an ambush.

The Collector obviously knew every section of this forest. He could be waiting anywhere for them. But Maggie didn't think that he would. He'd already accomplished what he set out to do. He wanted them gone. He wanted them to feel the sting and the panic. If he wanted them dead she was certain he had the skill to make that happen. And he would have shot them while they were all scrambling around out in the open.

Although she wanted to believe all that, her eyes kept scanning inside the forest, searching for movement, looking for him hiding in the shadows. She strained to listen but it was impossible to hear over her own heart banging against her chest. They were making a lot of noise, shuffling to get footholds and sending loose dirt and pebbles skittering down. Minutes seemed to turn to hours. It was taking forever and yet, Maggie knew they were making good time. Then she'd get a glimpse of Cunningham's trousers and see all the blood.

They heard the voices and running engines before they could see the waiting paramedic team down on the service road. Sheriff Olson was there, too, with another team. Only this time each deputy carried his Remington 12-gauge Police Magnum shotgun. The sheriff had a map spread out on the hood of their SUV, and he was giving them directions when he heard them coming down the last stretch.

Maggie wanted to tell Olson it was too late. That his men would waste an afternoon searching. The Collector had too many shortcuts, too many hiding places and several escape routes. The K9 unit had shown them the most used and the most recent path, but didn't the handler even admit there were many more?

Somewhere the Collector had another entrance into the forest so he could avoid using this service road. Maybe a dirt path he'd found through one of the pastures that butted up against the forest property. He was good at noticing what others took for granted.

The paramedics had taken over and in seconds they had Cunningham in the back of their unit, running IV lines and stabilizing his leg. His rag-tag rescue crew – Ganza and his two techs, Turner and Maggie – stood back and watched. They were spent from exhaustion, drenched in sweat and trying to catch their breath.

'He gonna be okay?' Olson asked.

No one responded.

Then Ganza said, 'I think he'll be okay. I'm not so sure his leg will be.'

77

Stucky took Back Road all the way to Highway 48. When he pulled onto the interstate he could hear the sirens exiting. The rage was clawing its way out. There wasn't anything he could do to stop it. He hadn't felt this way since his father. The man could derail him with one simple backhanded compliment.

'I would have thought you could blast that buck between the eyes with how tight you had those puny fingers of yours wrapped around the trigger.'

At fourteen, his father expected him to be man enough to move on from nailing deer to nailing the whores he brought home. And of course, there were more backhanded compliments that quickly turned into vulgar scoldings when Stucky didn't live up to being his father's 'little man.'

Stucky thought he had squelched that rage years ago. Or at least, he had tamped it down when he shut his father up for good. A yachting accident. That was the official report of the Bristol County sheriff's department. They had a difficult enough time believing anyone would want to murder Dr Allan Stucky, a pillar of New Bedford society, least of all his only son who he had raised on his own.

Even now it made Stucky smile to think about the irony of his father drowning in Buzzards Bay.

He used the money he collected from his father's estate to create a multi-million dollar computer company, one of the first that developed online stock trading. But Stucky's true love was the segment of the company that created video games. In the early days those creations gave him a pleasure he'd never experienced before. It was quite wonderful until it became quite boring.

Then he sold the company and started playing different games. His computer savvy made it easy to develop as many identities as he wanted, depositing his millions in various accounts, acquiring documents – driver's licenses, credit cards, property purchases – in each name. It wasn't until later he realized he was a master of disguises. Simple ones, really. He studied and observed as he sat in cafes or roamed the aisles of grocery stores, always watching and learning what it took to become invisible, to look ordinary, to elicit trust.

He was proud of how organized he was. He worked hard to become a part of a community, getting a good job, creating a backstory, all the while blending in and not being noticed. He planned and prepared, he anticipated then he executed his game – a video game in real time, in real life.

If anyone were to ask him why he killed he knew the answer without hesitation. He didn't need to psychoanalyse the reasoning. It didn't matter what his childhood had been or that his father had emasculated him. The truth was, Stucky did it because he enjoyed it. Each kill became a challenge to best the last one.

And now Stucky was surprised that despite everything he had controlled and created there was still this anger that simmered just beneath the surface. He didn't like his hiding place being discovered. He didn't like his plans being upended. He'd only just begun his game with Agent Maggie and she'd ruined it by bringing all those men to his secret place.

He'd need to start all over again. Find a way to remove her

from all those men, where she couldn't count on them for protection. He'd need to lure her away to someplace where she had no safety net. Where it would be only her and him.

In less than an hour he started brewing another plan. He wanted to move quickly. He knew he needed to leave. Go to an area they'd never think to look. Immediately, he thought of the perfect place, far enough away that no one could follow. A property he'd never used before. In fact, he bought it several years ago because it was secluded in an abandoned warehouse district. The building was huge and empty, and it swallowed up sound like the belly of a whale.

He was already concocting his plan. This time it had to be something that aimed at the heart. Everyone had a trigger, a soft spot, something that made them jump instinctively. He'd watched her protect the guy he knew was her boss. She'd shielded him with her own body. He meant something to her. There were others who meant a great deal to her as well. But she was an FBI agent. How deep was her obligation to save an innocent person she didn't know?

From everything he had observed, from all that he had learned in the last week, Stucky believed he knew exactly how to lure Maggie O'Dell down into the belly of his whale.

78

It was late by the time Maggie left Warren Memorial Hospital. Cunningham was conscious but groggy and already annoyed by the attention and restrictions. The surgeon expected a full recovery but wanted him overnight for observation. Gwen was still by his side and Maggie found herself thinking that Cunningham was lucky to have someone as dedicated as Dr Gwen Patterson. Whatever their relationship, she was a good and trusted friend.

Maggie wondered: if something had happened to her in the forest would she even call Greg? Their relationship had become so strained.

'See, I told you this job is too dangerous.'

She could already hear his reaction. He'd probably not come to the hospital just to teach her a lesson.

No, that's not true. Of course he would come to the hospital.

And of course, he'd give her a lecture about how dangerous her job was. Fact was, she wasn't sure she'd want him there. Already she'd made up her mind that she wouldn't tell him about Cunningham. About the madman with a crossbow hunting humans in the forest. Nor would she tell him about the bodies in the ravine.

When Maggie asked Turner if they should contact Cunningham's wife, he gave her a strange look. Then he said he'd let Delaney make that decision, since he had actually met Mrs Cunningham. But Turner said he was sure the two had been separated for quite some time. Of course, he admitted Cunningham hadn't actually told anyone that, but Turner had caught him spending all night in his office and using the locker room to shower early in the mornings.

Maggie immediately wondered if Gwen knew about any of this. Then quickly she decided it certainly wasn't her place to tell her.

At the moment, she just wanted to feel the relief. She hadn't realized until they were hauling Cunningham out of the forest how much she thought of him as a father figure. Recently Greg had complained that Maggie had started dressing like a guy and she realized he could be right.

She took her cue from Cunningham, searching out classic but boxy style blazers and straight-legged trousers that hid her figure but gave her a professional look. She even found herself choosing colors he favored – copper, bronze, dark emerald green. She admired the man as much as she respected him. For several brutal hours, while she tried to block out all the blood leaking out of his body, she kept remembering that day her father didn't come home.

Turner was the one who convinced her to go home, get some rest, and sleep in her own bed. By then she had little energy to argue. Cunningham was literally out of the woods. The drive home was almost two hours. She had too much time to think. She had spent the day keeping her emotions in check. Now, with her guard down, the feelings rushed out like a spigot had been turned on.

The one that surprised her most was anger. Anger with herself for not being any closer to knowing who the hell the Collector was. Even knowing his name was Albert Stucky had gotten her nowhere. And then there was the anger toward

Stucky for what he had done to all those poor women. Anger for his arrogance to shoot a federal officer and think he could get away with it. Anger for making her feel as though she was a part of his stupid cruel game.

She'd figure out who he was and what hole he slithered into every night. There had to be a way to turn the tables on him. There had to be a way to stop him.

Of course, she would have been more convincing if she hadn't just missed her exit and needed to backtrack five miles.

It was just after midnight when she dropped her go-bag in their small laundry room. She stepped carefully, knowing where all the floorboards were that creaked. She didn't want to wake Greg. With a glance down the hallway she could see their bedroom door was closed.

She turned on a lamp in the living room and tried to remember when she had eaten last. Suddenly she was starving. But she pulled out her cell phone first. She hadn't checked messages during the two-hour drive home. It had been twelve hours since Cunningham had been shot. He had been fine when she left the hospital.

And yet when she saw the message from Gwen, her pulse started to race. Was something wrong? Her fingers flew over the necessary buttons to retrieve her voice messages. She punched the last one and pressed the phone to her ear.

'Maggie, it's Gwen. Everything's fine. Cunningham's fine. I was just thinking that you might be reassured to know that. Also, I wanted to let you have my cell phone number. Call anytime. I know you're dealing with your mom and all of this. If you ever need anything, just let me know, okay? Do try to get some rest.'

Maggie smiled. If she wasn't mistaken, she and Gwen were becoming friends. She'd never had someone who called just to put her mind at peace. She tried to remember if she'd ever had anyone genuinely care whether or not she got enough rest. As if on cue the next voice message activated and began.

'Mag-pie, this is your mother. I thought I might hear from you today, but I guess not. I swear I spent more time talking to the repairman this afternoon than I've talked to you all week. Call me.'

Maggie closed her eyes. The phone stayed pressed to her ear but there were no other messages. She felt the weight heavy against her chest. How was it possible for the woman to make her feel this way with a short voice message? What was it that Gwen had said? Something about of course her mother knew how to push Maggie's buttons because she helped install them.

Okay, that made her smile again.

And she was still hungry.

Neither she nor Greg were good about grocery shopping, but Maggie opened the refrigerator door anyway and stared at the sparsely filled shelves. She started to grab the pizza box from the bottom shelf when she saw the takeout container on the top one. It was plain, white, and foam. Just like all the others.

Maggie's stomach dropped and her knees felt spongy.

It could be nothing, she told herself.

Greg could have ordered takeout. She hadn't been home last night. Of course, it was his leftovers.

Yet when she picked up the container and slid it off the shelf, transferring it to the kitchen counter, she did so carefully, using the palms of her hands on both sides. She was already treating it like evidence.

There were no smears on the outside. No signs of blood. She was going to be embarrassed when she opened it and found a cannoli or cinnamon roll from his favorite pastry shop.

Maggie eased the tab out and let the lid snap open.

Inside was a lock of blond hair curled over a piece of paper with an address. Without touching it she could read the note:

ONLY YOU CAN SAVE HER. TELL NO ONE.
COME ALONE OR THE NEXT CONTAINER
WILL HAVE HER HEART INSIDE.

79

Maggie's hands were still shaking when she woke up Greg.

Before she woke him, she had slid the lock of hair into a plastic bag and the note into another. Then she marched to the laundry room, emptying the dirty clothes from her go-bag. She put both items at the bottom. She'd already committed the address to memory. She needed to pack fresh clothes without Greg seeing her panic. And in order to do that she needed to remove the urgency that had started her pulse to race and her heartbeat to gallop against her ribcage.

'You just getting in?' He rolled over at the touch of her hand to his shoulder.

'Yeah, I needed to pick up some fresh clothes and head back out.'

He rubbed a hand over his face then pushed himself up onto his elbows.

'Seriously?'

'We think we found a serial killer's burial spot in Devil's Backbone State Forest.' She had decided to tell him this because in comparison to what she was getting ready to do, a mass grave of victims seemed like child's play.

'Holy crap! Devil's what?'

'Backbone. It's northwest of here. At the foot of the Appalachians. Technically it's a state forest but there's no public access. We think he may have been using the forest as a dumping ground for a year. Maybe longer.'

She had turned on a lamp in the corner so she could see well enough to pull what she needed from her drawers. Greg watched, but he wasn't really interested in what she was doing. He was still trying to process what she had told him. Her instinct had been right. Throwing out something shocking for him to think about had derailed him . . . momentarily.

'Hey, did someone come into the apartment today?' she asked.

She was still trying to figure out how Stucky had managed to get the container into their refrigerator.

'Not that I know of,' he said. 'So you're driving all the way back tonight?'

'The crew wants to get started first thing in the morning. We'll probably be there for a few days.' She folded and tucked clothes into her bag. 'I just wondered because sometimes maintenance comes in while we're both gone. I've been wanting them to check the icemaker on the frig.' The icemaker hadn't been working for over six months. She was counting on Greg being too groggy to mention that.

'Nope. No refrigerator guy.' He smashed his pillow into a ball behind him and sat back against it. 'There was an air conditioner guy showed up when I got home about six. He was checking units throughout the apartment complex. He didn't find anything wrong.'

She swallowed hard and ignored the knot that had started tightening in her stomach. A repairman. That had to be the Collector. For an appearance changer, this would have been a piece of cake for him.

Then suddenly Maggie remembered her mother's phone message. Didn't she say she had spent the afternoon with a repairman?

80

INTERSTATE 95, FLORIDA
Thursday

Stucky had driven all night. He was wired and hopped up on adrenaline. Everything had gone so well. Even better than he expected.

He couldn't stop grinning, thinking about Agent Maggie's husband letting him into their apartment. The guy remained on the phone the entire time and paid no attention to him. He was standing with his back to Stucky, less than twenty feet away when Stucky opened the refrigerator and placed the takeout container inside.

It couldn't have gone any smoother.

Now, even the small catering van ran smoothly despite getting few breaks to cool down in the last nine hours. Sleek and new, Gibson had barely used it. He'd asked Stucky to park it in storage just a few days ago, and his boss didn't notice whether he returned the keys to the utility drawer. Unlike the florist van, this one had no wrap or graphics on the outside. The panels were polished white. Perfect in case Gibson suddenly noticed the van missing. Just for good measure, Stucky took the extra time to swing by the Richmond Airport. No one was around in long-term parking when he switched license plates with a black SUV.

The sun had been up for a couple of hours, and already he

could feel the Florida heat. He cranked up the air conditioning and checked his rearview mirror. No movement. She wouldn't need another injection for several more hours. She should be thanking him that he decided to use the van or she'd be smoldering inside the trunk of a car. Poor thing looked so terrified, he doubted that he would need to use a full dose next time.

Where was all that vibrant energy that teenagers usually had? When he met her at the art gallery she appeared to be the spitfire image of her mother, not just in looks but in attitude – spirited and independent. That was, in fact, what he had seen when he pulled up beside her on the street and rolled down his car window.

'You want a lift?' he'd asked casually.

He knew she took this route every day and that she had at least six more blocks to get to the restaurant. She usually stopped and checked in with her mother then headed over to the gallery where she worked the evening shift. Yes, he did listen to what Rita told him, though he knew Rita didn't think so. He remembered her telling him how excited Carly was to get the part-time summer job, and how the job had led to her being featured in her own showing.

'You work with my mom,' she said and still hesitated.

'That's right. We met at your art show. I'm headed to the restaurant now if you want a ride.'

He clicked the locks open for her and pushed up his sun-glasses, trying to make it look like it was no skin off his nose if she'd rather walk. She glanced at her wristwatch then came around the front of the car and slid in with her clunky box that looked like an old-fashioned lunch box. It was even metal and had a similar handle.

When she saw him notice it she said, 'My art kit. If we're not busy they let me work on my project in the back.'

He nodded. He didn't really care. It looked like the pocket of her smock was filled with art tools, too. A small brush stuck up out of the top. He remembered how pretty the girl was, but now, with little makeup, she was stunning. A younger version of Rita. Most importantly, he knew how much Carly meant to her mother. He knew she'd do anything to get her back. He was counting on it.

He waited for her to put on her seatbelt. Other cars drove past, but he was idling along the sidewalk where he knew no one would notice. He'd purposely rigged the seatbelt to make her turn and take extra time with it.

'So I can't remember your name,' she said, looking down between the seat and door while she fished out the seatbelt.

He slipped the syringe out of his pocket, flicked off the cap.

'Call me Drew,' he said as he poked the needle into her arm.

81

Maggie called Ganza because she needed to check in with someone.

'I'm headed back out with Wagner,' he told her. 'Sheriff Olson and his posse are meeting us.'

She actually smiled at that. She remembered yesterday, the sheriff and his men with their shotguns. Posse seemed appropriate.

'I'm spending the day checking on a couple things,' she told him. Then she changed the subject immediately so he couldn't ask what those things were. 'Have you heard how Cunningham is doing?'

'He's trying to get himself discharged. I think they're making him wait for a physical therapist to give him instructions. You know that's got to be driving him crazy.'

Somehow she had managed to end the conversation without giving Ganza any more details about what she was doing. Or where she was. Because she wasn't sure how she'd explain that she was at a rest area in South Carolina getting ready to cross the border to Florida.

Last night, after finding out that her mother was fine – annoyed at being awakened, but otherwise fine – Maggie realized if Stucky had pretended to be a repairman in order to meet her mother, it was only to rattle her. Which he had succeeded in doing.

Maybe he also wanted to buy some time. The Florida address he had left for her in the takeout container was thirteen to fourteen hours away. Greg said the repairman had been at their apartment around 6:00 p.m. That meant Stucky had about an eight- to ten-hour head start. Adrenaline pushed her to hurry though she knew he'd wait for her. Why bother with such an elaborate plan and then not wait?

Now as she climbed back into her vehicle her phone rang again. She thought about shutting it off. She didn't want to explain anything more to Ganza or Turner or even Gwen. She didn't recognize the caller's number. If Albert Stucky could get inside her apartment there was nothing to stop him from getting her phone number.

'This is Maggie O'Dell.'

'Agent O'Dell?' It was a woman's voice. And she sounded panicked.

'Yes?'

'I don't know if you'll remember me. I'm a waitress from Gibson's Restaurant and Pub? I was the one who ... you know, who opened that container.'

'Of course, I remember. Rita, right?'

'My daughter's missing.' The woman's voice hitched and she could barely get the next sentence out. 'I'm just so frantic. I don't know what to do. Who to call. I think she's been taken.'

'Rita, does your daughter have blond hair?'

'Yes. How did you know?'

82

Stucky had collected all kinds of items from the vehicles of his victims. Actually he didn't like to refer to them as victims. Prey was a better term. After all, most of them were given a chance to escape. Before he returned any of the vehicles to their original place he went through the center console, the glove compartment, any purse or duffle. Sometimes he even checked under the seats.

One of the treasures he'd taken was from Paige Barnett's car. She had a stack of mail on the passenger seat. And in that stack was a letter from her sister. In the letter she gave Paige her new phone number. The envelope included Lydia Barnett's home address. In Fort Lauderdale, Florida. He kept such things just in case he needed to change territories. And here he was. He'd just passed a road sign. Twenty-five more miles to Fort Lauderdale and less than an hour from his final destination.

Stucky pulled off Interstate 95 to get some lunch and fill the gas tank. He couldn't resist the opportunity. He pulled out the letter and dialed.

'Hello?'

'Is this Lydia Barnett?'

'Yes?'

'This is Deputy Steele with the Warren County sheriff's department in Virginia.'

'Oh my God! Do you have information about Paige?'

'I'm down in Florida following up on a lead.'

'In Florida?'

'Yes, in the Miami area. There's someone who may know what happened to your sister. I'm wondering if you might be available to meet me and check this out.'

'Of course. Anything. Oh my God! I can't believe we might finally know something.'

He gave her the address and ended the call.

Stucky shook his head.

Much too easy.

Then he glanced up in the rearview mirror. Carly's eyes were staring up at him. Somehow she had rolled onto her side.

Time for another injection.

83

MIAMI, FLORIDA
Late Thursday afternoon

Maggie had made several stops during the long drive. Mostly to refuel and stretch her legs. Once to stock up on items she thought she'd need, including a cooler with ice to keep her Diet Pepsis and water bottles cold. Virginia weather had been cooler and wetter than normal but the Florida sun was unrelenting. Each time she stepped out of the car she could feel the heat hit her in the face, steaming up her sunglasses and rising up from the asphalt as if in waves.

Though she wasn't hungry she ate, making sure she had plenty of protein. The weight of her exhaustion was lifted only by the constant flow of adrenaline. She wouldn't allow herself to sleep even if she thought she could. Right now being sleep deprived would play to her advantage. Or so she hoped.

By the time she arrived she knew what she had to do.

On a map the address looked like an ordinary warehouse district. Now Maggie tried to examine the area from a highway overpass. She had already driven by three times. Although the buildings looked dilapidated and abandoned she felt slightly relieved that he wasn't leading her to a trailhead into another forest.

One thing that did bother her was the total absence of life. Loading docks were empty. There were no vehicles, no people.

Roads in between the buildings were cracked and crumbing. Palm trees sprouted out of small patches of grass. Electrical lines dangled from pole to pole. A chain link fence surrounded the property, with a security gate that was now broken off its tracks and shoved aside. There was nothing left inside the warehouses to secure and protect.

A railroad track ran along the backside of the property. Across the street was another abandoned building.

During her second pass she saw a bright white paneled van in front of the largest warehouse. On the third pass a black SUV had pulled up beside it. Maggie wanted to drive by again but there wasn't enough traffic for her to risk it. She found a parking lot on the other side of the highway.

According to Susan Fuller – the only woman to survive – Stucky used an injection that paralyzed his victims almost instantly. Maggie and Ganza had speculated that the drug he used was Ketamine or something similar.

Ketamine had hallucinogenic, tranquilizing and dissociative effects. It was used to induce relaxation and a loss of consciousness when used as an anesthetic. As Ganza had pointed out, the drug had also gained popularity as an illicit party drug. It produced an abrupt high, a sort of euphoria, along with feelings of floating and other out of body experiences. Hallucinations, similar to LSD, were common.

Maggie had learned that higher doses of Ketamine could result in more extreme and dangerous effects known as K-holing. That's when users became unable to move, a sense of being paralyzed. Communication was difficult if not impossible. The intense feeling of being separated from your body and no longer in control, was no longer euphoric but rather, became terrifying.

Maggie believed that Stucky was injecting his victims with high doses of Ketamine. If she was going to walk into his trap and hoped to survive, she'd need to be prepared for that injection.

Before she left Richmond she had looked up everything she could find about the drug, including what could interrupt its effectiveness. Being sleep deprived and drinking too much caffeine were mentioned. Also listed were benzodiazepines such as Diazepam or Valium. She still had the bottle of Valium she had taken from her mother's hiding place.

Maggie still wasn't sure she could bring herself to take the pills, though she knew they might be her best protection against the full effect of Ketamine. She feared the Valium would lessen her reaction time, and she knew she'd have only one opportunity for one kill shot.

The idea of being disarmed and not in control of the situation was unsettling. The idea of not being in control of her own body simply terrified her.

She needed to tap into the anger she had felt after Cunningham had been shot. So she filled her memory with the sight and smells of that mass grave. Stucky had used those women as prey. Then he'd taken his trophies and shoved the rest of them down a ravine, discarding their bodies like they were containers he no longer had any use for.

He was going to do the same with Carly. Unless Maggie could stop him.

84

The white van and the black SUV were nowhere in sight when Maggie walked up the railroad tracks behind the warehouse. There were no windows back here. The only ones she had seen were in the front, their glass broken out, leaving gaping holes alongside the huge garage door.

She found a break in the chain link fence and crawled through it. Sweat already drenched her body. She had removed her holster and left it in the car. She didn't want anything that might encumber her. She tucked her weapon into the waistband of her jeans and pulled the hem of her T-shirt over it.

Deep breaths, she told herself.

She felt calm despite the surge of adrenaline. She was going to stop the bastard. That's what she needed to concentrate on. One opportunity. One chance. Aim for center mass.

Other than the huge garage door at the front, Maggie had counted three entrances. The one that faced the railroad tracks was up on the loading dock. She'd almost missed it because of the stacks of old crates in front of it. As she climbed the concrete steps to the platform she saw that the door was hanging from one hinge. The bottom of the door was jammed against the floor and tilted halfway open. No one had used it for a very long time.

Maggie stopped and listened. Traffic on the overpass was a distant hum. A couple of seagulls flew overhead. She inched her way closer to the door and now she saw that she could squeeze through it, hopefully without much noise. She pulled out her Smith & Wesson, pleased that there was no tremble in her fingers. She squatted low to where the door opening was widest, took another deep breath and went in.

Dust motes streamed from a hole in the roof. There were aisles and aisles of stacked crates that made it impossible to see what was on the other side. But Maggie also realized she could sneak in without being noticed.

With the van and SUV gone, she wondered if he hadn't expected her to arrive so quickly. Was it possible he had left Carly here while he went off to get something? Could she be that lucky?

Maggie tried to listen over the thumping of her heartbeat. She took small steps, careful not to make a sound. Then suddenly she stopped and flattened herself against the crates behind her.

She could hear something. A moan. Like a wounded animal. Low and quiet and staggered. She had to wait for it. Seconds lapsed before she heard it again. And now it sounded like it was coming from the front of the building.

She increased her pace and gripped her weapon, holding it ready to take aim and fire. The closer she crept the more she became convinced that someone was injured. But she couldn't see a thing. At the end of each aisle was yet another. She paused and tried to look between the crates.

Nothing.

She finally came to the end of an aisle but stayed put. Off to her left she saw the black SUV. The passenger door was flung open but she couldn't see inside the vehicle from this angle. The door's window looked like it had been shattered.

Maggie inched closer to the end of the aisle. She still hadn't located the sound though she was definitely closer. She kept her eye on the opened door of the vehicle, anticipating movement from inside. She was so focused on what was in front of her that she didn't realize her mistake. There was movement, but it wasn't from the interior of the vehicle. It was in the side mirror.

Just as Maggie started to turn around she felt the needle plunge into her arm.

85

'I want you to watch how I do it.'

The voice sounded like it was coming from a different room. Maggie wasn't sure how she ended up on the floor or how much time had passed. The SUV was in front of her and now she could see inside. There were twisted limbs – arms and legs overlapping. Blood dripped down the seat. Tossed to the side was a baseball bat with more blood.

A young blond girl sat propped against the vehicle, Her eyes were wide and looking at Maggie as though something she was seeing was terrifying her.

If only Maggie could focus on what that was.

And then, almost as if she were floating along the ceiling, she saw him. A tall, lean figure with dark hair and dark eyes kneeling over a body with a shiny scalpel. He was slicing slowly, delicately into the skin, beads of blood popping up in the wake of the blade.

And he was talking. It was his voice that she heard, and it still sounded so far away.

'You people always want to know why I do it,' the man was saying. 'I'd say enjoying it is a good enough reason.'

He lifted his head and she could see his eyes, so dark and empty, but he was smiling.

'What do you think about that? I do it because I enjoy it.'

He didn't seem to need her answer. In fact, he looked pleased just to have her watch. Although it was difficult to see clearly while she floated above him.

'I don't like the rages,' he gestured toward the open car door. 'It's a waste of energy. But she shouldn't have brought someone with her. I hate when they're unpredictable like that.'

He wiped the blade as he tilted his head and stared at her.

'It takes a great deal of precision. That's why I want you watch. I've never removed a heart before.' And he pointed at the blond-haired girl who had now slipped farther down. As if on cue there was a tiny moan that came from her mouth, though her lips weren't moving.

He bent over the torso and began cutting again.

This time Maggie felt a sting.

Her vision started to shift. She was seeing things from a different perspective. Suddenly she was back on the floor instead of up above. Her vision was still foggy, but now she could see that the torso he was slicing into was hers.

She didn't feel panic. Instead, there was strange calmness. Her heart didn't race. Her breathing was steady.

She remembered the needle. The drug. It was supposed to paralyze her, make her feel numb, cause the floating sensation. She had no idea how much time had gone by. Were the effects wearing off or had the Valium helped counter them?

No more floating, but she could definitely feel the scalpel's sharp blade. He cut only enough to make her bleed. It wasn't deep. It wasn't so bad. Maybe she was still a bit paralyzed and not feeling the full effect. Was that possible?

Her hands were placed up under her chin. She saw them, and she could feel that her wrists were bound together. His head was bent over her, so he didn't see her testing her fingers. She could move them. Her legs were stretched out in front of her. Inside her shoes, she tested her toes. Yes, she could curl them easily. But now it was becoming difficult to not flinch from the pain of the blade.

Don't cringe, she told herself. He can't know. Play along. The Valium was working. The Ketamine was not.

When he looked up at her, she simply stared, not moving anything. She didn't dare to blink or speak.

'That's just a start,' he told her. 'I can gut you later.'

He said it as casually as a butcher who'd finished slicing a cut of meat.

'I need to prepare and get everything ready. This should be a treat. I've never extracted a heart before.'

He stood up and looked down at her. This time he was studying her. Could he tell that she was coming around? Maggie stared straight ahead. She didn't move. How long did he expect the drug to work? She couldn't afford for him to inject her again. She'd never be able to ward off the effects if she had another dose shot into her system.

But then Stucky turned around and disappeared behind the back of the black SUV.

Maggie listened.

He hadn't gone far. He was close. Somewhere on the other side of the SUV. She heard clicks and clacks like he was opening and closing metal drawers. He was preparing. He was getting the necessary tools to extract a heart.

Maggie flexed her knees, pleased to have control of them. Her mind, her vision were still playing catch-up. She scanned the concrete floor for her Smith & Wesson. Of course, he wouldn't leave it out even if he thought she was drugged.

Maggie strained to see where Stucky had gone. Just how close was he? At the same time she tested her hands. The cord he'd used to tie her wrists wasn't tight. He'd gotten sloppy, taking the drug for granted. He hadn't bothered to tie her feet together. She started twisting her wrists back and forth.

She rolled over onto her side and pain burned across her abdomen. The girl's terrified eyes followed her, but now she didn't make a sound. Nor did she move. Maggie plastered her face against the dusty floor so she could look under the SUV. She saw Stucky from his ankles down. He was standing by a cart with rollers.

Click and clack. Open and close.

He was gathering tools, preparing and equipping himself. So sure, so confident, so arrogant, that he didn't hear Maggie stagger to her feet. Suddenly dizzy, she thought for sure she'd fall back down. He'd definitely hear that. It was more difficult than she thought it would be to make her legs work.

The Valium was wearing off, too, and now she could feel her pulse ticking up. The calm was being replaced by adrenaline. But there was still such a fog clouding her vision. And she could hear him slam the drawers like he was finished. Like he finally had everything he needed.

The girl's eyes were still following her. She'd give Maggie away no matter where she hid. Maggie shoved the last of the cord away from her wrists and let it drop.

Seconds. That's all she had.

And then she realized she wasn't wearing any more clicks or clacks.

86

Stucky came back around the vehicle. His hands were filled with various tools. From her hiding spot, Maggie could only see a sliver of him in the side mirror. She couldn't see Carly, but silently she implored the girl, *please don't give me away*.

In the mirror, Maggie watched Stucky. Before he even looked toward the girl he noticed that Maggie was gone.

'What the hell?'

She rushed up behind him just as he started to turn. The first swing of the bat caught his shoulder.

Not a good hit.

But it knocked him off balance and took him by surprise. The tools in his arms clattered to the concrete floor.

'Damn it, you bitch!'

He started to bend over to pick something up. Maggie tightened her grip and swung again. This one hit him in the side of the head.

He wiped at the blood and when his eyes looked at her, there was rage.

He tried to block the next hit with his arm. But there was a sickening crack and it wasn't the bat. It was bone.

The shriek sounded like a wild animal. An angry, wild animal. When he came at her, she didn't hesitate. She pulled back and swung again.

Somebody had to stop him.

That's what she told herself every time he got back up and

came at her. Each time his growls sounded more and more fierce as he continued to lunge at her. Maggie kept swinging the bat again…and again.

When he finally didn't get back up, she stopped.

She wasn't sure how many times she had hit him. Nor was she sure how much of the blood on her T-shirt and jeans was hers and how much was his.

Later, as she helped a paramedic load Carly into the back of the ambulance, Maggie could barely remember tying Stucky up. Carly had helped her. She did remember that. The girl moved slowly but with purpose. The cops who had responded to her 911 call believed she was just another of his victims. They hadn't asked any questions … yet. And she hadn't offered any information … yet.

But she heard them talking to each other and into their radios, about how the guy had been hogtied after getting the crap beat out of him.

'Looks like he got what he deserved.'

'We've got two waiting for ambulances.'

'And two dead.'

Stucky, however, was still alive. He was now handcuffed, on a gurney and inside another ambulance along with police guards.

Maggie waved off a paramedic when he tried to look at her wounds. She wasn't bleeding and right now she didn't feel any pain.

'I'll wait for the next ambulance,' she told him.

She managed to call Rita. She told her where they were taking Carly, and she tried to reassure her that the girl didn't seem to be injured, other than being drugged.

Maggie was surprised that Stucky hadn't bothered to take her cell phone, though she had no idea where her weapon was.

A CSU van arrived. Another police cruiser, too, adding more blinking red and blue lights just as the sun disappeared. She heard more sirens in the distance. There was a lot to process, and they'd probably be here most of the night. No one even noticed as Maggie slipped away. She followed the railroad tracks and crossed the highway under the overpass. She found her car where she'd left it, slid in behind the wheel and locked the doors.

There would be dozens of questions, but they could wait until tomorrow.

She was tired, so tremendously tired. She put her arms on the steering wheel and rested her head on top of them. She could still hear sirens. Finally, she sat back. She grabbed a bottle of water from her cooler. She twisted the cap off and gulped it down. Then she pulled out her cell phone again.

All she wanted right now was to talk to someone who wouldn't ask a lot of questions. Who wouldn't give her a lecture or ask why she had shut her phone off. Someone who'd only want to know how she was doing. That she was okay.

Maggie found the number and dialed. It took only two rings.

'This is Gwen Patterson.'

'Gwen, it's Maggie.'

'Oh my God, we were so worried about you? Are you okay?'

Maggie closed her eyes, leaned her head against the backrest and said, 'I got him. I stopped the bastard.'

Silence. Long enough for Maggie to second-guess her decision to call. She braced herself for the barrage of questions along with a stern lecture.

But then Gwen said, 'Tell me where you are. I'm going to come get you.'

FIVE DAYS LATER

FIVE DAYS LATER

87

Maggie waited. The hardback chair in front of Cunningham's desk felt incredibly uncomfortable. Anita had told her to go ahead and wait for him inside his office. He'd only be a few minutes.

'Make yourself comfortable,' Anita said. 'Can I get you anything to drink?'

Maggie shook her head.

'You sure? Maybe some water?'

Maggie shook her head a second time then wondered if the assistant knew something she didn't know. Would having a glass of water make this summons more comfortable?

No, she doubted anything would.

Now Maggie wondered how much Gwen had told Cunningham. Did her allegiance to him override her promise to Maggie? She suspected that she was about to find out.

Maggie was still surprised that Gwen had even shown up. So much of what happened after the warehouse remained a blur. She knew it was partly because of the Ketamine and the Valium. Ketamine could cause blackouts and memory loss as well as hallucinations. At times Maggie questioned how much of what she remembered was real and how much was simply the side effect of the drug.

Did she really beat Albert Stucky with a baseball bat?

In the nightmares that already haunted her sleep, she could see him cutting her as she watched from somewhere up above. But that was real. The wound still oozed a bit.

When Gwen had arrived, Maggie forgot to tell her about it. *No, that wasn't true.*

She hadn't forgotten. She never intended to tell Gwen.

But five or six hours into their trip home to Virginia, Gwen noticed before Maggie did. The wound was seeping through her T-shirt.

'You're bleeding!'

Even the detour to an emergency room was a blur. Was it Daytona Beach? Jacksonville? She wasn't sure. But she did remember how concerned Gwen looked. Concern that didn't come with a lecture or a scolding. That was a new concept for Maggie.

But she suspected she was in for lecture now from Cunningham. A lecture and a reprimand.

'Agent O'Dell.'

He startled her from behind, coming into his office. She turned but tried not to stare. She hadn't seen him yet with his cane. The temporary limp wasn't pronounced but it was enough to make him look more vulnerable than she was prepared for.

'I see you made it home safely.'

'Yes, sir.'

She focused on her hands in her lap and how much effort it took to keep them from balling up into fists. She didn't want to watch how much effort it took for Cunningham to get settled into his desk chair.

He opened a drawer and brought out several files.

Was one of them her file, again?

She had no idea what to expect. Nor did she know what exactly happened to an agent when she was insubordinate. Although insubordinate would mean that she had simply disobeyed orders. This wasn't as simple that.

No one knew she had followed Stucky down to Florida. She hadn't reported the container he'd left in her refrigerator, let alone told anyone about the note. Cunningham had still been in the hospital. Had she waited for approval, Carly Burke might be dead.

But that wasn't the point, and she knew it. It was more than disobeying orders. Despite being a novice in fieldwork, she knew the rules. She knew protocol. Going rogue wasn't acceptable.

'Paige Barnett's sister was one of the victims,' Cunningham said as he sorted through a file folder. 'Lydia Barnett. The other woman was a friend she'd brought along. I'm guessing Stucky pretended to have information about her sister and lured her to the warehouse.'

'The bodies in the SUV?' Maggie asked.

Cunningham nodded.

'I saw the vehicle when it was outside the warehouse. They must have just gotten there. If I'd just been a little sooner, I could have—'

'Stop.' He said it with his hand up as if physically stopping her and the gesture made her sit up straight. 'You risked your life and your career to save this young girl. I understand that. I get that. But that's where it stops. You can't get into the mindset that you could have saved them. We can't save them all.'

He stared at her. Maggie had no idea what response he expected, so she stayed silent.

'Because of those two murders, he'll remain in Florida. For now. He's being charged with kidnapping as well. They'll need your testimony when the time comes. In the meantime, you and Ganza will need to work together on these other victims. Have you talked to Keith yet?'

'No, sir.'

'He and Wagner have the body count up to five just from that ravine.'

Five and still counting. That didn't include the Boston councilwoman. Maggie knew there were others.

She noticed that Cunningham had sat back and crossed his arms over his chest. He shifted his weight in the chair, and she realized his wound was making him a whole lot more uncomfortable than she was.

'According to Rita Burke he was a bartender at Gibson's Restaurant and Pub. Started a few months ago. Said he was going to culinary school.'

'Culinary school?'

'She said that he was smart and charming. And attractive.'

Maggie nodded. That didn't surprise her. Ted Bundy had been described as handsome and charming. Although culinary school was something she would have never guessed.

'He went by Drew but on his application he used Dennis Andrew Nilsen. Do you recognize that name?'

It took her a few seconds and she nodded. 'Handsome, charming and clever.'

Dennis Andrew Nilsen was a notorious serial killer who murdered at least a dozen young men in London between 1978 and 1983.

'Albert Stucky made millions of dollars over a decade ago,' Cunningham told her, 'before he walked away from his computer business. As far as I can tell, he just disappeared one day.'

'And became someone else.'

'I think once you start digging in, you'll find he has several aliases. And I'm afraid we'll find even more victims.'

He looked at her again, studying her. She didn't flinch under his scrutiny.

'I understand you did what you believed was right. You have good instincts, Agent O'Dell, but instinct is not enough in this job. You could have gotten yourself killed. That's unacceptable. Is that clear?'

She nodded and was waiting for the reprimand when he reached to another desk drawer. This time he pulled out a revolver and placed it in the middle of his desk. It was her Smith & Wesson service revolver.

'Miami officers found this in the warehouse. Traced the serial number. They were curious because they said there wasn't an FBI agent on the scene. Two deceased victims. Two alive. But no FBI agent.'

Here it was. She felt her back straighten as if preparing for the punishment. She had already decided that she wouldn't argue with him.

Cunningham slid the revolver closer to her, giving it to her, as he said, 'They told me the weapon hadn't been fired. If it had, that would trigger an internal disciplinary investigation. But in fact, they said, there was no gunfire. No gunshot wounds. I have their full report.' And he tapped the file folder but his eyes never left Maggie's. He paused as if giving her a chance to explain. Maggie kept quiet.

'I'll expect to see your report by the end of the week. Is that clear?'

But it wasn't too clear at all. Was he really giving her weapon back instead of taking it away?

'Agent O'Dell?' He waited for her eyes to meet his, then said, 'Do you have a problem with that?'

'No, sir.'

'Then get back to work.'